TAILWAVERS

Sally Watson

TAILWAVERS

SALLY WATSON

iUniverse, Inc.
New York   Bloomington

TAILWAVERS

iUniverse books may be ordered through booksellers or by contacting:

iUniverse
1663 Liberty Drive
Bloomington, IN 47403
www.iuniverse.com
1-800-Authors (1-800-288-4677)

Because of the dynamic nature of the Internet, any Web addresses or links contained in this book may have changed since publication and may no longer be valid. The views expressed in this work are solely those of the author and do not necessarily reflect the views of the publisher, and the publisher hereby disclaims any responsibility for them.

ISBN: 978-1-4502-5377-2 (sc)
ISBN: 978-1-4502-5378-9 (ebk)

Printed in the United States of America

iUniverse rev. date: 09/03/2010

AILUROPHILE means
cat-lover.
Literally, Tail-waver-lover.
*From the Greek **ailuros: tailwaver.***

Can't you visualize it?
An Egyptian cat, the first that Greece has ever seen, goes ashore
gently waving a friendly caudal appendage aloft.
Instantly a dozen fingers point excitedly.
"Oh, look! Ailuros!"

This is dedicated to the friends and fellow-ailurophiles
who lived through these events with me and checked on my memory:
firstly, Jenny Maxwell, fellow author and protagonist,
who wrote her own part and that of her family;
to Constance Swinton, Arlene and Dan Szabo, Sandy Bevivino and
Chris Bell,
to Veterinarians Grant Patrick and Russ Gurevitch,
to the memory of dear Fred, Dad, Marilyn and Cattery Kate,
to my cousin Leslie Taft Treanor,
who runs Forgotten Felines on her own in Seattle.

And to all the cats, living and dead, who are the real stars--
--almost all of whom can be found on the cover.
Domino dancing with her red rag, Deirdre standing on the door--
Felicity eating string or grinning diabolically at Elinor--
the calico twins and their eager brother Tuffet--
Elinor sulking behind the sofa, Cameo enjoying the roof--
Lorelei with her head in a water glass and Onyx sporting his fox tail--
Fuji playing with baby Felicity--
even the raccoon and Little Dorrit the skunk.

And my enormous thanks to Caryn Cameron for the cover design!

TABLE OF CONTENTS

PART ONE: CATS IN CAHOOTS

1. The Frustrated Ailurophile 3
2. The Coming of the Cats .19
3. Double Trouble. 39
4. To the Winds, March!. 49
5. Frenetic Felines. 58
6. New Territory 63
7. The Black-Paw Gang. 74
8. Earthquake!. 84
9. Wildlife. 91
10. Farewell to Fred 98

PART TWO: CATS IN THE BELFRY

11. Catnippers 111
12. Requiem for a Shadow 117
13. The Ruddy 'Orrible Half-year. 121
14. The Cataclysmic Summer 132
15. The Coming of Elinor. 138
16. Mia and her Children 142
17. Scallywag 148
18. Orphanage for Skunklets 154
19. A Burmese Virago. .161
20. Bootsie 165
21. Chandi 172
22. Oboe. 180
23. Tuffet 195
24. Lorelei. 204
25. The Catastasis 220
26. Epilogue 226

PART ONE: CATS IN CAHOOTS

CHAPTER ONE

THE FRUSTRATED AILUROPHILE

I think I was born wanting kitty-cats.

No one understood this for some time--including me. A much-loved first-child, I received all sorts of lovely cuddly toys named Woof-woof Doggy, Kitty Meow and Mr. Quack-quack Ducky--which bored me because they were only pretend--and baby-dolls, which puzzled me as well. What was I supposed to *do* with them? (Maternity was apparently omitted from my make-up.) When one of them bleated MAMA at me, I was scandalized. "Don't you call *me* mama!" I snarled, clapping my hand over its cheeky mouth.

Eventually, they presented me with a fox-terrier. "Sally, this is your new little puppy. His name is Pet." (Choosing Each Other was an unknown concept in the days of President Hoover.) Pet and I regarded each other affably but without adoration. He was nice--but not what I craved. Nor was Jack the canary. So I began to come home trailing or carrying stray cats--usually old, scruffy, feral or flea-ridden--whom I insisted had followed me.

Sometimes they actually had.

I staggered home one day under the weight of large cat who was really *really* sick, with a plaster cast on his back leg, and a bad smell and

3

sticky stuff coming out around the edges. Poor Mother was horrified, but Dad was an ailurophile too.

"Oh, for crying out loud! It's a compound fracture, and infected!"

This was a poser. It clearly required a vet, but in those Depression days going to a vet was as inconceivable as a limousine or *paté de foie gras*--or for that matter, piano lessons for Sally or meat on week-days. So Dad, both clever and ingenious, bought some ether and iodine and other stuff, and did surgery on the kitchen table while I--violently allergic to ether--hung whoopsing out the upstairs window thinking of names. He was, I decided, Throckmorton J. Chowderhead Jr.

He survived nicely, but was old and lived only a few more years. So we acquired Lucifer; but he got too nosy with the birds' nests. Blue jays, at that. Vengeful and unforgiving, they hounded him and dive-bombed him until at last after two or three years of abject hiding, he fled to some other home. Third was Heathcliff, who--as certain facts emerged one by one--became Kathy and then, hastily, Mrs Cat (to give her the benefit of the doubt, said Dad).

I always danced to a different piper. Not waltzes but Highland Fling. No friends: nothing but age in common with my classmates. No dreams of mommy-hood. Mommies did housework instead of reading or climbing trees, and tended to babies instead of cats. I wanted none of it. Especially housework, cooking, or sharing a bedroom. (Our house had two parents, one son, four daughters and three bedrooms. QED.) In the '30's this attitude was tantamount to rejecting Jehovah, the Flag, Motherhood and baseball: in fact, it was. Nor would I consider any of the only other options available to girls: nurse, schoolteacher, secretary.

What *did* I want? Well--kitties, for starters. And my very own bedroom. Books about girls having adventures. Going to England where all my favorite books and history took place, and a friendly robin like in 'Secret Garden'. I might even write another book...

I had already written my first. When I was four. Mother saved it. It was a masterpiece of literature, lavishly illustrated, brilliantly plotted.

It read: *The sun roze up. The littul girl got up and dresed and had brefruss and went out to play with her kitty. The End.* Then, having temporarily exhausted my genius--and also realizing that I had no idea how to make a really truly book with covers, I rested on my laurels for 25 years. And planned my future.

It might cost more than my two-cents allowance, I realized. But I figured *that* one out! I was five when the Crash hit. By the time I was ten, without even reading David Copperfield, I had invented the whole of Economics. Simple. Always spend less than your allowance and save what's left. Worked very well, too--after a slow start.

With the help of Figgy.

She's my Faery Godmother (F.G.: Figgy for short). Sunday School said she was my guardian angel. Clearly I needed one, being a difficult child who asked awkward questions, usually about cats going to Heaven. (On being told No, I said then *I* wasn't going, either. I think they were fairly sure I wouldn't be invited. So *that* was all right, then.) But Figgy was never a Biblical angel! No feathered wings and harps for *that* one! Rather, iridescent wings and bagpipes. A spirit with a warped sense of humor, addicted to wildly implausible Coincidences that would make any fiction editor shudder--but effective. Together we managed most of my aims and a few unexpected ones--

Well, who'd have expected Pearl Harbor?

So I joined the WAVES and spent a challenging six months at boot camp and training school learning how to repair and calibrate aircraft instruments, and then two years at a very bad base learning to grit my teeth and endure, and never to sign away my autonomy. There was no equipment for my training, either; so I wasted it at A&R, barracks detail, and as runner for arguably the worst Exec in the Navy. I was totally alien: made not a single friend--and there weren't even any stray cats to befriend. (They'd not have lasted long, anyway.) But as the song said, "You can get into the Navy, but just try to get out". Still there was a library--so I spent my spare time there and saved virtually all of my pay.

Free at last, I used that and the GI Bill and part-time work to get my degree. Augmented goal: write books *and* cross the ocean; *and* buy a country cottage in England with cats *and* robins. By a roundabout route. Wrote books in S.F., L.A., Berkeley, Oakland for starters; made fleeting visits to most of Europe and the Near East, spent five years helping Mother develop and produce *Listen & Learn with Phonics*. (No cats any of those places, either.)

And somehow, another twenty-five years on, there I was in England, unencumbered by debts, husband, children (or, alas, cats), living on royalties and bank interest in my very own cottage complete with English robin, in a non-village called Headley Down, spread between Headley Village and Headley Common. The houses had no numbers, only names; because much of rural England still do it that way--which is charming, quaint, and totally confusing. Distraught travelers kept pulling up on narrow dirt Fairview Road, to glare at my sign, and beg to know where they could find Hacienda, or Twin Pines, or Mum's Dream. Usually I didn't know.

My house, when I bought it for a song, was named--ugh!--Hazeldene! I promptly re-named it Sutemi, a judo term wherein you hurl yourself to the ground in order to throw your opponent--making sure, of course, that he hits first. Means 'Full commitment'. (Well, you can hardly change your mind halfway down, can you?)

Sutemi had four rooms strung side by side, with a roofed veranda in front of two of them. It made my bedroom very dark and gloomy inside even after I had a window put in the veranda roof (which didn't help much, but did cause polite head-scratching. Odd folks they Americans, mm?)

At the back, a hall with doors to each front room ran clear across from study through the kitchen to the bathroom. (I never saw an open plan in England. Every room is separate, kept closed so you can heat just that room and let the rest of the house sulk in damp cold. Tradition. Often, no central heating.)

I chose room 4 as my bedroom because it was nearer the loo, (toilet to Americans) in case I needed it at 2 AM. (How could I guess that Mother would regularly phone at 2 AM because she always thought it was 8 hours the *other* way, so I'd have to run even further over icy floors to the living room?)

Sutemi was surrounded by the requisite high thick laurel hedge (the English do love their privacy) and contained in its quarter-acre a shy hedgehog with many fleas, a garden with arbor, a song thrush with a lovely repertoire and the required cheeky resident robin straight from The Secret Garden, who sometimes sat on my fingers or trowel. His bright intelligent black eyes with a narrow rim of brown were friendly, trusting and alert for any nice worms. All the neighbors were friendly, too--except the recluse beyond my west hedge, whom I had never so much as glimpsed in seven years--but none were Kindred Spirits, of course. Neighbors had never had anything in common with my Different Drummer.

Never mind, I made wonderful friends all over England: just not in Headley Down. First thing I did on arrival was gather all my courage and take the Mensa test. Bravest thing I ever did. You had to have 154 IQ--and I was sure mine was nowhere near that--which of course, was why I had to have a go. I'd have been crushed if I failed--but a coward not to try. To my amazement, I came out at 158--and I walked into the most delightful friends I had ever imagined, who, since I didn't drive, met me in London and drove me on to meetings all over England. Alas, none lived anywhere near me.

I took up judo. Every village has its club, and there were week-end courses accessible by British Rail. More wonderful friends. I even went all the way up to London every week for a class at the Ministry of Defence [sic] taught by my dear friend Ivy.

Which was one way I learned about National Health.

It's a story in itself--worth telling, perhaps, to readers who live under Capitalized Medicine. I busted my ankle in judo class. Badly. The ambulance rushed me (free) from the London judo class to St.Thomas Hospital, where they took one look, an X-ray, my name and address and whom to notify. No nonsense about insurance or even whether I was a British citizen, which I wasn't. Looked at the X-ray, sent for the top surgeon and the next thing I knew I was waking up in traction, in an airy, spacious four-bed ward where a watching nurse sent at once for the Sister who sent for Matron who sent for the surgeon, who grinned sympathetically. Said I had certainly done it brown, hadn't I? I had the most--er--*smashing* Potts fracture he had ever seen. Like a jigsaw puzzle in there, he said: took a couple of hours to sort out the bits and put them back where they belonged. But not to worry: it'd be as good as new.

I asked when I could go for my Brown Belt. He said not to rush it. I'd be in traction for three weeks, then plaster for six, then get the muscles strong again--and I could expect it to hurt decreasingly for 7 or 8 months. But in--5 months, say?--all the jigsaw bits would be perfectly *healed* and I could get back on a judo mat--but this time try not to practice with large chaps of lower grades.

Testosterone sets in," he told me ruefully. "When they're losing to a tiny woman, and have run out of skill, they fall back on brute strength without even realizing what they're doing."

I said I'd noticed that. We grinned at each other.

So I was their guest for three weeks. Literally. Didn't cost a penny. Lots of TLC. No TV or private phones, but no one expected or missed them, and BBC radio with headphones had everything anyone could want. And the librarian came daily and asked if she could order any special book.

"Japanese 17th Century martial arts?" I suggested tentatively.

She didn't even flinch. "Might take a day or two, luv."

From my bed I had an uninterrupted view through a wide window reaching from window-seat to ceiling, across Westminster Bridge to the Houses of Parliament and Big Ben, whose quarter-hour chimes comforted me during the nights when pain kept me awake. (They quickly discovered what no one else ever had: that my liver is odd, and normal pain medication has on me about as much affect as does alcohol. Which is nil.) So they found something that worked a bit better and never mind how often. Needs of patients, they said, trumped rules. They kept a sharp eye on me, too.

"Hurting again, luv? You must *tell* us! We don't *want* you in pain: it isn't good for you!"

At night Matron would wander through all the wards, sharp-eyed, knowing when I was awake even if my eyes were closed. She'd send for tea: that infinitely delicious and comforting national drink, which I never did learn how to make properly. And she arranged that if ever I fancied a Cuppa, even at 3AM, just ring twice and they'd bring it.

I was almost sorry to leave. They made a celebration of it: scones and clotted cream for tea, everyone gathering, the surgeon in to wish me my Black Belt soon. I could have had a free ambulance ride the fifty miles back to Sutemi--but Mensa and judo friends were there to take me, so I thanked everyone, flourished my newly-plastered leg, demonstrated my brilliance on crutches, hugged matron and the surgeon, waved goodbye at the desk, waltzed--well actually hobbled--out and went home to precisely the dénouement the surgeon had predicted.

The Brighton judo week-end, five months later, was my first serious venture on the mat again and I couldn't do *anything* any more, and feared--not getting hurt, but making a fool of myself and shaming my Blue Belt. And then I saw a gorgeous ginger-headed young woman across the tatami. Not pretty like movies stars or my sister, but-- I, the writer, fished for words. Couldn't find 'em. She wore beauty as unconsciously as does May or a cat. She was far too good for her Orange Belt: Green at least. Even Blue? I suspected she was better than I--even allowing for Potts fractures. In any event, I knew her at once for an Old Friend, and edged over to her. She gave me a lovely smile and took me under her wing while pretending it was the other way around. Asked me earnestly for instruction (which I could do very well in theory, and she never asked me to *demonstrate*, bless her!) and kept telling me how very brilliant and skilled I was (which I wasn't really: only in groundwork). And she has maintained that fiction ever since.

But she lived in Hove and I in Headley Down, so we virtually never saw each other for the next few years, and I still had no real friends living near. By now I had a score of medals in Scottish Dance, had reached 3rd Dan Black Belt, County Coach, National Referee and International Examiner in Judo, taken up copper enameling and acquired Special Friends at Reed College, British Mensa, Great Books and judo, living all over the world and Great Britain--except in Headley Down. I'd had a dozen books published. I had my house in England. I had travelled a lot. I had most of my ambitions, in fact--except the cat.

My fault, that. Well, it hadn't been practical, had it? 'Fancy-free' involved 'foot-loose'; and I kept going off to Paris, Israel, Greece, Denmark, Malta, Kenya, Yugoslavia. My regular visits to California were always for at least a month--and I sometimes returned via freighter through the Panama Canal, which was another four weeks. Actually, I was just back from a long-saved-for six-week freighter cruise with Mom, around the Pacific to the Antipodes--during which time, it now became clear, the recluse had been replaced!

How did I know this? Elementary, my dear--er--Holmes. The Recluse was known to dislike cats. But now a stalwart black and white cat emerged from the west hedge and paused to look around possessively. Delighted, I spoke to him! He turned on all his heels and stalked back through the hedge. My feelings were deeply wounded. Cats usually love me. What had I done to make this one act as if I were a vivisectionist? He kept on doing it, too! For weeks!

Then one day an elderly man drove along to my gate, walked up to my door, knocked and said diffidently that he was Fred who now lived next door, and he'd heard I had no car, so would I like to join him on his shopping excursions?

I was delighted. The village was six hilly miles away, busses ran hourly and bikes were limited both in carrying-space and protection from rain. Returning from our first trip, I thanked him and then voiced my complaint.

"If that's your black and white cat who keeps running away, he's hurt my feelings."

"Oh," said Fred. "Come along, then, and I'll introduce you." At which he turned into his driveway, and when the cat rushed up, he said "Sooty, this is Sally; she's a friend."

Sooty said Oh, why hadn't anyone said so? and *that* was all right, then; and rubbed himself against my legs. And meant it. Henceforth he was as much at my place as at Fred's. In fact, it was the start of two beautiful friendships. Figgy arranged it. I had no relatives in England, and Fred had none in the world. I think he had never had a girl friend, either. Scared of females, so his coming to my door was incredibly brave. But when it became clear that we both firmly eschewed romance, a blissfully platonic friendship bloomed.

And at last I had a cat. Sort of. Sooty loved me. I had him and Fred over for dinner at least once a week, plus all British *and* American holidays. Fred appreciated that. His home diet was traditional English stodge, like steak-and-kidney pie, spotted dick (a boiled suet pudding) toad-in-the-hole (sausage baked in batter) bangers and mash (sausages buried in mashed potato) Cornish pasties, and the ubiquitous baked-beans-on-toast with chips. I introduced him to a lot of American food, and it was a great credit to him that he tried everything and liked most. The British are wildly unadventurous in eating, and Fred was a particularly conservative (and Conservative) Englishman. But he did enjoy our holiday meals. All the American ones, plus Boxing Day, Hogmanay, Guy Fawkes day, Good Friday, and four Bank Holidays. We celebrated them all, and birthdays. When I got a tiny English freezer (two cubic feet, which was considered large) we celebrated again with that uniquely American dish fried chicken.

After I had lived there a dozen years or so, the authorities apparently decided that as a resident I had not only the right but the duty to vote, citizen or not; so they began sending me a ballot, and Fred would drive us down, as he now drove me everywhere I needed to go. The poll-takers would greet us, ask us how we were voting (perfectly legal there) and we would smile benignly and announce that we had come to cancel each other out.

Inside, we were each presented with a 3x4 slip of paper bearing two words: 'Conservative' and 'Liberal'. (I wanted to vote Labour, but it was such a Conservative district that Labour never bothered to run there.) We checked our respective squares--always for the party, never the person, in England--and left.

Fred was so hide-bound that it really amounted to bigotry. No tolerance for lefties, foreigners, gays, lovers, other races, other religions, Yids or Wogs. Not in theory. In person he was infinitely kind and incredibly tolerant--of me, anyway. Here was I, foreign, left-wing, practically a heathen--or at least not Church of England: an opinionated woman who more than once told Fred that I couldn't call him reactionary, really, because that word implied some sort of movement.

He would just smile benignly, taking no offense because I meant none and he liked me. He was the only person except Dad with whom I could indulge in no-holds-barred argument without, ever, anger on either side. He was, I realized, quite like Dad: both carefully-taught racists and anti-Semites whose minds held prejudices that their hearts simply did not get. Tongue deep, it was. I never knew either of them to do anything cruel... And both loved cats. And vice-versa. QED!

But when I got a washing machine (taking out the only kitchen pan-cupboards to crowd it in beside the sink because Sutemi was not made for washers *anywhere)* and offered to do Fred's washing, he blushingly refused. Dear Fred: kind, shy, generous: infinitely tolerant of my American heresies--if of little else. He and Dad were--I think--about the only adults I've known who loved me almost as cats do, unconditionally.

Dad visited me every few years. He and Fred quite took to each other. And Sooty. And Dad was for the first time bitten by the travel bug. We went to Malta together, and for his next two visits I had a brilliant idea on how to treat Dad's skin-deep (I hoped!) bigotry.

First I took him to Israel. He loved it. He took to the Israelis at once, and, innocent that he was, would chat happily, using terms like *kike*--without even suspecting it was offensive! And, realizing this, they smiled and didn't take offense. So next time I took him to Kenya, and he loved it there, too. I *knew* it!

Fred started having dizzy spells that worried him--mainly, bless his heart! lest he should be unable to take me to judo, which I was now teaching in Haslemere, twelve miles away. (*Every* English village has its pub, church, village hall, news-shop, yearly panto--and judo club.) It occurred to us that perhaps I had better overcome my poor judgment of distances and learn to drive Fred's mini-van, just in case. So I did.

Driving tests there are--interesting. To start, L (learner) plates on the car and a qualified driver with you are compulsory and strictly enforced. And a learner can't go on a motorway under any circumstances until he passes the test. No written exam--but my instructor warned me that no one ever passes the first time, and the young, the old, and females seldom the second or third. (I didn't ask why. I wouldn't have liked the answer.) Moreover, once you've duly failed, you must wait six months before trying again. Need a *lot* more practice, you do.

They never tell you why you've failed--but my instructor knew the examiner, who confided it to him. I had (a) failed to put on the *hand brake* at a stop sign, and (b) when turning a corner I had stopped for the pedestrians on the cross walk.

I asked bitterly if I was supposed to run them down. Got no answer. Nor did Swanage reply when I wrote them with the same question. I did pass the second attempt, thank goodness! Just in time to drive to spend Christmas with my dear Judo friends Ivy and Len. They lived about 70 miles north-east, across the Thames, in Essex; and the bus-train-Underground-train-bus trip was a long cold nightmare even if you got seats, which at holiday times you usually didn't.

So off I started in the mini-van: buoyant, careful, assiduously avoiding the motorway. I had not yet driven on one, and I planned to start with Fred aboard--a*nd* in good weather, which this was not. It started to snow. And the signposting confused me. Especially when I came to a T-crossing which was coy about what was to the left, but definite about the right. Guildford, it said. Having driven through Guildford half an hour ago, I turned left--and found myself on the motorway! *Going in the wrong direction,* south, to Gatwick Airport! And there were no off-ramps for the whole 25 miles. I wept as I drove implacably away from Ivy and Len; less because I was lost and late than from sheer fury. When I finally got there, two or three hours later, they hugged me and commiserated. Neither of them drove. (Well, working-class Londoners usually didn't.) But they had, they said, found a bottle of that exotic and rare American drink, bourbon, as a treat for me, and they proudly poured me a glass. I beamed and sipped.

It was Southern Comfort.

The shop had assured them--doubtless in innocent ignorance of untraditional foreign booze--that it was a brand of bourbon. I never disillusioned them, of course, so they saved it for all my future visits. Bless their hearts, it must have cost a bomb.

Somewhen in the next few months, when Fred no longer dared drive, he quietly deeded his little mini-van over to me, and when I found out, wouldn't even let me pay him for it.

Meanwhile, National Health took Fred to hospital for a fortnight while they tried in vain to discover the cause of those dizzy spells; so naturally he asked me to feed Sooty. "At my house: I doubt if he'll want to leave it."

So I did. For two days. Then I returned from judo on a nasty wet November night to find Sooty waiting frantically at my door. His Human had Deserted him, he cried piteously, and would I take him in?

I did, of course. He checked to make sure Fred wasn't there, then followed his New Human all over the house, clearly intending to spend the night in the bedroom--

--until he reached the doorway. Froze, he did, fur standing on end, staring wild-eyed at the innocent-looking far left corner of the ceiling. Hissed, yowled, spat, backed out. Nothing, he said firmly, would induce him to stay in *there.* He meant it, too. Only at the end of the fortnight did he sidle in, glaring warily, and arrange himself on the furthest corner of the bed--eyes wide open facing the enemy.

(I never did figure out what he was seeing. But three years later my own cats were fascinated by the same corner, standing up on the furniture and leaping up to bat excitedly at Whateveritwas.)

When Fred arrived home, Sooty nearly went bonkers. Had two Humans again, he purred, head-pushing Fred all over and then rushing back to love me as well. Fred, bless him, wasn't at all jealous. Just beamed like a successful matchmaker.

Friendship flourished even more after that. We cut a passage in the five-foot-wide wide myrtle hedge between us, because it was idiotic to keep rushing all the way around. Fred had a full half-acre, mine was a quarter-acre, and both our houses were set well back, so it was a considerable hike around. Fred could now see my back door from his kitchen window; and often reported without reproach that Sooty had spent two hours shouting at my door in the rain, but apparently I hadn't heard him.

It was a terrible shock to both of us when Sooty suddenly died. By then I was popping over nightly, ostensibly to visit, but also because I was uneasy about those dizzy spells, which still baffled the doctors. And his house was as old as mine, but without 'modern' heating like mine: no heat at all, in fact, except the coal-burning Aga stove in the kitchen--which became of necessity his sitting room; so I wanted to be sure he was all right. Sooty used to leap joyfully from Fred's lap to mine as soon as I sat down.

But one Friday, Sooty crawled instead of leaping, and Fred said worriedly that he hadn't felt well all day. I was to leave next morning for a two-day craft market way up in Norfolk, but I said we'd take him to the vet first if he didn't feel better.

He didn't. So we took him in at nine A.M.--and buried him at ten. It was a kind of galloping kidney failure, we gathered. He shrank almost visibly on the examination table, and the vet said instant euthanasia was the only kind thing.

We drove home with the little body, both sobbing with no pretense at Stiff Upper Lips. Needless to say, I didn't go to Norfolk. Poor Fred had lost his only family, and needed someone to grieve with and to participate in the funeral--and dig the grave, too; for Fred really wasn't up to it. When I'd finished, he called me in to see Sooty. He had wrapped him lovingly in his dead mother's best lace tablecloth, and put in his paws the catnip mouse I'd given him. It nearly broke my heart. I put a heavy stone on the grave so the foxes couldn't get at him, realizing for the first time what the probable original reason for gravestones might be.

It may have been about then that Figgy returned from some *peri* vacation or other, and got into the act, which was how Fred got Fluffer and I got Domino and Deirdre.

His grief was dreadful. It was bad enough for me--and Sooty hadn't even been mine. Fred mourned that he could never bear to have another cat. I knew I had to do something, at once.

"Of *course* no one will ever replace Sooty, Fred; but you will always need a furry loving little friend. And what's more--" (the clincher) "--somewhere in some cattery is a cat who needs *you* most awfully."

That did it, of course. Off we went to the catteries. In England most villages also has a cat-lover who is kept supplied by the RSPCA with moggies to be cherished until someone adopts them. (Euthanasia merely for not being adopted is unknown.) Figgy probably went along for the kicks. And of course it was *just* coincidence that we went all around the villages without finding the Cat Who Truly Needed Fred, until we got to Liss. There Kate, the strong-minded cattery lady, took one look at us and beamed. She had *just* the ones for us, she announced: one each.

"Not me," I said firmly. "I haven't finished traveling yet. Just Fred."

Kate ignored this. She took us out back and showed us a bouncing, tail-waving little calico, just right for Fred. (She wasn't, of course, and everyone but Kate knew it, including the cat, who trotted off on business of her own.) And over in that shed, Kate added, buoyant, was Sally's. I followed her finger inside and beheld a sorrowful tortie who hissed at me half-heartedly. One of four cats, Kate called from without, whose owner had died. She had never had Her Very Own Human.

Right! I backed out and pushed Fred in. There was quite a long silence. Then he emerged. "When can I take her home?"

So that was fine. Fred asked what the adoption fee was, and Kate said Oh, that was up to him. Whatever he wished--*if* he wished. He did, of course, and off we went. He named her Fluffer, and she was very sweet--for about three days. Then she realized that Fred really *was* Her Very Own, and promptly became so totally possessive that she went for everyone who wasn't Fred. Especially me, because Fred liked me. This grieved me, because the last time a cat had seriously taken against me was when I was three and put Blueboy in the dresser drawer--and *he* was annoyed only briefly. Moreover, this wasn't to be solved by an introduction from Fred.

Enter Figgy again. I went back to Kate's to get something-or-other for Fred. Kate said hallo and how was Fluffer? I said she adored Fred and hissed at me. Kate said that just showed I needed one of my own. I said sorrowfully, not *yet*. I hadn't yet been to Portugal, the Scilly Isles, Gibraltar, Zimbabwe or even York. Or even on a canal-boat trip. Kate said never mind, but I must see the four-month-old feral kittens they'd just trapped in the wilds of the Common. In the long low cage in that shed, she said, and she'd be right back with the something-or-other.

So I went in, and there was a small black triangle in the furthest corner of the cage with flattened ears, showing pink tonsils and sounding like a despairing adder. I said I'd had enough of being hissed at, thank you very much, and where was the other one?

Creeping bravely toward my corner, that's where it was. Scared but game. Like Fred approaching my door that first time. Black tail clinging so hard to the little white tummy it was almost invisible, huge ears, golden eyes round with apprehension--and the most adorable perfect black teardrop covering its little white nose.

Kate returned with the something-or-other to find me staring helplessly at the little baggage. "It says its name is Domino and what took me so long?"

"She," said Kate, looking like Jehovah at the end of the Sixth Day. "They're both females. When can you take them?"

"I can't!" I wailed regretfully. "It wouldn't be fair! I'm away too much. I'll be away most of December and over Christmas, and--" The penny dropped belatedly. "*THEM!?!*" I stared at the pink tonsils in horror. "No *fear*! I really *can't*..."

After Christmas would be fine, said Kate and Domino affably. The pink tonsils hissed.

CHAPTER TWO

THE COMING OF THE CATS

And then Jenny wrote. We'd been independently busy since that meeting in '69: I with judo and travel (I'd virtually stopped writing), and she was even busier, divesting herself of a thoroughly unsatisfactory husband and raising her two small sons on her own. Then she moved north and married an Oxford professor named Max, and produced two more sons--identical twins named Jay and Lee. Or possibly Lee and Jay? Who knew but Jenny?

I visited them in Oxford once, in '79 after the twins were born, and six or eight times, later, in Reading. Max was almost a stereotypical Oxford don: suave, elegant, kindly, with a smart black beard and a brilliant mind apparently 90% in ancient India. Aside from those few visits there was just the occasional note or phone call. But it was one of those rare friendships that blossomed at first sight and flourished without need of propinquity.

And now Figgy became a busy little faery godmother again.

Reading
25th Nov, '82
Dear Sally,

You might remember that when I told you I was going to marry Max, there was a four-second deadly hush before you went into your rather unconvincing "Whoopee, isn't that great?" act. Well, eat your heart out, you cynical Colonial Cousin, you.

Guess what I'm getting for Christmas from "My God, what does she want with another man, wasn't the first one enough for anybody?"

A Siamese kitten.

I spent my childhood with them, of course, since Mother bred them, and so have a rough idea of how to handle them. But Max's sole experience of Siamese cats was when a couple with whom he was staying went out shopping leaving him alone in their London flat. Alone, that is, apart from two Siamese cats. Who took a scunner (get out the Scots dictionary) to him, and the afternoon ended up with Max locking himself in the kitchen (the only room in the flat with a door that they couldn't open) with two angry Siamese outside it wailing and wauling that they were going to tear him apart when they got at him.

It really is enough to put one off cats in general, and Siamese in particular, for life, isn't it? And never mind the fact that, if they really HAD been after his blood, they would have got it, without any of this fore-warning nonsense. An angry Siamese will go straight for your face, Buster, and you'd better be a quick blinker if you value your sight. Luckily for mankind, they usually love people. But it is not so very long ago that they guarded temples and palaces in Thailand, and did a very good job, too.

So when Max asked me what I wanted for Christmas, and I told him, and he drew a deep breath and said "All right"-- I call that courage. And love.

Eat your heart out.

Anyway, I'll keep you posted about this new Aristocrat.

Love, Jenny

PS: Please stop breaking bits of yourself.

PPS: You've had a dozen novels published. Would you read the one I've finished and tell me honestly what you think? I just don't KNOW if it's any good.

Sutemi, Fairview Road,
Headley Down, Hants.
Dec. 2, 1982
Dear Jenny,

How super! I might have considered marriage myself, if I'd thought he'd give me a kitten. Siamese, too! I never knew your mum bred them. But then there were lots of things we never got around to discussing while hurling each other around the judo tatami that week-end, weren't there? Like cats.

You *didn't* know I'd always longed to have my very own cat one day when I've finished traveling, did you? Thought not. It's Figgy, that's what. I've mentioned her? The Faery Godmother who doesn't do much about keeping me from breaking bits of myself, but mucks about in my life like a dime-thriller novelist. So now I have an urgent question. Has Figgy been nudging *you*? Because though I think it's marvelous of dear Max, I find the timing of all this very suspicious indeed.

I guess what I'm trying to say is, if you wait too long, I may, like it or not, get a cat before you do. Two, if Kate has anything to say about it. Kate and Figgy.

In a nutshell, I'm being pushed on all sides to adopt **two** cats when I'm not sure I'm even ready for one. I was like the innocent in a gothic novel. Good old Sally, doing Fred a kindly turn--only to get hit with two feral kittens. One, who says her name is Domino, went straight to my heart, and I'm really tempted. Actually, I've about decided to give up travel so I can take her. But she has this angry black sister, all tonsils and hisses, and Kate says it's a package deal, that Poor Little Smudge is so needful and dependent on her sister, and she'll just pine away if separated-- Which is all very well, but even one scares me. It's a lot of responsibility, and I don't know enough, and I learned in judo not to try throws before you can breakfall.

Besides, I'm fed up with being hissed at. Fluffer is quite enough, thank you.

So I've said I absolutely draw the line at those tonsils--but it's been nearly a week, and they're all on at me. Fred says she *needs* me (deliberately quoting what I kept saying to him, the stinker) and Kate phones almost daily to tell me how happy Domino is, and *she* knows her name already, but poor little Smudge doesn't respond to hers at all.

I tell her, with a name like Smudge, neither would I.

Jenny, how could I possibly take on *two* kittens? *Feral!* I've never had anything to do with actually *feral* cats! I think I'm crazy to consider even *one*.

Keep me in touch about your coming aristocrat. Where will you get it? Give Max my love and tell him I'm almost sorry I didn't see him first. (Well-- sort of-- in a way--) And if you see Figgy, send her packing.

Also-- Sure, I'll read your ms. for you. *And* be honest. But remember, I'm a writer, not an editor. And I've no pull with publishers even for my own books. If they like it, they like it.

Love, Sally

PS: I've broken hardly any bits lately. Only the dislocated thumb when Nigel forgot that he weighs 16 stone to my eight.

(Actually, I was--as always--dismayed at being asked to read a friend's manuscript! Every single one so far had been truly dreadful, beyond hope--and how do you tell friends that? People think *anyone* can write: it's just words, isn't it? No exotic techniques like music or dance: you just write it down and let a friend In the Know get it published for you. (And, alas, however much writers--or would-be writers--say they really want people to Be Honest, the fact is, we don't. We want people to say how marvelous it is.)

Then are the ones--inevitably male--who don't know the difference between a writer and a free hack, and order me to write their books for them. "You need the work and I need the money," proclaimed one arrogantly. (But at least I didn't care about hurting *his* feelings.)

10 Dec. '82

Dear Sally,

Are you trying to steal my thunder or something? Getting two kittens to my one? Or are you really going to leave that pathetic, frightened little creature in a rescue centre, no longer merely pathetic and frightened but also lonely? Damned right, she'll pine away. Poor little thing. Poor little you, with that on your conscience.

Well, we've found Dustanna Samantha. My Siamese kitten. Max sent off a deposit last week, and we are to collect her in a couple of weeks. I've not seen her yet, but a copy of her pedigree arrived today, bristling with grand champions, and a letter from the breeder who says he hopes we'll love her and take her before she tears the house apart. Rather daunting, really. I've been shopping for litter and trays, brushes and combs, food, dishes, and so on. It all adds up! (Or have you found that out?) Also, the only possible way to get to Samantha's current abode is by car, and I haven't got one. I phoned the hire company, and when they told me how much it costs to hire a car, I thought they had misunderstood, and were trying to sell me one.

Still, well-bred Seal Point Siamese are not thick on the ground these days. You take anything there is, fast, before someone else gets it. We telephoned I don't know how many breeders before we found Sam, and they had all sold all theirs. They really did try to help, especially when they found I'd had Siamese: they are chary of selling to the unwary! "Are you houseproud?" is a question I have never been asked before, and I got it every ten minutes. I would love to be houseproud, but I haven't got the time, and anyway, I hate housework.

Max is claiming to be doing overtime to pay for her, so I have to stop now and feed the twins.

Love, Jenny

P.S. How are you getting on with Fluffer?

Sutemi

Boxing Day, 1982

Dear Jenny,

Now don't you start, too! I'm being bullied, that's what. By everyone. By Fred looking sorrowful. By Kate and Domino. By Figgy. By dreams of pink tonsils. I'd hoped the month's delay would sort things out, and some soppy nut would adopt Smudge or she'd get less Dependent, but Kate's just been on at me again.

I said No Smudge. I said Smudge simply hates me, just as Fluffer does; and I couldn't stand *two* of them spitting at me all the time. Nobody listens. I'm nervous enough taking *one*, and I hate being pushed, and *everyone's* pushing me. No. *No*, **NO**, *NO*!

---Combs? And so forth? I'm afraid to ask-- What is And so forth?

Love and Happy New Year to Max and the boys, but I'm not sure I'm speaking to you.

Sally

Jan. 3, 1983

Dear Jenny,

Yes, I know you probably haven't even had my last letter, with Christmas mail so slow and all, but I do have a bone to pick with you. Two, in fact. *And* with Fred, Domino, Kate, Smudge and Figgy. I *told* you all I didn't *want* two cats, not even two friendly ones, let alone ferals and another hisser. I *told* you no, and *no*, and **no**, and *NO!*...

...So they sat together in the carrier coming home, on Fred's lap: Fred looking intolerably smug, Figgy probably smirking with Kate, Domino peering anxiously through the bars (she takes life very seriously, she does. A worrier) and Smudge-Tonsils sitting round-eyed and quiet--except just once when she undertook a very professional examination of the carrier latch.

"That's going to be your lively one," Fred commented judiciously.

I almost ran off the road. "NO! That's the timid helpless quiet one! Kate said so! She *promised*!"

Fred says he distinctly heard Figgy guffaw at that point.

Anyhow, we got home, and I'd got everything, even And So Forth, but nobody had mentioned the wisdom of keeping them in one room until they got used to things; especially ferals. So I didn't. And almost at once it was too late. We opened the cat box in the kitchen. Domino, tail and ears apprehensively low, tip-toed out, and slunk cautiously along the wall to the sand box. From behind her an impetuous furry black bullet shot out and vanished.

It took a long time to find her. Wedged into about three inches behind the dressing table. "Let her stay there: she'll be all right," Fred suggested.

But Smudge was having none of *that*. We had found her, therefore she was no longer safe. So she moved and I was scared not to know where she was, so we started over. That's how it's been ever since: her hiding in simply impossible places that *have* to be narrower than her tiny elegant head. And then hissing and going to find another even more impossible one. Like squeezed behind my noisy old washer, where she sat firmly through an incredibly violent complete cycle. Said she preferred that monster to the two-legged one.

I said why didn't she go explore with Domino?

She said Bother Domino.

She is now holed up under the bathtub. You may recall, my tub is on cast-iron claws, with particle board all around. Only now it has a large gap at the outer corner, which is how I found her. Having looked everywhere else except the loft, which I didn't want even to think about. Shone in the flashlight (torch to you) and there was a pair of glowing emerald eyes at the very back corner, defying me to reach her *there*. Which I couldn't, of course.

She's been there ever since, hissing when I appear at the corner crack and talk to her. Says she's *never* coming out. I believe her.

Maybe it's just as well. If I could get my hands on her right now, I'd take her straight back to Kate. Or you. Or Figgy. Or Fred! (See how Fluffer'd like *that*.)

In the meantime, Domino is settling in. Sort of. She really is a worry-wart! Lives by my contribution to the Beatitudes, which I call the 13th, and goes "Blessed are they who expect the worst, for they shall not be disappointed."

She spent the whole of the first night creeping around the house, commenting in a series of tiny nervous yelps which I translate into "Does it BITE?" Never saw a Common like this before, she said. Where were the gorse and pines and yummy voles? Was it going to turn out all right? Had she made a mistake in Choosing me?

As for having a nice cuddly cat in my lap, forget it. I can't even stroke her, much less cuddle. If I try even moving a fingertip gently down her back, the back drops and slithers away like water. In fact, the only time I can touch her at all is to curl fingers around her tail *en passant* and let it flow through as she moves on. Still, I think she *wants* to trust me. She comes and leans engagingly against my ankles now and then, her front paws going up and down like little white pistons. I don't know where she sleeps: certainly not on me. But at least she knows about sand boxes. And while I'm far from house-proud myself, I-- Well, the thing is, I don't know where Not-Smudge is going potty. (To the loo, as you Brits so elegantly put it.) If she's doing it under that tub, I'll *never* be able to get at it. So far there's no smell, but--

Meanwhile, keep me posted about Samantha. At least I *saw* what I was getting. You're just getting a pig in a poke? If there is any justice, those faint misgivings I detect in your last letter will turn to horrid reality, and she'll do a Not-Smudge, or something similar on you.

Love to Max and the boys. I was going to ask Max to marry me and get me a Siamese kitten, but I think I've already got more in that line than I can handle. I'm thinking of going off cats and trying for hedgehogs or ferrets. Or English robins.

Love, Sally

PS: Fluffer still hisses and spits. Not too proud to accept goodies from me, of course--but having snatched them out of my hand, she savages me neatly before I can jerk away. So now I do have broken bits.

Reading
Dear Sally,

Heh-heh-heh! ONE cat is so banal and boring (unless it's a Siamese).

Yes, she's here, and nobody is going to be allowed to forget it. WE damned nearly got two, as well. Samantha and Solitaire, because Max fell for Solitaire, too. The breeders even offered us a discount! But the bank manager is twiddling his eyebrows at us these days, so I put my foot down. If we want more we'll breed them. But I think one is enough.[1]

These breeders live in the middle of nowhere, no trains or buses, only taxis. And the car I hired cost almost as much as she did, and I'm not saying how much either were. First we met Mum Cat, a lovely person with a wise face and an intelligently questioning voice. Then we were assaulted by three kittens, who launched themselves at us, shouting. Sam, Solitaire, and their small blue-point brother Simmie, who was leaving for his new home that afternoon.

Once the riot had run its course, Simmie went to sleep behind the cat-proof fireguard. (I DON'T KNOW! One minute he was standing on the bookshelf yelling at his sisters and the next minute he was behind the fireguard fast asleep. I think he teleported but I didn't see him do it.) Sam came over and chewed a button off my anorak and then stuck a paw in my eye to see if I blinked (I did!) and Solitaire climbed onto the back of the sofa behind Max and tried to hook off his toupee. Once she discovered that all that hair really did grow out of his head, she sat down and made personal remarks about it in a loud and penetrating voice. When did he last have a haircut? she wanted to know. Why is it so thick and black? Is he a Persian?

We were both so entertained by this that we didn't notice Sam, and when I next looked she had emptied my handbag and eaten half my driving licence. She is the type who takes advantage of a moment's inattention. I shall have to remember that.

Anyway, having firmly and regretfully said we could NOT take Solitaire

---

1 Famous last words!

too, we brought Sam home. She was rather subdued in the car. But once we got back, she livened up.

I shall never forget her first meeting with the twins. I had told them they were to be very good and quiet, and wait for her to come to them. So they sat in the hall, good as gold, and waited, and waited, and waited, hardly daring to breathe. Finally I went to investigate, and found Sons Numbers One and Two downstairs, playing with her. So I beat them up a bit, and said they were to let Sam come upstairs to meet Lee and Jay. A few minutes later, she came tearing up the stairs, shot round the corner, and came face to face with the twins. She stopped dead, and looked absolutely astonished. Then up went her tail, and she came forward.

"Hullo," she said, "I'm Sam. Why are you two?" (Well, it was a reasonable question, they being identical.)

Ten minutes later, they were all galloping around the flat playing a version of musical-chairs-without-the-music that the twins insist Sam invented.

You know the rule about allowing a new kitten plenty of peace and quiet in order to settle in to her new home. (Or perhaps you don't. You seem to have harried poor Not-Smudge a bit.) Well, speaking of peace and quiet, I wish Sam would give me some.

I mean, three o'clock in the morning I woke up to find Max throwing ping pong balls for her. He told me she couldn't sleep. And it was he who had said we should put a hot water bottle in her box in case she was cold or lonely. Box be damned! That kitten has not set foot in that box. She sleeps where people are meant to sleep, in bed. On his chest under the duvet, and he'd better not fidget, otherwise she wakes up and lectures him. It's his own fault. I told him he should be firm with her, and he looked at me as though I had suggested frying her.

Oh yes. Those curtains you liked. Well. . .

Have your two found curtains yet? Don't try to stop them if they do, because Feline Revenge is not something to be taken lightly. I looped up the curtains and told her she was a ruddy nuisance and would she please use her scratching post and her climbing tree, and she slitted up those blazing blue eyes and looked at me. A long, considering look. And she didn't half teach me.

She got into the wardrobe. Just as much fun as curtains. Max's academic gown for his lectures at Oxford that cost the bank a packet, my last decent evening dress, two rather good summer skirts, and my car coat. All the jumble sale stuff and the things I was thinking of chucking out were left strictly alone.

So I let the curtains down again. And I don't think you would like them any more. Not unless your taste runs to soft furnishings in the Clawed String style. I think I would rather have your problems with the bath. Or what may or may not be under it. It would be cheaper. Am bunging off my finished manuscript to you before Sam eats that, too.

I do feel you are going to have to do something about a name. Unsmudge and Not-smudge are hardly elegant, are they? What about Boudicca? Since she is such a dependent and helpless little thing?

Love, Jenny

PS. Max says he's sorry, he would love to marry you too, but he can't manage three cats.

Sutemi

Jan. 15, 1983

JENNY!

Of all the gol-danged cotton-picking side-winding *polecats*! Here you goad and nag *me* into taking two, and then chicken out yourself! What about pore li'l Solitaire pining for her sister? And that bit about bankers' eyebrows would have been a lot more effective if you hadn't blown it with the next line about One being Enough.

YES, she's still under the bathtub!

Pining away, she says. The Common and even the cage were ever so much nicer than here, she says. She doesn't *want* to be my cat and why did I make her come with Domino? she says.

Actually Boudicca would be an appropriate name and serve her right

to be called Boody for short. I thought of Antigonë, too. Something
to do with self-righteous intractable obstinacy. But then both of them
came to very sticky ends, and I didn't really want to hex her. I thought of
something like Nelson's Column, which she is about is spineless as. But
a couple of days ago, while crooning dulcet remarks through the crack
in the skirting to a pair of implacably terrified green eyes, I bethought
me of the Irish queen of legend who was, I seemed to recall, green-eyed,
beautiful, feisty, tragic and solitary? Though I don't suppose she was
these things under anyone's bathtub. And I may have misremembered.
Regardless, Not-Smudge is now Deirdre. I've been telling her so, over
and over, through the gap in the skirting. She doesn't answer to it, but at
least she doesn't hiss at it either, which I suppose is an improvement.

The only one.

No, I take it back. I've found where she goes potty. In the sandbox,
of course, as any civilized cat does even if she did spend her infancy
in the wilderness. (I had begun to suspect as much because Someone
always covers everything tidily, and Another Someone doesn't. Claws
the newspaper under the sandbox, instead.) I was sure when I got up the
other night to go potty myself, and got between Deirdre and Sanctuary,
so she simply ran me down.

She comes out to play then, too. While I lie awake listening to
the gentle sounds of Cowboys and-- No, these are English cats, aren't
they? Well, then, Normans and Saxons, or Vikings and Danes, or
Roundheads and Cavaliers, or even IRA and UDI. Anyhow, it involves
thunderous charges from one end of my mostly-uncarpeted house to
the other. Bathroom, back hall, kitchen, front hall, study. I think one
is chasee going west and then they reverse going east. What I want to
know is who shod them and whoever started that silly notion about
silent little cat feet? I expect the Battle of Culloden was quieter, with all
those skin-shod Highlanders on the heathery moors.

I am pleased that Samantha is living up to my hopes. Serves you
right, though I don't think those lovely curtains deserved their fate. *My*
two don't even *think* about climbing curtains. So far. In fact, Domino

hasn't climbed anything at all, not even chairs or tables. Either very virtuous, very cautious (which she is) or just can't climb. Deirdre is still anybody's guess.

I suppose Sam cuddles? I wanted a cuddly cat. I haven't got one. Kate says she *warned* me they were wild. I say she did no such thing. Kate says to be patient. I ask her how long. Stroking a tail *en passant* is definitely not a cuddle, even though Domino has begun to pause and raise it expectantly. And I did get her to eat some munchies out of my hand today, very doubtfully, ears flat, explaining that she wouldn't, only they were so yummy.

I think she's put one over on me about food, though. When I gave her what Kate said they always ate, she sniffed it in horror, backed up, stared at me with hurt reproach, and turned away in martyred desolation, resigned to starving before eating *that,* though she didn't want to be rude, of course... Said they had *never* eaten stuff like that when they lived on the Common.

I rallied a little. I said I *bet* they hadn't! More like bugs and spiders and the occasional vole. She said those were quite tasty, actually; and anyhow, they hadn't been Civilized when they lived on the Common, had they?

So I rushed all the way to the village (nearly six miles) and bought some expensive food. When I got back, *some one* had gobbled up most of the Kate food.

Domino insisted it wasn't she. I looked toward the bathroom, fancying I'd heard a satisfied burp from under the tub. I looked at Domino, tiny, worried, entirely at my mercy, trusting me to Feed her Properly, small face lifted to show that snowy chin and the red lips beneath that engaging teardrop-nose... So I opened the new food. But I suspect I've been had.

Tell Max he wouldn't have to manage three cats; only two. I'm going to send Deirdre back to be helpless and dependent for Kate. Or Fred. Or You. Or Figgy. Except that I can't get hold of her.

<u>Jan. 18:</u> All right, I've had it! Enough is too much. Me still trying to Win Deirdre's Trust, and all those things Kate talks of so glibly. (I've stopped talking to Kate, by the way. There's a very sympathetic cattery named Val down the road.) Anyhow, my life is spent on my knees, rear waving, ear to the floor and nose stuck in the skirting, murmuring "*Dear* Deirdre!" into black silence. And I go on doing it. Because Kate says to, because Mum's astrologer said I had "a jackass obstinacy that never knows when it is beaten and consequently seldom is" (which may be what wins me more judo contests than my skill deserves, and I suspect you suspect it too), and also because I'm really sorry for the poor scared little thing when I'm not furious with her.

But this morning that black silence was--well, *empty*. So I shone the torch in. No emerald eyes. She was Out!

But out where?

Not behind the dresser or under the book cases or in the washer. Not in the cupboards or Domino's favorite spot behind the books. Not in the drawers. Worry set in. I *knew* she couldn't have got outside--*could she?* I started over. Went through the house a room at a time, closing every door behind me. When worry became panic, I rang Fred and we did it together. I even went to the loft and spent an hour on my face across the beams. Down again, cobwebby, blank and disbelieving. I started around the house again, in a kind of hopeless denial. Bathtub. Towel shelf. Blouse cupboard. I felt around the emptiness behind the blouses, then ran my hands across them: the white lawn, the rose dacron, the black fur, the blue--

Black fur? I did a double-take. I reached. The black fur blouse-- (No one is *ever* going to believe this, but Fred is my witness!) --the black fur blouse hanging neat and flat between the others, presumably by its front paws, squalled, let go, and bolted under the tub again.

Firmly. Still saying she's *never* coming out.

I'm not telling you what I've been saying to Figgy.

Love--sort of-- Sally

Somewhen in Jan, 83
Dear Sally,

Don't nag! Siamese are Not Like Other Cats. Half a Siamese is equal to six others. I sometimes feel we have six cats anyway, I cannot count Sam, she moves too fast. What on earth am I going to do when she has kittens? It is a daunting thought, I can tell you.

Remember this flat? A bit like a coal mine, with that central well in the middle from the front door at the bottom, stairs winding up to the bedrooms, then living room, and on to the skylight? And the hanging plants suspended from the skylight? Well guess who is playing Tarzan, twenty feet above a concrete floor, giving me heart attacks at the rate of three an hour?

It all started with Sam and the twins playing football with the catnip mouse you sent her for Christmas (thank you) and she kicked it over the railing into one of my macrami pots. With a wild Siamese yell, she followed it! I heard a sort of swooshing noise, and one of the twins bawling "Goal!" I galloped out, to see Sam, mouse in teeth, clinging determinedly to the ropes and staring wide-eyed down at the floor. She was definitely thinking rather hard. So I shouted at her to Hold On Darling, Mummy's Coming, and grabbed my shepherd's crook and pulled the hanging basket to safety.

You'd think that would Larn Her, wouldn't you? Well, it did. Now, Goal! is the signal for me to go and collect her. "Rescue" is not the correct word. When the basket is within about four feet of the railing, she soars past me, carrying the mouse (which is looking a little tired now) and flashing one glinting blue glance at me. I am absolutely terrified that she will miss her footing, but there is nothing I can do, short of moving. There are twin-proof nets above the railings, of course, but Sam can get through those like you and I could get through an open barn door; she doesn't even slow down.

She is a teen-ager now, with legs so long she doesn't always know what to do with them, incredibly slick and slim, and rather self-conscious. You would not believe how blue her eyes are! Like extra-dark sapphires. Her tail is like a whip, and when she is angry, she lashes it so hard it almost cracks!

She, too, goes under the bath, but she comes straight out again, making rude remarks about the dust, with cobwebs draped between her ears, like a rather fetching mantilla!

I think the Battle of Culloden is quite a good simile, since many of those skin-shod Highlanders were mounted on fast little ponies, which didn't sink up to their hocks in the mud the way the English horses did, poor things.

Yes, Sam likes to be cuddled. But there's none of this nonsense about waiting for me to settle down and then jumping onto my lap. If Sam wants a cuddle, she comes and tells me so, and I had better put down the wooden spoon or the washing-up brush, and cuddle her! Or there'll be trouble, and Letters to the Times, and so on.

She always wants to join in. Making beds is her favorite, she gets under the bottom sheet and grabs at my hand. Sometimes she just won't come out, so I leave her there, and wait for her indignant yell. Or she sits on the draining board dabbing at the foam in the washing-up bowl, completely nonplussed by this peculiar activity.

But at nights she sleeps in our bed, between our heads, or snuggled down under the duvet, purring, and telling us how much she loves us and how pleased she is that we chose her and not Solitaire.

I had forgotten what Siamese were like. Now I'm remembering.

I don't know how you can get Deirdre out from under the bath. Of course, you could block it off if you could get in while she was being the Battle of Culloden, but then she would find somewhere else, even more inaccessible if possible, and it would shake her confidence. What she has of it. At least she is coming out occasionally, even if only to keep you awake or to be a blouse (oh, yes, I believe it!) or eat when you're not there. Have you got a tame butcher in the village? You might get cheap scraps of raw meat (not pork) and see if that tempts them. After all, for the first five months of their lives I doubt if they ever had anything cooked.

I have entered Sam for a show next month. I am not sure how she is going to take to this, but we have to start sometime.

                                        Love, Jenny

Sutemi

Jan. 29, 1983

Dear Jenny,

Well, neither are mine like any other cats! Not that I ever heard of, anyhow. Still, I'll concede you a point on Sam's trapeze act. Domino seems totally uninterested in flying.

I do indeed remember your flat, and it must be *more* than twenty feet down! Yoiks! Has your hair gone gray yet? Pity: I always envied you that gorgeous Scots red.

Domino hasn't grayed my hair at all. Yet. Leaves that to her sister. She's a dear little thing. Still very shy and wary, but trots everywhere after me, now, leaning against my ankle when I stop. Lifting her tail in invitation, waving it slightly, wanting to encourage me but not too much. I'm beginning to wonder about their past. There had been a whole litter out on that common. Three survived. And these are both terrified of anything long like a broom that might have been used to drive them away from an unloving home...

Domino kneads a lot, too. Not casually, but in terrible earnest, leaning her full weight into it with a kind of sober intensity. She keeps on and on, as if doing a Mummy-conjuring magic. She definitely can frown, by the way, and smile, too. I'll send photos.

She has a strong sense of Propriety. Even prudery. If she comes to the loo while I'm using it, she shows every sign of acute embarrassment, gives a funny little muffled whimper, averts her head, rushes out, and seats herself just outside the door, back pointedly turned.

Eating is different. Propriety dictates that I sit right there, being attentive, while she eats. Otherwise, she says, I might run away while she's not looking. Even if I read, it makes her insecure. And she *hates* anything being changed in any way. Move a chair two inches, put my purse (handbag to you) on the floor, and there she is, prowling around it warily, inching her nose toward it, low, with neck outstretched, ready to leap three feet up and back if anything so much as *twitches*. You can virtually hear her: "Does it BITE?"

She doesn't purr. Chirps when loving, whimpers when her feelings are hurt, twitters, groans in her sleep, yelps worriedly when exploring, and occasionally under deep stress says "Wowowow". But no purr. (Deirdre, silly clot, purred like crazy every time we found her hiding that first day, and she was scared mindless.)

Domino learned about Beds in the first week. Not snuggling in or near my arms, alas. Using my right ankle as a pillow--so I can't escape while she's asleep? She's learning to play on the bed. Soberly, as she kneads. Pouncing earnestly if I twitch my toes under the covers, leaping straight up if I twitch under her warm pointy little behind. (It really is pointed!) Now if only Deirdre would Emerge--

Meanwhile, your ms., <u>The Nemesis Club</u>, arrived and I confess now, despite the super title, I started reading with misgivings. Because *every time* a friend has *ever* asked me to read a ms, it's *always* been simply painfully awful--and what can I tell them? They *know* I could get it published for them if I really *wanted* to, and what kind of friend am I?

I decided you really did want honesty--but I was really depressed about it, all the same.

What a super surprise! Jenny, it's *good! Very* good! Great style (well, I *knew* you had that), good structure, suspense, and what I call *shape*. (Don't know another word for it.) You need only to sharpen your plot and characters a bit--and I'll recommend you to my English agent--who hasn't done a bloomin' thing for me, but should love this.

Thank you for not putting me on the spot! What a gut-wrencher, though! Wow!

Next day. Hold the Press and all that sort of thing. Guess wot? **Deirdre is out!**

This was not voluntary, I assure you. I was on the phone, which means, if you recall my house, I was well hidden behind the open living room door, phoning Kate to tell her to send an excavation team to dig the little monster out and remove her. While I waited for her to answer, in rushed the Battle of Hastings. Thought I was out, it did.

Quick as a wink, I slammed the door.

The posse--no, I mean the cavalry--froze in mid-skirmish and stared at me with very round eyes. Domino said oh there I was, and why had I done that? Deirdre did not, as I'd expected, go into what you Brits call a flap. She just gave me a long green look, marched up to the door, and gave it the same professional examination she had the carrier fastener on that first day. Pushed it, had a little dig at the floor, eyed the knob speculatively; then came over and fixed me with the hardest scrutiny I've undergone since my Captain's Mast. About as scared as old Willie the Conquerer himself.

I glared at her. Then Kate answered. I changed my message.

"Kate, if I were to lock that pernicious little baggage out of the bathroom, do you think it would permanently warp her little personality?"

"Crikey, is she still there?"

"Until two minutes ago."

"Lock her out!"

So I edged out of the living room, shutting the door nearly on Deirdre's whiskers, sprinted for the bath, and firmly closed the door, resolved to stay dirty for years if necessary.

Deirdre promptly vanished again, as you predicted. This time I refused to hunt for her. Presently those green eyes began to appear like the Cheshire Cat's grin, from around corners, under chairs, behind furniture and books, even the top of a door, yet! It was ages before I spotted her there! I think she was missing all the attention she'd been getting. So I pretended not to notice. Paid special attention to Domino and her delighted tail.

Bedtime. Domino as usual draped on my ankle while I settled myself in bed to read. Presently there was a small inquiring chirp from the floor at the foot of the bed. Domino leaned over and chirped back, obviously saying oh, yes, it was lovely here; come on up.

So Deirdre did. Briefly. I got one quick glimpse of shimmery black fur and horrified emerald eyes when she saw who else was there, and then blank space.

Domino and I shrugged. I turned out the light and settled down in the blissful silence of the countryside...

Silence? Where was that ruddy bulldozer I could plainly hear? Irritated and puzzled, I came up on my elbow and listened. *Not* from out on that narrow and deserted dirt road. Not from the dark and silent garden. Not from outside at all, in fact. From--*underneath my bed?* Not the foot, either. From under the *head* of my bed! An extremely contented-sounding bulldozer, purring loudly enough for two.

"Why, you rotten little fraud, you!" I said to it.

The purr got louder, if anything.

Okay, your turn. Going to one-up me again?

Love to you, Max, the boys and Sam.

                                                Sally

CHAPTER THREE

DOUBLE TROUBLE

Jenny's book, *The Nemesis Club,* was avidly accepted by the agent who didn't like my juveniles, and was not only published, but translated into about nine languages. Then we both got writers' blocks that went on for years.

We didn't see each other much, partly due to other distractions like twins, cats, judo, unemployed husbands, craft markets and gardens. But this time we kept contact. We phoned, even visited now and then. Mostly, I did. (Jenny had her two older boys *and* the Twins *and* Max to cook for.) Still, Reading was reasonably close to Headley Down even for a rather recent driver like me.

And if Reading seems an odd place for an Oxford Professor to live--well he wasn't, any longer. An Oxford professor, that is. Max, though a World Expert in some esoteric aspect of the mythology of ancient India, was also a sweet, naive, unworldly and impractical man. He had innocently supposed that because he knew more than practically anyone in the world about his subject, that gave him some authority in the University, or at least the Department.

Wrong.

So now he was unemployed and they lived in Reading; and the

twins, passing through Terrible Two's to Frenetic Fours, combined with Sam to lead Jenny a merry chase. Max was a background presence whenever I visited: always there, charming, and with his attention still focused on India. I assumed Jenny and he had some savings--but I didn't like to ask.

I did buy a new car, though, when the mini-van got senile. A Ford Fiesta. I had never heard of them in America. It was a dream to drive, and got 53 mpg, which, even allowing for the imperial gallon being a fifth larger than the American ones, seemed pretty good--but then, what did I know? I had never druv in America.

Sam was not a show cat, it turned out. They took her to one show, and she hated every minute of it so that was that. Jenny forgot all about One Being Enough, and bred her, and she produced half a dozen gorgeous rascals with eyes of astonishingly deep blue just like hers. I think Jenny brought herself to sell two or three--but the bug had her by then. Max produced from his India lore the breeder's name of Suryasun (India's sun god) for Sam and her descendants. (The first litter all had names beginning with A, and so forth, ultimately at least through the J's with Jamaica). It was, presently, a name to be reckoned with in cat shows.

Meanwhile, Domino and Deirdre didn't precisely become normal cats, themselves--that being an oxymoron to start with, isn't it? They didn't even become normal *for* cats. I did dimly suspect this, but I had no idea how *very* unusual they were. How was I to know that most cats don't toe out like little ballerinas (Deirdre) or give Roman salutes (Domino), or offer a permanent view of their little ass-holes (both of them). I decided, as they stood on my lap, backs in my face, tails aloft and forward, that though odd it seemed trustful. I had no notion how very trustful it was. I just stroked them in happy ignorance, wondering when they'd get to Cuddly.

Cuddly never happened, actually. But I was having such fun, this dawned only gradually. They really were *very* unsocialized kittens. (They were five months when I took them home, which is extremely late for taming ferals, so we did remarkably well, the three of us.) It had been a major project just to get even *Domino* to eat from my hand. Poor baby, in addition to being nervous about the whole thing, she had no notion what we were doing, and kept chewing my fingerpads manfully, thinking they were the food I was offering.

But Domino was a walkover compared to Deirdre, who wasn't having it. It wasn't my hand she objected to: it was the rest of me. So I spent a lot of time looking like a demented corkscrew: kneeling and trying to feed Domino with one hand stretched behind, while the other arm tried to make a 270-degree bend around two right-angle doorways where Deirdre lurked with what was nothing if not a negative attitude. Didn't like the look of it, she said. All those fingers! Up to No Good, she predicted, with her huge ears and snaky tail erect. (I didn't yet know the significance of erect ears and tail, or I'd have done a lot less scrooching.) Not going to take any chances, she decided, and in one of those lightning Oriental boxing acts, batted all the Munchies out of my hand and went and ate them at her leisure. After that she got organized. She would simply stuff her mouth to bursting point and go off to consume her loot in privacy. And then return for another load.

The next step was using Munchies as a bribe to let me stroke their heads while they ate. This scared them to death at first. Then Domino, always the more passive, decided simply to endure it. Like rape. Anything for a Munchy she said, screwing her eyes shut and flinching her body away from my intrusive hand.

Deirdre, to start with, did the old one-two on my hand. Until the first time I actually managed to stroke her head. She stopped. Oooh, *luvverly!* she said, pushing her head ecstatically against my hand. All Over, please, with *both* hands, she insisted from then on, grabbing and pulling any hand lazy enough not to be in active service. I was over the moon!

About then I realized that this was a cat who firmly believed she had fingers. Sometimes I thought so, too. Whereas Southpaw (literally)

Domino clawed and scraped Munchies out of the jar, Fingers would reach in, grab a handful in her fist, and then proceed to eat them out of her palm. I mean paw. If a thing was really too tricky to manage, she would stare at her paw in puzzlement as if she could *remember* having fingers there once, and whatever became of them?

(That's how she got her first nickname: Fingers. No, come to think of it, that was the second. Deirdre Quivertail Fingers Greedygut Squeakypurr. Her sister by then was Domino Worrywart Southpaw Curlytoes Sobersides.)

Poor Domino always remained schizophrenic about being fondled. I think she was a Puritan at heart and felt all this sensuous stuff to be sinful. So her back always dipped away from my caressing hand even while her raised tail gave it the lie. But though Deirdre adored being fondled, she wouldn't tolerate being picked up. Went berserk, she did. Exploded out of my hands like Mount St. Helens. And turned around almost in mid-air to return for more caresses.

Quivering her tail.

That snaky black tail of Deirdre's is a tale in itself. It was not only double-jointed; I think it was mounted on ball-bearings. While any normal cat raises its tail like a mast to express pleasure or greeting, sometimes waving it lazily as well, hers went all the way forward to lie along her back. Or shot out sideways. It reminded me of an excited earthworm. When she greeted me lovingly, it snapped forward to her ears, and her body contracted until her belly stuck out as round and tight as a balloon. Then the tail would suddenly stiffen into a letter-S-- and *quiver* like a cross between a dish of Jello and a belly-dancer

Soon the dancing tail was accompanied by a piercing soprano. Going to the vet, it became a prolonged aria punctuated from time to time by a despairing and equally piercing contralto wail from Domino. It made quite a duet, and usually got awed attention from everyone else in the waiting room.

Domino usually had very little in the way of volume, but she was a linguist. Learned a number of English words, and taught me some of hers. Mews, wows, chirps, twitters, all distinct, and, I began to discover, each with a specific meaning. She even developed a couple of three-syllable words, one of which, (prrr-yow-woop), always meant "Come quick! Deirdre's done it again!" There was a kind of "woohhah" that meant water. And she also knew English for water. (That is, *waw-tah*, as opposed to the American *wotter*). One of us would make her own water sound, and the other would come running. I would pick up the dish, and she would trot along at my left ankle, flower face turned up to me, explaining in her tiny voice how she *did* like it fresh.

She also used body language. There was The Attitude, when she would sit with paws neatly together, tail curled around them, and stare straight at me with an expression comprised of trusting expectancy and sorrowful disappointment when I failed to understand whatever it was she was telling me.

"I'm sorry," I would say humbly. "I *don't* understand, Domino."

She would sigh, and either rotate ten degrees or pull herself more erect. *Now* do you understand?

Usually not, alas.

Domino's markings were absolutely symmetrical--which I learned much later is exceedingly rare. (*"The Bicolor British Shorthair Show Standard originally specified that the markings should be symmetrical: a standard almost impossible to meet, and a revision had to be made to relax the Standard."*) Domino would have cleaned up at every cat show--if you could have drug her out of hiding. White face, perfect black teardrop on nose, a black head and body except for white chest, front slippers and rear boots. Her fur glittered in the light: every separate hair effulgent. Her legs went on forever: I think her mum was scared by a giraffe. And she walked distinctively, like a model or a fox, one front foot placed directly before the hind, lifted slightly when she paused, in a stylish pose of casual elegance. Her eyes were deep gold, her ears enormous.

Deirdre's ears were even bigger. She was all black with green eyes. Soft fur gleamed like silk velvet: no glitter. And in summer sunshine it acquired overtones of bronze. Short legs, tiny dancer's feet always turned

out, and when she ran scared--which was often--she crouched so low
that she looked like a speedy black turtle ballerina--with back and front
legs actually appearing to go at different speeds!

But short-legged little Deirdre was the climber and knew it. She
leaped to the tops of doors with a single bound and walked along them.[2]
Domino with her long legs and lithe body couldn't climb worth a bean,
and it embarrassed her. Once she managed to get about five feet up
the rose trellis, so I praised her to the skies. Sharp-ears heard me from
goodness knows where, shot around the corner of the house, gave us both
one comprehensive and scathing glance, and disappeared around the back
where there was a seven-foot shed some six feet from the house. A moment
later I heard her call. I looked up. She wasn't just on the house roof. She
wasn't even just on the chimney. The English have these tall skinny terra-
cotta chimney-pots with open sides and curved tops that sit on top of the
tall narrow chimneys to keep the ubiquitous rain from falling into the
fireplace. Deirdre was *on the chimney pot!* Virtually balancing on one foot,
waving the others, shouting "Wot about *this,* then?

The first time Fred's Fluffer threatened them from the veranda table
outside my bedroom window, it scared them spitless. Sound asleep,
they were, sweetly curled together on the inside window ledge, when a
Horrible Apparition, easily bigger then both of them together, suddenly
roared terrible threats at them through the glass two inches away.

They literally teleported across the entire room to where I was
sitting on my bed. Deirdre kept going, across and then under my bed:
Sanctuary ever since her first night out from under the tub. Domino
darted behind me, paused, peeked cautiously around at the menacing
window, saw who it was--and for virtually the only time in her life,
completely lost her temper. With a screech that laid my own ears back,
she teleported back to the window and tried to claw through the glass to
get at the shocked Fluffer, using language she never learned from *me.*

---

2   See cover

Fluffer backed up with what I can only describe as an apologetic grin. Said she hadn't really meant it; couldn't Domino take a joke?

Domino said she couldn't, and let loose a few more blistering threats. It went on for a good three minutes, and then Fluffer got back into the spirit of the thing, and they went on that way for the rest of Fluffer's life. Every morning they would take up their respective positions on either side of the glass and have a blood-curdling fight, standing on their hind legs, attacking the window with front ones, and yelling insults in a fine double frenzy.

Fluffer had the advantage of ending it whenever she chose just by going home. Then Domino developed tactics. The minute Fluffer jumped off the veranda, Domino would scoot to the cat door which Fluffer had to pass, and lurk with one eye peering out, so she could yell a parting shot from the safety of inside.

Deirdre never got into that act. She hid, moaning like a ghost in the wind. Just once in a while she would get terribly aggressive--for her--and go sharpen her claws meaningfully.

Deirdre was far the more timid with humans and other animals. But when it came to *things,* Domino was the cautious one, Deirdre the reckless. Their first snow, for instance. When I opened the door, Domino stood frozen with astonishment for a very long moment. And while she was still reaching out a wary paw to test the stuff, (Does it BITE?) guess who catapulted over her sister's head into the nearest drift, poked up a delighted head, vanished again, and began burrowing excitedly?

I didn't hear much from Figgy those years. I think she was resting on her laurels. Neglect of duty, I told her sternly, after Domino started a curious regime with the sandbox. First she stopped covering her urine. When I didn't get it, she first gave me The Attitude, then piddled outside the box, and finally, in exasperation, she *led* me to it and piddled the floor. '*Now* do you understand?'

Dim-wit me! Belatedly, I took her to the vet, who diagnosed

ineffective kidneys. Not diseased, he assured me as I stared aghast: just too small. So it would take a bit longer to kill her? Oh, great! There was little to do, but I did it all, and she seemed to feel well, mostly. When she didn't, there was her code for how bad it was: uncovered, outside the box, or in the middle of the room.

Three years after Fred got her, Fluffer also died of renal failure; almost as suddenly as had Sooty. Once again I reminded Fred of how much happiness he'd given Fluffer, and that another cat needed him now. This time *he* virtually dragged *me* to the car, and we went back to Kate. This time he was enchanted by a sturdy six-month old gray and white male who loved everyone. I strongly doubted the need. More so when we arrived back at Fred's and the kitten tried to go home with *me*, thinking *I* was his new mum.

Fred said he thought he'd name him Snowflake. Wincing, I hastily suggested alternatives: good upper-class boys' names (as opposed to Alfie, Wilfie, Bert or Len.[3]) Colin or Justin? Anthony? James? Timothy or Tobin?--

"I don't approve of human names for cats," Fred said austerely.

I fished frantically. "What about Tigger, then?"

It wasn't madly original, but Tigger and Fred approved. However, Tigger still wasn't sure where he lived or who was his human; and maintained that alarming tendency to think it might be me. A week passed that way. Then I got bossy again. Not only did Tigger need someone to keep him home, but Fred's devastation--twice!--at losing his only cat, told me something about eggs and baskets.

"Look what fun I have with two, Fred! I'm sure there's another who needs you--"

Fred was quite willing. Back to Kate we went. And there was a charming little brown tabby female, just the same age as Tigger.

---

3   Upper-class girls would be Emma, Daphne, Elizabeth or Sophie as opposed to Doreen, Linda, Myra or Lily.

"What will you name her?" I asked on the way home.

"Lucy," he said blandly. I gave him one brief startled sideways glance, and looked quickly back to the road. Neither of us ever said another word about human names for cats. And when we arrived in Fred's kitchen Tigger took one look at Lucy and fell instantly in love, and there was never again any nonsense about going to live with Sally.

There were no more fights through the veranda window: these two were much too peaceable--but there was no feline friendship, either. I realized that mine were devout practicing ailurophobes, and the sight of another cat--even a tiny kitten--sent them into frenzies of growling, hissing, and hiding behind furniture wailing to be Rescued from the Monsters. They accepted Fred as much as they could anyone who was not me. Which was not, I admit, much. Just once he ecstatically stroked Deirdre over the side of the armchair where she couldn't see him. Chuffed, he was. Over the moon!

I went away for just two days. Fred would have taken care of them--but it would have worried us both, lest they get out and run off to find me, which was altogether possible. So I arranged with a cat hotel called *Bon Repos* to keep them safely in a wee private room with a view, with lots of privacy, lovely food and loving visits from Angela.

We went via the vet, just to check Domino's kidneys. They performed their usual duet there, but had no notion that I was about to Abandon them until I took them on to *Bon Repos* and to their lovely private room, and started to leave. The shocked desolation in those two scared pairs of eyes was awful. I almost changed my mind.

Arriving home, I rushed off to retrieve them instantly--to learn that they firmly hidden under the book case the whole time, and eaten nothing. Poor babies! I felt dreadful. But they forgave me almost instantly, so I forgot about it.

Three months later I had cause to take Deirdre to the vet. No aria. She crouched in the carrier and trembled, as I had never seen her do in her life. I couldn't think why. It didn't dawn on me until later that she remembered what had happened immediately after her last visit there.

The way home was through one of those narrow English lanes just wide enough for one car. If you met another car, one of you must back up into a lay-by provided for such occasions. Naturally I met another. It was a dismal November dusk. I opened the car window to peer back for the lay-by I had just passed--

--and Fingers had the carrier open and was out of the window. That professional study of the cat-proof fastener the very first day, had paid off. Leaving the other car sitting there, I hurled myself out of the door and followed Deirdre back down the road, calling and coaxing. She said she *knew* I was taking her back to the cattery, and she wasn't going. Then she shot up the eight-foot bank and through the hedgerow on top.

Nearly crying, I went back, explained things to the patient driver of the other car, said no, thanks, he couldn't help, backed into the lay-by, and climbed up the bank to the thorny hawthorns on top, calling and calling in the cold drizzle.

Mercifully, Deirdre was by then as dismayed by the whole thing as I was. She answered at once, and after some twenty minutes of no-abandonment promises, permitted herself to be taken back to the car.

A good thing, too. I'd have been there yet.

CHAPTER FOUR

TO THE WINDS, MARCH!

And then I had an unexpected letter.

Dear Sally,

If you want to see Sam and the twins again in the reasonable future, you'd best get up to Reading soonish. We're moving to Germany. Yes, I KNOW; but it isn't practical to teach at a university from two countries away, and Max has found a university (Bonn) that appreciates his expertise on his subject, and they want him, so there it is.

You remember how Max resigned his teaching post at Oxford (on the good but impractical grounds that he was right and they were wrong, and don't ask me what it was all about because though he's explained, it's all too esoteric for me). I'm actually inclined to think he really was right, because he does know his subject, which practically no one else in the world does, but it was certainly a terrible tactical blunder because he seems to have been blackballed (if that's the word) and can't get a post to match his expertise. Well, not in Britain. But it turns out, Bonn would be delighted to have him. Next term, actually.

Sons Number One and Two opt to stay here, as they're both out of school and have jobs. The twins of course come along. It's all a bit fraught; you'd best come visit again before we go.

Love, Jenny

I had the instant horrid conviction that "the reasonable future" would be never![4] I wasn't being psychic, just logical. Especially if I were one day to head seven thousand miles in the opposite direction, back to California and All That Sunshine-- But Jenny had no choice: she'd given away her autonomy. (Catch me ever doing that!) And her insouciance about her move seemed decidedly forced, so I rallied and tried to write a chipper reply.

Sutemi

June 20,

Dear Jenny,

Well, for crying out loud! (as Dad would say). I've no words! Except that I think it's absolutely rotten for you to go off like that! But-- I must confess that I've been thinking (just fleetingly, mind) of moving back to California after 20 years. I thought I was here forever, but-- Mom and Dad are nearing their 90's. And I think I've been suppressing the little things that bug me here, damming them up. I do miss material conveniences like screw-in light bulbs of a mere 110 volts, sensible plumbing with the hot water tank in the basement instead of up on a shelf in the kitchen, real brooms instead of those push-things, food like corn on the cob, proper smoked bacon with the rind trimmed off, ripe olives, and proper salads. Bread-and-butter pickles instead of onions and unripe walnuts pickled in vinegar. Squash, pumpkin pie-- (Ivy liked that so much that I gave her the recipe, but forgot to mention that being basically a custard, it would be soupy before cooking. She thought she'd done something wrong, and thickened it with flour!) Real

---

4   It was.

walk-in closets, with lights in them. Screen doors! Oh, and California informality like hugging and using first names and grown-ups dressing up for Halloween.

On the other hand, there are things *you* can't appreciate, never having lived without them. BBC. Really *good* programs and *no commercials!* English birdsong. Village fêtes and plays and pantomimes. Electric kettles. Subtle deadpan humor. The general knowledge of history and lit and music, so you can quote a few words *en passant* of anything from G&S to Alice in Wonderland to Noel Coward to Shakespeare, and receive appreciative smiles and a perhaps an answering quote-- Special friends. You'll be gone--but Fred, Ivy and Len--and Gill--and all my dear Kindred Spirits in British Mensa! The fluorescent May foliage, like nowhere else I've seen. No guns. *National Health!* I'd forgotten about having to pay for medical services--though I hear the US now has things like Medicare and Health Insurance, so it might be a bit better. (On the other hand Blue Cross came up with health insurance in '48 while I was at Reed. Al Bragdon subscribed--and when he slipped on the ice and broke his leg, they called it a Pre-existing Condition and refused to pay a penny. He said it was one kind of education Reed didn't offer.)

I'd have to think it over. *Carefully!*

Fred says nothing when I hint at the idea, bless him. I know he'd miss me terribly; I'm the nearest thing he has to a family, and I'd feel awfully guilty. Oh, I know he gets Home Help as part of the Welfare State; and Marjorie-and-Maurice, and Colin Smith-and-family along the road are fond of him and would visit and shop for him, and of course he gets around very well--if slowly--in his invalid car-- But I'm his Best Friend, the beloved sister he never had.

And I'd miss him, too. Awfully...

Well, I shall indeed come to Reading again soonish, and we can talk about it.

Hugs and imprecations, Sally

Jenny and family settled in Bonn, and we began writing again, both missing our visits badly. Her beloved Samantha had a second litter, and then they had her spayed--and she died of it. It sometimes happens, but I think Jenny has never forgiven the German vets. All of them. But the Suryasun line continued, and they soon were cleaning up at all the German, French, Belgian and Dutch cat shows. All her cats, of course, had very posh names--but were inevitably known by nicknames. Toot, the most forward of Sam's first litter was, I think, the one I had watched climbing over the barricade that was supposed to hold them for at least 2 weeks longer.

The twins went to German school, and of course became bilingual in no time, while poor Jenny was still struggling. (Max, of course, was completely fluent in that and a number of other languages, or he wouldn't have got the position.) Being a moron at other languages myself, I felt for Jenny!

We wrote voluminous letters. Jenny's were filled with the growing Black Paw Gang and the cat-shows they increasingly dominated, amusing accounts of the trials of a new German *hausfrau* who couldn't speak German, coping with landlords, twins, drunken truck drivers, vets, bureaucracy, and incomprehensible laws and customs. She never complained--but somehow Max never seemed to appear as the Man of the House (which in Germany, it seems, is the only one to be respected), or even the helpmeet. Or advisor. Or even there.

I rather dropped the idea of moving. It was too daunting. I truly loved England. I had lived there for over a third of my life; including 18 years at Sutemi: nearly twice as long as I had ever stayed in one house before. I loved the birds (especially *real* robins--both the summer and winter songs--and the song thrush and the Birdie with a Yellow Bill--English blackbird--with a song like a boxwood flute.) Oh-- so many things! I really *did* intend to end my life right there, even though I had sadly discovered that, as it says in <u>White Cliffs of Dover,</u> "only the English are really her own." Still-- I had always been a misfit in America, too, so-- Oh, forget it, I decided.

About then who came out of apparent retirement and started meddling again? Who nagged about Getting a New Start, and comfy warm American Houses, and convenience and My Family? And when I proved resistant, who persuaded me that a cruise up the Rhine with a stop at Bonn to visit Jenny and the Black Paws would be a splendid thing?

You bet she did! And it was a fiasco. To begin with, at the last minute Jenny and the boys *had* to go off somewhere with Max *just that exact week. And she had no autonomy.* My last chance to see her! *Ever!*

Second, it was a lousy cruise, featuring all the very worst of everything British. I was reduced to sulking on the hard window seat of a wee cabin too small for a chair or even a stool, (*and* they charged me extra for "single occupancy of a double cabin"!) because there was no room in the lounge, and no one would talk to That Colonial American, and anyway you couldn't see the castles from the low seats through the high windows; and the half dozen "deck chairs" were upright unpadded cast-iron, and it was cold out there. (We jeer at English weather, but it seems that German is worse and colder.) I was feeling particularly ill-fed and ill-treated because one of the lovely things about a cruise is always the food--and it was dreadful! No choice at all: no menu, in fact: they just stuck a plateful of British stodge in front of you. On a *cruise!* An expensive one, too. All were Brits but me, and they ate the stuff with apparent relish. Perfectly good English Food, mm?

No! It *was* stodge. Stewed steak. Literally. Boiled to gray mush. So were the Brussels sprouts. The ubiquitous English salad, which, everywhere in the UK always consisted of precisely two leaves of limp lettuce, two slices of tomato, two slices of cold boiled beet--beet-root, they call it--two slices of hard-boiled egg, two slices of cucumber, two slices of radish, a sprinkle of watercress--and salad cream!

In America, salad cream would be considered cruel and unusual punishment.

And the cruise had apparently collected all the thoroughly offensive English snobs from at least six counties. Where did they *get* them? I had met only one in the whole of my twenty-three years in England. (On a ship, come to think of it--) So there I sat, glowering, watching the castles go by and muttering darkly that I was going home to America, where when people were rude it was either from anger or ignorance; they didn't make a bloody *virtue* of it. I meant it, too. Got back to Sutemi, fetched my pining cats out of the lovely cat hotel which they still hated, and put Sutemi on the market. After all, I remembered, my life had so far been a whole series of new starts, and it was clearly time for another.

Dear Fred put a brave face on it and never tried to talk me out of it--but couldn't hide the sorrow in his eyes--which made me feel so remorseful I almost changed my mind. But Figgy was actively pushing now, and the urge was too great--even though I knew what was eating me.

"Greener grass syndrome," I told him ruefully. "I never lived more than ten years in one place before, and that was when I was a kid. Itchy feet. Just wait; once I'm back I'll remember all the awful things I hated over there, and start missing England as much as I miss California now. Except for the rain, maybe--"

Fred smiled sadly, and forbore to point out the obvious solution.

So I decided, and wrote Jenny. Twice. And eventually got an answer. Two, actually: the first one very severe indeed. The second was better.

29 Sept,86
Bonn
Dear Sally,

I owe you two letters now, because my last one was a bossy note - do this, don't do that, etc. Sorry about the tone of it, it wasn't meant that way, but I'm a bit cross because I don't want you to go (any more than you did when we moved to Germany. Now I've said it so you needn't.) But seven thousand miles (I looked it up) is overdoing it a bit, don't you think?

But since you will do it, being as stubborn as I, I do have a few suggestions about getting the cats there.

First, I assume you needn't put them in quarantine. I don't think you'd go, otherwise.

So, for the trip, first get them used to a sponge in their drinking water. YES, I DID say SPONGE. Gradually reduce the amount of water until they get used to coping with it. Then, when they are en route they can have water without slopping it all over their nice warm blankets and getting wet and chilled. As for sandbox, what I do is make a small one out of a low-sided carton, & stick it down at the back of the box with Velcro. Also, I recommend that you leave their traveling box, with a warm blanket in it, where they can explore it, for as long as possible before the trip - and DON'T use it for trips to the vet. Encourage them to sleep in it during the day, perhaps by putting a hot water bottle in it during cold weather. Get their water container (the sort that clips to the cage) and put it in; in short, make it as familiar as possible for them. As for tranquilizers, I never do, but ask a vet, and also Kate, who knows them.

Please give my love to Fred, and Lucy and Tigger. MUCH better to have two! I know how he still grieves for Fluffer, I still mourn Sam, but getting those two was his best tonic, if not cure.

Toot sends her love. She's beginning to look more rounded now, but I don't think she'll have as many kittens this time. Five was really too much for her. I'm enclosing a sketch of all of them.

The twins are being impossible because they still have to translate for me lots of the time. I shall practice my judo on them one of these days. I'm not <u>that</u> out of training.

Love, Jenny

I put Sutemi up for sale in the autumn of '86, coincidentally (?) just after the Council changed our density rules from a quarter-acre minimum to six houses per acre--*average!* This meant you could build on a postage stamp and still average out! It was about to become a Headley Down I no longer much cared for. The builders went into a feeding frenzy. And the estate agents were all in league with them, so no one would offer for Sutemi as a house with garden, but only as a piece of land with a building to be replaced. Especially when they grasped that I was in a hurry! Had it all sewed up, they did: my quarter-acre was to be joined with that on the corner, to squeeze in six houses on *half* an acre, at a huge profit. And I would accept their price willy-nilly; they made that perfectly clear.

"This is the top price anyone will give you," they told me, smirking.

Oh, yeah? I suddenly became bolshy, as the English say. Shirty. Went spare! Got my knickers in a twist! Sutemi was a perfectly good house, with all sorts of modern improvements like a roofed connection between main house and loo, and a sort of vague central heating fed twice daily by coal, and a kind of shower attachment that you could shove on to the tap and it stayed if you didn't turn the water on too hard-- Well, it was a *much* better house than--

Inspiration hit me. Or Figgy did. Whatever.

"Look," I said to Fred. "They think they have me over a barrel, so let's fox 'em."

And we did. They all offered for land only, not a penny for the house. So Fred offered me a bit more and then sold *his* land (twice the size of mine) to the neighbor behind who was glad to pay him what it was worth. I came out with £75,000: twenty times what I'd paid for it back in '67: surely enough to buy a house *and* car in California outright. (Without a mortgage, of course. Else I wouldn't have done it! Sally's Economics was still working fine.) And Fred would have the luxury of my semi-central heating (instead of living in his kitchen, because *his* only heat was still his coal-burning Aga stove!) plus the washing machine and 2-cubic-foot fridge already in my house; and he would have enough profit on the sale of *his* land to live very comfortably indeed for a change.

As for the realtors and builders, they suddenly stopped smirking.

I still felt guilty about leaving Fred, though--not to mention sad at parting from such a good friend.

But it turned out Figgy probably saved his life.

It was Thursday, Jan. 7th, 1987. It started to snow as the taxi took my cats and me to Heath Row. So hard, the flight was held up for two hours. On Friday Fred left his barely-heated kitchen, moved into my house during what was about to become the worst blizzard in years, and filled up the coal hopper to get warm. On Saturday the roof of his old house collapsed with the weight of snow. Right over the kitchen.

CHAPTER FIVE

FRENETIC FELINES

Oakland, California
Jan. 26, 1987
Dearest Fred.

Sorry it's been so long, but I've had a thing or two on my mind. I'm staying in Dad's house, which has two resident cats, so mine are holed up in the bedroom and terribly upset abut the whole thing.

Well, I can see their point. That trip was fifteen hours, counting delay for the blizzard. I wasn't allowed to bring my girls in the cabin: hadn't even been allowed to see them loaded or check that their quarters were warm enough! I threatened not to go at all--only then the captain said *they* were going to San Francisco, cats and all, whether I did or not. So I fretted and muttered the whole way because I knew my kidlets thought I had abandoned them again--if they were even aboard! At San Francisco I crouched like a cat at a mouse hole by the door where they should emerge. Had they made it? Had they got left behind? Or frozen *en route?* Had someone jimmied the padlocks I had put on their cages (visualizing either of *them* escaping into the hold)?

After eternities, the double wooden carrier emerged. Not a movement, not a sound, from within. Panic! I rushed toward them, calling--

The effect was electric. Two wee figures leaped into life, shrieking their little heads off for me to Come Rescue Them from the Kidnappers. It was so loud and tireless that when I got them to Customs-combined-with-Passport, the man glanced perfunctorily at my passport and waved me through. "Take the poor little things home," he said.

What a pity I wasn't smuggling anything!

Now I'm frantically house-hunting. I need to have my own house, for the three of us. We aren't used to sharing. My autonomy is crippled. Marilyn and I turn out to have a bit of sibling rivalry. And she and Dad have two cats, so mine have to be shut in my bedroom, which, they point out bitterly, they never had to do before, and they don't like it and want to go Back Home or at least Outside.

So it's all a bit dicey, and I want out. Say, by about yesterday. Trouble is, I don't want to live in Oakland, but 50 to 80 miles north in a more rural area. Up in Sonoma County, which is known both as wine country *and* the Redwood Empire (what a combination, mm?). But not having a car yet makes it awkward getting there to look.

My dear Scottish Dance friend Alice has been driving me up, and has also helped me find a car. I wanted another Ford Fiesta, but the dealers said there was no such thing. I said not to be daft: I'd *owned* one in England, hadn't I? Oh, England, they said. They made special cars for Europe. Not sold here. I asked why. They wouldn't say. Tried to sell me an expensive gas-guzzler, *and* on the never-never. Their mistake. I simply walked out. Finally bought one (Not a Ford) from a car-fleet, bound to be in good condition because they have to keep them up for the renters. It's ok. But--smaller than the Fiesta--it gets about 20 mpg! Small U.S. gallons! Alice, surprised, said that's about average here! (Makes you think, dunnit?) But Alice will go on driving me up to house-hunt, since I've never driven in the US before and want to practice before venturing on a US freeway!

It's 87 degrees today! All this gorgeous *hot* sunshine! In January! I can't believe it!

I miss you abominably already!

Love to you, Tig and Lucy, Sally

Sienna

Feb. 27, '87

Dearest Jenny,

Sorry about the delay. Things got on top of me. Finally found a house, in a little city named Sienna, and moved in last week. Thank goodness! A charming small house with a large back garden, and a cat-friendly redwood fence.

And owners who, when they heard of my plight (*and* that I was paying cash) arranged to vacate in just three weeks! Leaving extra goodies like all the garden tools, *besides* the usual carpets, fridge, cooker, curtains, drapes, shelving, light bulbs, etc.-- (Yes, honestly! It's customary. One leaves *all* those things! And of course the screens. Window and door. I'd almost forgotten about screens after all these years! Remind me to explain them to you some day.)

It's spring! I have grape hyacinth, pansies, violets, daffs and narcissus blooming now. My crape myrtle trees, apples and pear aren't yet blooming; the plum, peach and magnolia are. Holly and camellia are both higher than the house, and the geraniums (*Outside!*) and roses are higher than my head! Chirping crickets in the dry-wall terrace have quite bemused my cats, who sit for hours in front of it, watching and listening.

Moving in was easy. Sort of. Anyway, there wasn't much to move. The stuff I shipped--a thousand or so books after I'd weeded lots out, and the odds and ends of irreplaceable furniture--won't arrive for months. So I paid Dad's neighbor to drive one small rented van up from Oakland to Sienna, with all my current household effects: a kitchen chair and table from a yard sale (car boot sale to you), a floral bed-sofa weighing a ton or two donated by Mum, and my old childhood bed snatched back from the family, with bedding and a fifty-year-old mattress that sags like a hammock and is very comfortable indeed.

I don't know how the van got here. Marilyn and I lost them early on. I do know that I drove her and the cats in my new used car, via Vallejo, and she was supposed to know the way and/or map-read, because I'd never been in Vallejo in my life and was still coming to grips with driving on the right, and unfamiliar street signs, and lane markings being the wrong colors.

Turned out she didn't know the way, after all, and couldn't (or at least didn't) map-read. Her contribution was *yelling* at me for being too far to the left. Which I wasn't. So I found the police station in Vallejo and drove in.

"Halp halp," I said to the first cop I saw, "We're lost."

Marilyn yelled at me for that, too, afterwards. Said they might have shot me or something. I still haven't figured that one out--but that's Marilyn. *I* write novels, *she* should have been an actress. Is, in fact. Unpaid. (*Exactly* the same age as Liz Taylor, and looks much like her, too, except that her gorgeous eyes are velvet brown.)

Anyway, by the time we arrived we were barely speaking at all, both cats were complaining loudly, and I had vowed *never* to drive Marilyn *anywhere* again--which she didn't take seriously. I meant it. I think--

Still, we did get here in the end, and so did the van, with Dad and his neighbor. They briskly unloaded, deposited everything (including the two-ton bed-sofa, which took three of us) just barely inside the living room door, collected Marilyn, the money for the rental and gas, an extra $50.00 so they could stop for a posh meal on the way home-- and happily drove off.

I looked at the bed-sofa, the brooding cat crate, suitcases, dismantled bed, and the pile of mattress, bedding and odd bits. I leaned against the door--my very own door!--took a deep breath of relief at being my own undisputed mistress after six interminable weeks, went and released the disgruntled cats, and started shoving furniture.

Happily.

Moving the bed-sofa over long shag carpet just enough to unblock the door nearly did me in. I decided to find a wall for it later. After finding, buying and arranging some large bookcases. Then I heaved the bed parts into the front bedroom and set up the frame.

By then the February night had settled in, so I fed the girls, dragged the heavy box springs and mattress on to the bed, and made it up. Then I discovered that the street lights and park noises invaded my solitude, so I dismantled the bed, moved it into the back bedroom overlooking that lovely garden, set it up again (with D&D demanding to know Why I was Doing That) and went to bed. Deirdre promptly vanished under the head, with an almost audible purr of relief. Sanctuary! I crawled under the covers. Domino spent the entire night just as she had at Sutemi, slinking along every inch of wall, corner and closet with those little yelps of "Wow? Wow?" She seemed puzzled by the closets (not water-closets: but what you Brits call walk-in wardrobes), never having seen one before. Also intrigued by the crickets, who chirped charmingly all night.

I think we're going to like it here. The sale of Sutemi bought the house and car handily--paid in full, with plenty left to remove the wood stove, add insulation and central heating, and replace the ugly small-paned living room windows with a big bay. Perhaps a deck in back. And, mind you, still not going into my savings! It all seems much nicer than your patch in Bonn sounds (even aside from your ruddy 'orrible landlord). Wish Max could get a professorship at one of the local colleges--but I don't think they could afford him, and I'm not sure your Scots blood would really like the climate--much less the politics.

Anyway, my girls and I send you all masses of love and good will.

Sally

CHAPTER SIX

NEW TERRITORY

Sutemi
March, '87
My dearest Sally,

We're all settled cozily in Sutemi now, which withstood the blizzard nicely as I told you on the blower. Tig and Lucy are very much at home but still a little puzzled at not seeing you or your kidlets. Lucy has become a great collector especially of pine cones, which she piles up just outside their cat door and then brings one in every time she comes and hides them somewhere but I haven't yet discovered where.

Tig has been bringing in live goldfish lately. I don't know where he gets them and am afraid to ask around.

Sounds as if you and the kidlets have settled in happily too. I'm glad even though we miss you very much around here

Love, Fred

Sienna
April, 1987
Dear Jenny,

This is really a continuation of my last letter. I was a bit busy at the time, as you can imagine. Now we're all settling in to what D&D now realize is our New Territory. They've explored it, and decided that it includes that of my lovely next door neighbor Grace, who, I think, must be roughly my age. Grace confessed that she doesn't really much like cats, but she's being a very good sport about it: not a word of complaint. I told her if they bug her in any way, a squirt with the hose can be very effective. From her faintly shocked expression, I doubt if she will.

Anyway, the kidlets have settled in happily.

I think the crickets are less happy, though. If you remember, Domino's vocabulary includes chirping. Well, a cricket got in the other day, sat down more or less beside her as far as I could tell, and began a duet. I think it thought Domino was a lady cricket. I won't say what Domino thought, but it was not benign. Her little mouth pulled down into her very most sourpuss look as they sat there, both chirping like mad. Since then, she and Deirdre sit facing the terrace wall a good deal, and there's a certain challenging shape to their backs.

There's a resident scrub jay who thinks I'm his aunt or something. When I go out, he shouts "Yike?" I yike right back, and we have long conversations, though of course I've no clue what either of us is saying. The mocking bird is less affable. He dive bombs me and my cats, presumably for hairs to line his nest. Deirdre eyes the trajectory with narrowed eyes, the way she did the carrier fastener. I tell him, "You could do that just once too often, mate!" but he doesn't believe me. Says anyway, he was here first. She just slits her eyes and smacks her lips.

As for me, I keep going around talking to you *sotto voce* about the big walk-in closets with lights in them! (Eat your heart out every time you open one of those magical wardrobes that somehow fills half a wall, yet coat-hangers must be angled in sideways.) Hardwood floors *and* thick wall-to-wall carpet--all *plain unpatterned* earthy umber-bronze! Ivory drapes, also without stripes, flowers or tartan. The washer and hot water tank are sensibly down in the garage. And *no* water tanks in the loft 'so that the water can run down to the taps'. I did get so tired of telling people that in America water *truly* runs out of the taps *without* our having to send it aloft first.

"But water really *must* flow *down*, you know, Sally. It's basic science."

"Yes, Quentin, so now kindly tell me how it gets *up* to the loft in order to flow *down*."

"Not to fret about it, luv: females can't be expected to understand the Laws of Physics."

Tell me, Jenny: how are the laws of physics in Germany?

I also inherited a large wheelbarrow, garden tools, and a 90-gallon trash barrel (dustbin to you) on wheels, so high that when I tried to reach in for something, I leaned too hard on my ribs and--no, I didn't break them. Quite. It only felt like it.

Weather is gorgeous. Well, you probably wouldn't like it, being a Scot, but I do.

I still think it was a good move. Anyhow, I couldn't unburn my bridges now if I wanted to. (Aside from not being able to take my cats back in without the requisite 6 months in quarantine.) I'd forgotten a lot of things. Like commercials. Now I remember, alas! A *third* of program time is commercials! And medicine here is still For Profit, They *have* got Medicare now, for seniors, goes with Social Security, and is far better than most Americans get. It's probably the nearest we'll ever come to National Health--but it's *not* the same: not nearly! Still--thank goodness I'm eligible!

Always and always, Sally.

PS: Something has been Spraying on my front porch. Do I use something like dettol?

18 May,
Dear Sally,

Dettol is absolutely lethal to cats. Please throw it away. Use bleach, sensibly diluted (except on carpets, of course). I think you have a visiting tomcat.

I've never known crickets, but they sound marvelous. They are, as you know, super burglar alarms, because they fall silent if a stranger comes near, and the sudden silence wakes the house. But why don't the cats eat them? I don't understand.

Deirdre, you can tell your Mum from me that any birds (except fledgelings) that let themselves be caught by cats are incredibly stupid, incredibly unlucky--or ill and probably just about to spread that illness to all their neighbors. Cats help keep the bird population HEALTHY by wiping out the sick ones before they spread it all around.

In Finland a few years ago a certain type of partridge was found to be getting thin on the ground, so it was forbidden to shoot them and a bounty was placed on a sort of hawk that preyed on them. Then everyone sat back and waited for the partridge population explosion, and were all hurt and cross when the wretched birds almost vanished off the face of the earth. Why? Because they had a virus, that's why. The first symptom was that they got slow, easy prey for guns and hawks and cats. Then they got good and infectious. Then they died. Luckily the Finns are a reasonably intelligent and practical race, and realized their mistake in time.

Yes. About the plumbing. Despite what a series of English plumbers told me, we have hot water tanks DOWN in garage or basement in Germany, well below floor level, and NO tanks in the loft. When I tell them here about tanks in the loft, they think I'm having them on.

Luv, Jenny

June '87

Dear Jenny

Yes, they do here, too. Think I'm having them on. I mean pulling their legs.

It turns out the cats do eat the crickets. I hadn't known it was a thing they did. But--you know I mentioned that D&D were fascinated, sitting motionless staring at the terrace? Well, after the chirping competition they sit there even more--and lately there's less chirping. Oh, darn. I love the sound! (But I'd never wake up at the cessation of their chirping.

I never wake up even for earthquakes--which very much annoys me. I actually enjoy them.)

I *knew* I'd miss English birdsong horribly! Especially blackbirds, song thrushes and real robins. Ours seem confined to chirps. Even the mocking bird, who hasn't much but chirps to mock. What deeply puzzles me though, is that several times at night I've heard what I swear is a nightingale! Which we don't have here. Nor any sound-alikes. People tell me it must be a mocking bird. Yes? So what's it mocking? Am I 'round the twist?

(No! A neighbor says she's heard it too!")

And I miss not only BBC but English radios. Letting you play long, medium *or* short wave. (Here it's only AM and FM.) There, choose push-button-or-dial. Here, no push button at all except in car radios. And no plug-in-and-battery! You *can't* just unplug the radio and carry it around the house or garden without missing a note. Radio Shack (male chauvinists to a man) sneer that females don't understand science. Just like English plumbers--but more insulting.

I've some more crazy reversals for you. (a) In this land of clever invention, they all stare at the idea of electric kettles or porcelain-top stoves. But-- (b) You have idiotic British lawn-mowers with that clumsy 'reflector" behind to bounce the grass forward to a great clumsy catcher in front, which the grass mostly misses and which prevents mowing to the edge of the lawn! Not like us, who simply and logically put the catcher behind. But then you invented the fly-mo, which makes even our electric ones look primitive; and when I tell people it's like a small hover-craft mower, they never heard of that, either. And when I explain that it rides on a cushion of air, they think I'm having them on.

Love you! Sally

Dear Sally,

I have been in a permanent state of bewilderment over the Contra hearings. What makes North a hero? Being a liar, a traitor or a terrorist? Or all three?

Luv, Jenny

Dear Jenny,

Please don't ask embarrassing questions about our politics. I DON'T KNOW! Except that he is certainly all three and seems to consider it a virtue. (So does Reagan, of course.) Nor have I any idea why anyone should consider Reagan a Good President *or* his pal Maggie (of 'Ronnie and Clyde') a Good Prime Minister.

I've found a local Mensa group. Their 'greeter', Jeanne, lives only half a mile from me! We're good friends (though not, alas, Kindred Spirits) so we go to everything together. I must confess American Mensa isn't much like British Mensa, though.

Thanks so much for the gorgeous photos of your lot! No wonder they walk off with all the prizes! Do they enter many shows? Do they enjoy them? I assume so, or that would be that, mm? I asked mine if they'd like to be in a cat PHOTO contest, but they said unprintable things.

Which reminds me. I've lost track of Sam's descendants. They come too thick-and-fast, and have too many names. Is Didi short for Deedle which is short for an official posh For-Shows name? Is it Mall Madam or Small Madam, and who is she really? I do understand that the family pedigree name is Suryasun and that they have alphabetical show names, and different home names, but I lose track with each new generation.

Not that I'd trade D&D for all the Siamese in the world--but some day I'd love a Siamese, *too*. I've mentioned this to Figgy. Just a plain one will be fine. Not an aristocrat. And no coincidences needed.

Love to you, Max and all the felines. Bring me up to date on them.

Sally

Bonn
21 Aug. '87
Dear Sally,

I've now got seven cats. Oldest, Toot (European Premier Suryasun Ayutthia). Then (alphabetically) Boy and Percy (Suryasun Bayard and Suryasun Bhairava). Suryasun Chandi is all of three weeks older than

Deedle (Suryasun Daredevil) and then comes Scallywag: (European Grand Champion Suryasun Excaliber). And Mall Madam (Suryasun Enchantress). Each litter has its letter, and the next will be F. Perhaps Fleetwood? Flamenco? (Jay said Frying Pan and then ducked.)

Mall Madam has just honeymooned with her cousin Grand Champion International Suryasun Desperado (Henry). He lives with a friend of mine, who tells me that he adores Mall, so if love produces beautiful kittens we will have a litter of world-beaters.

Love, Jenny

Sienna

8 Sept.,

Dearest Fred,

You asked if we have hedgehogs. No, nor cuckoos (whose call I miss even though they *are* wicked) nor real robins. (Only a thrush that we call a robin, at least 3 times the size.) We do have cougars, raccoons, 'possums and skunks, all exotic aliens to you Brits. Some things are all too familiar, though. Remember me saying that at least I'd enjoy having no ivy, invasive blackberry or snails? Ha! This is heaven for all three. I've heard that some Frenchman a hundred years ago imported snails to raise for *escargot*--and I needn't tell you the rest, need I?

Well, I don't want to use anything on the snails that might harm D&D, so I got some expensive semi-liquid stuff they say is perfectly harmless--after the 2 minutes it takes to dry...

So you *know* who came dashing over to me as I applied it, thinking it was a new game, and walking through it with all four feet.

Remember how Deirdre won't be picked up? If I try to lift her, she becomes a berserk octopus and explodes out of my hands. And she's incredibly strong. Well, I managed to get her to the bathroom somehow, and shut the door, and what happened next made judo seem like a doll's tea party. They say to wrap them in a large towel. The shreds are lying across the toilet seat. She struggled like a crocodile, yelled like a banshee, hissed and squalled curses I never *dreamed* she know--*and*, I later realized, *never once aimed a tooth or claw at me.*

It took ages to be sure I had every paw scrubbed almost raw. When I finished, we were both limp as as battle heroes. When I let go, she instantly turned to quiver her tail at me lovingly, purring and head-pushing, saying as we were in there, why didn't we both use our sandboxes?

Deirdre, unlike Domino, has always been a sociable litterbox user. As I live alone, I seldom close the door, and if she's near, in she rushes, purring, to use hers too. If I do close the door--as I do when Dad visits--she's outraged. I told him once that it sounded as if she were banging on the door with both fists.

"She was," he said dryly.

Domino is still an embarrassed little prude about such things. Sits outside the door with her back politely turned.

Always and always, Sally

1 Oct. '87

Bonn

Dear Sally,

Cat shows. Yes, well, Chandi half ate another steward, which was nothing more nor less than sheer naughtiness, and if there were any justice in the cat world (which there ain't thank God) she'd have had her spoiled little bottom tanned good and proper for it. Instead she came home with a damned great rosette and a premier certificate. Mall Madam (who is really Small Madam, because that's what the little baggage is, but if you pronounce the 'S' she thinks you are spitting at her and is either hurt or offended or angry, which means bloody dangerous) simply swore at the judge and spat at the stewart, and was given only a first prize and a rosette, because she was too young to be in the adult class.

So I took her to another show last Sunday. Unfortunately, there weren't enough seal points for a Best of Breed nor enough Siamese for a Best of

Variety. So she decided to go to the top in one bound and walked off
with Best in Show. Against strong opposition, too! A large trophy, a brass
candlestick, a rather peculiar plaque and a rosette nearly twice as big as
herself, behind which she hid while on stage, so no one got a photo of her.
Max said never mind, I was grinning like a searchlight, so it wouldn't have
been a good one.

I'd better stop now and feed Max and the imps. Hug D&D for me.
Love, Jenny

Oct. 10, '87
Dearest Fred,

I'm never sure how to time the mail over there, but I hope your
birthday gift arrives right on the 14th. I hope, too, that you're really
doing as well as you insist you are. It worries me that you'll never
complain. Are the Strides and the Smiths keeping an eye on you as I
asked them to? Are you getting Home Help all right?

There's an orange and white neighbor cat named Pokey who lives
on the other side of Grace. He's decided to take over my cats' Territory.
Tries to drive them off so he can move in. Of course my little heroines
instantly run squalling to Mummy. Not a speck of fight in either of
them. Never was. (Unless you count Domino threatening Fluffer from
safely behind the closed window.) Pokey lives two houses down. I never
thought I would resort to chasing a cat away with imprecations-- but
he's depriving mine of their Very Own Jungle. Or it will be when I've
filled that relentless spread of featureless lawn with shrubs, agapanthus,
arches, flower-beds, a fig tree (I love figs!) and maybe one day a pond
and fountain.

I'm still surprised by things I'd forgotten about the US. No separate
grocers, meat markets, fishmongers, fruiterers or butchers: everything is
the supermarkets--which are open 24 hours a day 7 days a week. Lots of
stores open on Sundays, and we have no Early Closing Day, and meat-
markets are open on Mondays.

Virtually no rain--well a bit in April--since I came in Jan. They say it should start next month--perhaps-- Seems this is Unusual Weather. A three-year drought, in fact. I love it!

Domino seems to feel pretty good lately. I've asked Figgy to arrange for a few years more than the diagnosed two, if she could possibly manage?

Love to all of you, Sally

16, Oct '87
Sutemi
My dearest Sally,

Many many thanks for the birthday card & gifts which reached me just at the right time. The goodies and stationery were very nice, & Tiggy & Lucy loved their fuzzy mice.

My kids have now started getting in their winter store of cones & hiding them on top of the wardrobe, they also have some twigs, a plastic spoon & an assortment of dry leaves, they are worse than magpies for collecting things. It was a long time before i found where Lucy was taking all those cones, i had to spy on her. Of course it's the very tallest wardrobe, the one in the spare bedroom, which I of course I couldn't reach, but Mrs.P (I have a new home-help now) brought her nephew one day to have a look and there they all were.

I had a proper feast for their anniversary. A casserole of several kinds of meat with vegetables, beans & cabbage, potato crisps & jelly and blanc mange for afters.

Love, Fred

Sienna,
Dec. 19
Dearest Jenny, Max, & Black Paws,

I always said I have weird cats. Get this.

As soon as we came, I registered them with a lovely vet named Grant Patrick. Extremely caring and gentle, so that *even Deirdre* arches and purrs for him! He suggested a new food called Kidney Diet for Domino, and a quality dry food for Deirdre. They love the dry (which was only a treat for them in England) and say how lovely to have all the Munchies they want--though naturally each thinks her sister's is much tastier. They keep looking sideways at the other dish, longingly, but willing to let Mum have her way. I can't believe they're so good about it! One day I found Domino sitting patiently in front of her empty dish--*with Deirdre's full one right beside her!* Can anyone explain that?

Love, Sally

CHAPTER SEVEN

THE BLACK–PAW GANG

Bonn

Jan, '88

 First of all, thank you for the Christmas gifts, and Scallywag thanks you very much for his whateveritis. Photograph of him using it enclosed. He really does think it's the cat's whiskers, and he says he has been ordering one like it for months, only I was too thick to understand.

 Congratulations on teaching your two to respect each other's eating bowls. I woul--(short break to sort out Chandi) --dn't have thought it possible, but never tried.

 So glad Domino is still going strong. Very few vets realize the efficacy of plain old love where the healing of cats is concerned. If cats know you want them around, they'll stick around if they can.

 My lot, as you call them, are being a Pain in the Posterior at the moment, as 2AM is the favourite time for a full scale armed quarrel between Mall Madam and Deedle, with all sound effects at high volume, and heaviest clogs worn for flat-out gallops up and down wooden open-plan stairs. Nothing static about OUR warfare. Mall in good voice would flatten any mere banshee. Ever since she got her blasted trophy. And the twins are as bloody 'orrible as eight-year old boys usually are--doubled. And Max is in India. Again.

Love, Jenny

18 Feb, 1988
Sutemi
My dearest Sally,

We have just been through another week of terrific storms & floods but around here damage has not been too severe mostly telephone & power lines. Ours went again but not for long. The kids have been sticking very close to me, Tig became very vocal when he saw the rain, kept sticking his nose outside of his door to see if it was easing up, eventually gave up in disgust & joined Lucy under the sheet, of course they blame me entirely for the weather.

I don't think Tig or Lucy ever saw any judo but I did, once or twice when picking you up & I'm pretty sure that's what they've been doing on each other. Are you sure you didn't teach them before you went?

Love, Fred

March 2, '88
Dearest Fred,

Yes, cats do hold their human pets entirely responsible for food, quarters and weather, don't they?

You don't need to teach a cat Judo: I think *they* taught the Japanese to start with. Mine do it all the time. Just in fun, really, says Domino when Deirdre squalls about Being Picked On, and she should go beat up some other cat. Like Pokey.

I did tell you I'd soon be grumbling even more about *here* than *there*, didn't I? So mote it be. To match the infuriating British habit of turning a *fine-tooth comb* into a *fine tooth-comb,* Michigan to Mitchigan, and BBC saying, toffee-nosed, that they *know* 'pronunciation' is pronounced 'pronounciation' because their Pronounciation Department says so--

--Americans write 'Here here!' for 'Hear hear!' (apparently calling the dog, and never mind any logic). They tend to pronounce *all* double C words like double S: (assede, essentric, flassid, cossyx). (Well, schools chucked phonics long ago, didn't they?) So aside from 'nephew; the F sound in PH tends to vanish, creating words like, spinx, spere, spincter and diptheria. AW becomes short O: (dotter, jonty, nottical). Iraq is

Eye-rack; and Saudi, Sawdy. I used to be annoyed at people saying 'nooze' for 'news'. Now they've reversed it, and say 'newn' for noon. (I can't *help* being a purist about words, spoken and written: they're my business--or were when I was still writing books. And when we misuse them (Decimate, momentary, problematic, disinterested, enormity, nauseous--) we lose both meanings.)

Dad sends his love. Says he misses you. I drive down to Oakland at least once a month and bring him back to stay with me for a few days, then take him back. I hate the drive, especially a certain merger where all the predatory college hunks like to bully little cars--but who knows how much longer I'll have Dad? He's only 92--which in my family isn't all that old--and seems very fit-- Still--

He went for checkup while I was down there, complaining bitterly that he can no longer play 18 holes of golf every day. The doc sighed. "Mr Watson, at your age do you expect to be *perfect?*"

"Yes," said Dad simply.

Love, Sally

April, '88

Dear Jenny,

Domino still seems to feel pretty well. They're both on a kidney diet now.

I've started giving blood again. It's privatized, of course, and all posh. Instead of camp beds there are luxury leather armchairs that tip back, and TV to watch, and iron *and* blood-pressure tests, and fruit juice instead of tea (before *and* after) with cookies; and a little pin for every gallon, and goodies like T-shirts, and you can give every two months instead of six, and platelets oftener, and they don't cut you off at age 65. They gave me credit for the 46 pints I gave in England. And the *big* reward--*you get* <u>*credit*</u> *toward any blood you might need some day!* (!!)

No, stop gaping luv. Here nothing's for free. Not blood or ambulances or hospital stays. When I tell them about National Health, they look stunned, rally, say they don't believe it and anyway Socialized Medicine is a wicked system! "*We'd* never let the government tell us what treatment *we* can have!" (That from people who have Capitalized Medicine, and pay thousands to insurance companies to tell them what treatment they *can't* have. Like anything they need, and then up the premium or cancel their insurance for needing it.)

While I lived there, people used to ask me (wearing expressions appropriate to asking a cannibal about his diet) 'Do Americans *really* think socialism and communism are the same? Is it true that you have campaigns lasting more than four weeks? Declaw cats? Have for-profit hospitals? Pay for prescriptions?' I would counter that **we** have a written constitution, and sane plumbing and salads, and no royal primogeniture--but the other questions were embarrassing.

Actually we could hugely reform elections simply by adopting your system. Public financing of campaigns and no loop-holes. *No one could get any more media time or space no matter how much money he waved around.* Bingo! Lobbyists bankrupt (or in jail for bribery, which is what it is) and 3-5-week campaigns like yours. They'll never do it of course. They think being able to buy elections is in the Bill of Rights.

Your lot hunt innocent foxes, ours buy guns *Over the counter!* Even assault weapons which the NRA (which used to stand for National Recovery Act, but now is National Rifle Association) promote! Second Amendment, they say, and never mind the bit about militia.

On the other hand, Fred is right when he says I could never be a proper Brit because I lack reverence for the Royal Family. True. 'Born to rule' offends me to the core. Any kind of Privilege bugs me--but especially the sort where you think an accident of birth somehow makes you superior. My knees, which lock even in a Catholic or high Episcopalian church, no matter what I tell them about Doing in Rome, would stay just as implacably stiff if ever I should find myself facing Her Majesty (much less any of her considerable family).

Enough fuming. I'm a disillusioned idealist, which is A Bad Thing.
Love to you, Max, the twins and the Black Paw Gang.
Love, Sally

Obersdorfstr. 2a
53340 Meckenheim-Ersdorf, Germany
May 31, '88
Dear Sally,

Yes, that's pretty primitive, all right. And you do have dammed fool gun laws. We British just don't like them - they irritate us. There was a bank hold-up last year, with some dumb young thug with a pistol (turned out to be a toy but no one knew) threatening the customers and an old woman said "Don't you point that thing at me, young man!" and chased him out of the bank with her umbrella. And please don't tell me what would have happened there: I don't want to know.

I think it is absolutely impossible for anyone not born and bred in this briar patch to understand how the British feel about the Royal Family and particularly the Monarch. An American once asked me if I would jump off a cliff if ordered to by the Queen, and I said "Yes". He was quite baffled. I wouldn't, of course, do it for Elizabeth Saxe-Coburg-Gotha-Battenburg-Windsor, who won't allow cats in any of the royal houses and has a rather careful sense of humour. But that, and she, are beside the point. She is the Queen. The Duke of Edinburgh is a disaster, but he isn't Queen, so it doesn't matter. You can burn the Union Jack all you like. It means damn all to us - because our Monarch is our symbol, not our flag.

You still don't get it, do you?

I don't know what the procedure for giving blood is in Germany - I gather much like the U.S. without the luxuries, but I am rather put off by the fact that they actually INSIST on giving you 40 marks per pint! I don't want money for that. Personally, I feel a damned sight happier with the good old British way: stab you in the thumb for blood to test, glower at you suspiciously while demanding answers to personal questions, a thoroughly uncomfortable folding camp bed and an English cuppa tea. And you have to give at least 12 times before you get anything like a badge. Imperial pints, too.

Sorry I haven't written for ages. Reasons include moving, a holiday, hay fever, Scallywag's broken leg, and a poisoned hand, so I shan't drone on.

Note the new address, somewhat outside Bonn. Not a bit like England's Green and Pleasant Land--nor California, either, I gather. Please don't tell me any more about your gorgeous garden in perfect-climate Sienna. The ground here is a thoroughly tough sandy bog, surrounded by the fir trees so beloved by the Germans. I call the damned things wooden weeds; they are revolting, and they produce thick clouds of yellow pollen which cause hay fever, thank you very much. Especially the Austria Pine outside Max's balcony, but that tree is sacrosanct. It belongs to the cats, especially Percy, as they can climb it pretending they really do mean to CATCH that enormous pigeon.

Scallywag's leg is all healed up. By the way he is now an International Champion. And little Toot is a Grand Premier International. That is the equivalent of a Champion, but for neuters. She absolutely adores shows, purrs all the time, and kisses the judge, which, as I tell her, is nothing short of bribery! Quite a change from her behavior at home, where strangers are fair game, to be nipped good and hard. The only trouble is, she does not like the car, so going to shows and coming back is a bit stressful. And damned noisy, too!

Love, Jenny

Dear Jenny,

Now who's breaking bits of themselves?

Actually, I do absolutely get it. Your feelings about the monarch. But in mind and imagination, not gut. I love your description of Liz Battenburg (as opposed to The Queen.) 'No cats in her castles and a careful sense of humour!' (Flags are never guilty of that.) But it figures, dunnit? I mean, what careful sense of humor could possibly be an ailurophile? Or vice-versa?

What *you* many not get--or even know--is that here, though we *vote* for persons rather than parties, nobody swears allegiance to *any* human: royal, symbolic or political. People swear allegiance *to the flag* and Presidents swear to uphold *the Constitution* (though with the last three out of four this was 'honour'd more i' the breach than th'observance'). Interesting, innit? We vote for the person and swear allegiance to the symbol: you, vice-versa.

Domino's kidneys are suddenly acting up. Dr. Patrick gave me instructions and wherewithal for giving her sub-cutaneous fluid. But I couldn't get it right. Poor darling didn't run or hide or fight; just crouched on the sideboard, crying piteously because I was *hurting* her! After several tries I phoned in despair, and his partner actually made a house call to do it for me. To my amazement, dear placid little Domino turned on him like a fury. Said she'd tolerate him Doing Things to her on *his* territory, or me doing it on *mine*, but damned if he'd lay a finger on her on *her* territory! He had to retreat in abject defeat, firm in the conviction that she's really a very aggressive cat, and just didn't show it before. (And they didn't charge for the house call!)

That's the first time I've seen her lose her temper since Fluffer died. Wish she'd do it for Pokey, who still wants to move in. Says why don't they just go live with Linda and Chuck and leave this place to him?

But I still don't know how much treatment is acceptable to Domino.

Why are you going around poisoning your hand?

Love, Sally

P.S. They pay for blood In Germany? How off-putting!

9th Sept. '88
Dear Sally,

I'm sorry about Domino's kidneys. For now, I truly think she'll rally.

It wasn't me who poisoned my hand it was Mall Madam. You see, she took strong exception to our going on holiday for 4 weeks without her, and when we got back I tried to take her to the vet for her slightly overdue rabies shot. That was the final straw. She bit me. And apparently hadn't cleaned her teeth that morning.

Madam had her second litter. We've got to the H's now. I found Heartbreak's hernia the moment she was born, and knew she didn't have a chance, so I named her and left her there as she was. Not in pain, just dying quietly. Madam knew, though. Cats can count to two, perhaps three. One, two, three, lots. Which is why, when they move their kittens, they always go back after the last one to have a final look around. They know their limitations; wish people did. Madam hunted for her, making that heart-rending low roaring noise of a distraught mother cat searching for a lost baby. I showed her the dead kitten, and she just sniffed and stared and would not believe it. Went on for 2 days looking for her lost baby. Then she forgot. I sincerely hope.

Never was a kitten better named than Hell's Angel! Now he lives in a small village just outside Cologne and I wish it joy of him. Why go through a door if you can destroy it? No fun climbing curtains if you can't rip them to shreds on the way up. Human toes are for eating, particularly if the human attached to them is so unwise as to be asleep.

And once they come down from the ceiling, be there smiling sweetly and telling them how much you love them.

I took him to a cat show. He waited until the judge had written in his first-prize place on the form. reached out a paw, drew the unsuspecting judicial finger toward him, (Aach! Wie Suss!) and bit it to the bone.

And he stayed seal point. I should have known. Somebody told me Blue Points are inclined to be quieter. I don't think I shall ever breed again from this line!

Current cats: Toot, her daughter Chandi, Didi (Deedle) who is a bit thick--I think. But it's funny how he seems to have organized everything to his complete satisfaction while blinking slowly and looking bewildered). Scallywag (Excaliber) Never beaten in shows, stunningly beautiful, totally loving--and sprays like a demented skunk and has to be kept apart. Madam is now Champion Suryasun Enchantress. She and Scallywag are both Toot's.

And then Whiskey, whose name is rarely uttered without the preceding words "--and as for that--" Slim. elegant, suave and wicked. Cannot be kept in a garden. Two meters high, that fence, and he goes over it effortlessly. So I built an overhang. Two days that took him. Hook paws through net and climb along dangling underneath. I JOKE NOT, WATSON! Moreover, he treats my overhang as a hammock. He's a Grand Premium International, by the way, and judges and breeders have teeny weeny little tantrums when they learn that he is a neuter. Tough. To my mind, he s too extreme. I don't want to breed cats with ultra-long heads, it isn't healthy. He's healthy himself, but what if his kittens had even <u>longer</u> heads?

The Black Paw Gang sends love to the Cats in Cahoots, and so do I.

Jenny.

October, '88

Dear Jenny,

Deirdre can count to four. Her vitamin pills are so large I quarter them, feed her one at a time, and she counts as she eats. One, two three-- Waits for it. --Four. And she walks off.

Puzzle. Kittens have to learn to drink out of a dish because at first they dip their nose in, and sneeze, yes? And any normal respectable cat learns quickly how to do it, yes? No. Domino hasn't got the thing figured out yet. She realizes this, of course, and approaches the dish with a wary but determined air--much the same way as the blood bank approach my rolling vein. "Now, let's see-- If I just turn this way--" and then gets it wrong and sneezes.

Moreover, she really prefers a tumbler to a dish. Perhaps thinking it'll be easier keeping her nose out of the way? In any case, I now have tumblers, vases, tall dishes all over the place for her convenience, and she uses them all, even the vases containing flowers, *and* my iced tea (Yes, we do drink it iced!) which she loves. And if I've drunk too much out of the glass, she rams her whole little face down until I fear it'll get stuck.

Love you! Sally

Sutemi
5th of November, Guy Fawkes Day, 1988
Dearest Sally

Thank you very much for the birthday gifts for me and my kids which we all enjoyed very much. It's been a very wet October this year so we all stay inside a good deal and Colin's lads pop over to see if I need anything, which I usually don't but enjoy the company. Maurice and Marjory come almost every day as well.

The kiddies are as rambunctious as ever, Tigger keeps bringing me dead leaves and Lucy brings dead voles. I think they expect me to eat them for they sit watching me expectantly.

Love, Fred

Bonn
Dear Sally,

I don't KNOW why Domino gets water up her nose!

CHAPTER EIGHT

EARTHQUAKE!

Obersdorfstr. 2a
53340 Meckenheim-Ersdorf, Germany
3 Jan. '89

Happy New Year! May it bring peace, health, prosperity, happiness and purring.

Your nice Christmas gifts arrived, and many thanks. The ocarina has me completely baffled, but amused with it. I'm slightly less musical than Scallywag, who said "Let ME try," but I won't because he'll break it.

But listen. Next time you send this herb for cats, could you please wrap it in a bit of polythene or something? They love it so much they not only chew it up, spit it out, and strew it all over the living room, they also chew up, spit out and strew all over the living room the letter that came with it, the envelope that enclosed it and anything else that smells even slightly of it. Luckily I read one of the Christmas cards before they got to it, and the other one they allowed me to keep. But if there were any questions in your letter or first card, you'll have to ask them again.

But I have a question for your lovely Grant Patrick. Why do cats always do terrible things to themselves when all the vets are closed? I've just made another emergency run halfway across Germany to find a vet that was open.

Love, Jenny

Jan. 30, '89

Dear Jenny,

Don't they have catnip in Germany? Okay, I'll enclose some *seeds*--
but you'll have to put them inside steel barriers the minute the first leaf
pokes above ground, because they love it fresh even more than dried.

In the meantime, Domino has appropriated that long-furry-red cat
blanket you sent for Christmas, and thanks you very much. It's her Very
Own Not to Share, you know, because she has always adored red. And
never mind that myth about cats being scientifically proved color-blind.
(It's also scientifically impossible for bumblebees to fly.) If the experts
spent less time peering at rods and cones, and more on observing cats,
they'd do better.

Remember in England when you gave us five identical-but-for-color
fluffy squares? Deirdre was permitted the blue, they shared the gold and
the green, Domino appropriated the red and the white. She kept the red
on the low shelf of a table, and would take it out, drape herself over a
low stool, pick it up and put it down a few times in her left paw (she's a
Southpaw), then take it in her mouth and proceed to dance![5] On hind
legs, waving her arms, humming a little purr-hum. Finished, she would
put it carefully away. Twice I saw her Doing Reverence to the white one.
Secret hiding place. Brought it out, arranged it carefully on the floor,
sat squarely at one side, reverently reached out left paw and then right
to touch it, then moved to the next side and repeated the ritual. All the
way around, and she picked it up and returned to its secret altar. I KID
YOU NOT! I have a photo of her dancing with the red. Photographing
her with the white wasn't remotely possible.

As for color-blindness, granted she might not see the same color that I
do--but then neither do nurserymen. They inevitably classify purple, lilac,
violet, lavender, mauve, amethyst, even fuchsia and magenta--as blue. "It's
all in the eye of the beholder," one of them said snippily when I said I wanted
true blue. I retorted that in that case E flat was all in the ear of the hearer.

---

5   See front cover.

(In my case it is. Tin ear.)

Anything red automatically belongs to Domino, and Deirdre never argues the matter. She quite likes blue, herself, but not passionately. They both hate orange, though. They had an orange dish once. Always removed all the food from it, they did, and took it across the floor where they could eat with their back to the offending dish, Domino with a martyred air.

But I did ask Dr. Patrick about why cats need vets when the vets are closed. He pointed out that here there are emergency clinics that *never* close, so there's no drama in it.

Hugs--Sally

August, '89
Dearest Sally,

Oh, I believe it! Your cats--like mine--are not like other cats. But I hadn't thought anyone still believed that color-blind theory! It's been quite disproved, you know, especially in the red/yellow range. As any observant cat-owner knows.

I had forgotten cricket, what with living over here for so long, but now I've remembered. And it's a Test Match. England v. Pakistan, and a cracker.

The twins are being hellions. So are the cats, but I find I can tolerate that better. One doesn't expect them to do anything else. James and Alex (still back in England, you'll remember) are doing well. I think I'll send Jay and Lee to them. And stay here myself--though I've been thinking lately of doing it the other way around.

An idea for another book is finally drifting round in my mind. I'm just letting it drift. Does yours work that way, too?

Gotta go, Sally. Love to the kids.

Sept., '89

Dear Jenny,

Yup; that's the way it works with me, too. Ideas drifting-- Hmm... D'you suppose Figgy has started mucking about with you, as well? Because *I've* got a book idea drifting around *my* mind, too. Well, three, actually--which can be confusing.

1. A short story about a haunted school house that I wrote ages ago--in the Reed Prologue in '49!--is now saying it wants to be a whole book. That should be easy. It's all there--and I love expanding-- Especially the end? Make it less like an abrupt fall off a cliff?

2. Domino and Deirdre say shouldn't *they* be a book, too?

3. And I've JUST learned that in 1811 there were massive earthquakes in *Missouri(!)*, the biggest-ever in America; for over a year, and aftershocks for a decade or three!--and I'd never *heard* of them! Me, who loves quakes! Wotta challenge for a writer! I'd love to try it! How would different people react? Not merely *one* devastating 8 or 9-force quake, but 4 of them in 8 weeks! A hundred times more powerful than the S.F. quake? More? (Geometrical progression?) Felt for a million square miles: in Boston, northern Canada, Florida, the Rockies! And the Mississippi flowed backwards and formed waterfalls. Waves of earth like a sea, swooping past, the ground twitching like just-killed meat--on and on and on--months of constant quaking, living outside for 2 winters-- What did they *do*? How did they feel? *Why has virtually no one ever heard of those quakes!* I really must have a go, one day!

I miss you terribly! Do you realize how little we've actually *seen* of each other this whole twenty years? One judo week-end, a few visits in Reading, one to Oxford, and perhaps two or three to Sutemi, early on. And we seem to thrive on it, albeit frustratedly.

Love to you and the Black Paw Gang.

Sally

A month or so after writing that letter, I went to visit my friend Jeanne in hospital. I was sitting by her bed when suddenly my chair began sliding gently to the left. Then back. It felt like a wave moving a rowboat. But though I hadn't enjoyed an earthquake since--oh, since those lovely ones in the Bay Area back in '57--I knew what it was, all right! Jeanne said later that a beatific expression spread over my face. I know my voice became a happy croon.

"We're having an earthquake!"

The gentle swaying went on for--perhaps 15 seconds, they said. They're timeless for me. Utter silence in the hospital. Jeanne said her room mate (behind me) was preparing for hysterics, but when we just sat there placidly, she apparently changed her mind, disgruntled.

It ended. Still silence. Presently a nurse came in, looked at us, moved the overhead TV sets well away from the beds, and quietly went out. We sat on for a bit. I was still feeling blissful. I've always loved them. Not killers, mind: the ones I've known just knocked down chimneys (no one on the West Coast is silly enough to build brick houses) and smashed things around a bit and buckled ridge-poles, so it's easy to enjoy them. Even the big Seattle one in April of '49 that rocked Portland as well--

Sitting there, I told Jeanne the story of when I was a baby and we visited Dad's relatives in California, just in time for the '24 Long Beach earthquake. Mom said all the house fronts along the block fell off, leaving a row of stage sets. I was sleeping in my crib in the bedroom, and there were a series of horrific crashes in there. Mom and Dad staggered in--just as the head of my crib crashed again into a wall and instantly bounced back to smash against the opposite wall. Bang! Bang! Not a sound from baby Sally!

They lurched to seize and hold it. I didn't move. The quake ended. They reached for me, fearing the worst. I opened sleepy eyes, yawned, ascertained that my nap was not yet over, and went blissfully back to sleep. And I don't even remember it! Oh darn.

About then it occurred to me that Deirdre and Domino were English cats who had never felt even a mild quake, so I decided to go home and make sure they weren't upset. I went out, saw a man in a wheelchair who for some reason was in a terrible panic. Couldn't get up and run! he kept bleating. So I asked kindly where he thought he'd run *to* that was any safer than right there in the open? He calmed, I got in the car, turned on the radio to see if a small local quake warranted the newscast...

It *hadn't* been a small local quake! It had been far south--a hundred miles?--in Loma Prieta--and 6.9 or so! A freeway in Oakland had collapsed and the San Francisco Marina was ablaze.

I hurried home, irrationally more worried about my cats than before I had heard the news. Walked in. Domino, asleep on the sofa, opened one golden eye and said hullo, was I home, then? Deirdre sauntered in from the back yard to tell me something about the crickets being too spry to catch, but she'd almost got something that wasn't quite a mouse. I turned on the TV--and sat riveted for hours.

Jenny phoned.

"Sally! Are you all right? How could you go live in a dangerous place like that? Was it near you? Did you feel it? Come back at once!"

If I did, she added temptingly, maybe she would one day return to England and join me. She and Max were drifting apart--he to India in spirit, and she clean round the twist--and the twins were more bolshy than ever, and she's homesick for England, and sometimes fancies living on a boat there with only her cats for company--

Oh, I wished she could just come here! But she'd have hated it.

Sutemi
October '1989
My dearest Sally,

Thank you for getting to me on the blower so quickly, you knew I'd be worried. So were the Strides and Colin and his family, he went all the way to the public library and brought a really big map of California and we all sat around looking at it. We were surprised to see that the quake was a very long way on the other side of San Francisco, and San Francisco is about as far from Sienna as Headley Down is from London which was surprising as we didn't know earthquakes traveled that far. Anyway I was glad to hear that you and your father and sister are all right too, we were concerned about you all. It was ever so nice to hear your voice, hope the call didn't cost you too much. Wish it weren't so pricy to phone, we could do it more often.

We are all well here though a bit cold as this turns out to be one of the brilliant but icy Octobers. Colin's boys are well grown now, you'd be surprised, and one of them comes over twice a day now to fill the coal scuttle for me and feed the hopper which is a welcome help. Maurice is feeling his age lately.

Your welcome birthday gifts to me and the kidlets arrived today, you're always very clever about the timing. I'm going to enjoy the book, you seem always to know what I'd like and we all enjoyed the goodies.

Love, Fred and the kiddies

CHAPTER NINE

WILDLIFE

Jan. 12, 1990

Dearest Jenny,

What a truly super cat pillow! I assume you made it yourself? Deirdre says this one's hers because it *isn't* red, and about time, too. Well, Domino has no one to blame but herself. When I opened it, she promptly went into her DOES IT BITE? act, prowling around it at a safe distance (about three feet) until Deirdre appeared at the door, took one look, one leap and full possession, wrapping all four legs around it and rolling all over the carpet, entwined.

But she's an affable creature, and says she doesn't mind sharing, now Domino has decided it's safe to lie on even if it isn't red.

Domino is still with me--two full years lobger than she was given! I've asked her for still more. *Yes*, I'm greedy!

My current revision, Haunted Schoolhouse, is augmenting nicely, and I've done a few chapters of the cat one, still unnamed. Have tried to contact my old publishers--five top ones--who once adored me. Zilch. They've all merged or been taken over, and the new lot have never heard of me and prefer to leave it that way.

How's are things in Bonn? (I already know how they are in Kuwait, and why waste all that time fuming when we'd agree anyhow?)

Love to all of you, Sally

14 March, 1990
Sutemi
My dearest Sally,

I haven't much news, really. Don't get out much: only on my little chair with a motor, I have little ramps for them now and it works very well, If I need to go out and about, the neighbors take me, they're really very kind. I expect you're very busy these days with your garden and new friends and the exercise class you're teaching. No judo, though, not for your seniors? How are the insulation and bay window you put in? Is the drought any better? I wish we could send you a bit of our rain.

The kidlets are doing well and very naughty. They send their love.

Lovingly, Fred

May 20, '90
Dearest Fred,

I'm so sorry about not writing for so long. Things do get a bit on top of me. The senior exercise class I teach at the community center meets three mornings a week, and I'm hard on them. No aerobics though: I don't think that's good for the feet except bare, on a hundred thousand years of leaf mold. But tough stretches and coordination and isometrics, mostly. And spacial orientation in the form of simple Scottish country dances. My 'boss' came to see and gaped. "Migawd, Sally, *I* couldn't do that--and I teach exercise myself!"

I smirked. "*They* can. Look at them." (All right, so a few do it rather badly--but they all more or less *do* it, which makes me very proud of them. And they *shine* over certain men who swagger in just once, can't do it, mutter that it's too sissy and leave.)

I've learned that used copies of my books are selling for totally obscene prices--like $881.00 (honestly!) for a battered and probably stolen library copy. Oh, it's a compliment, in a way, but an outrage. Books should be to *read*, not as collector's items! Through a local librarian, I'm slowly getting in touch with grown-up but faithful readers who had thought I must be dead by now, but remained loyal. (They actually have a Sally Watson Yahoo [?] Group on this new-fangled thing called Internet!) Figgy insists that's one reason I *needed* to come back. It was time I faced new challenges, she says, and *past* time I started writing again, after a 20-year block when I wasn't even *thinking* about writing: just peacefully living there at Sutemi.

All *right!* So I'm writing again. On a computer, heaven help me. (So far, a quill pen would be faster and less frustrating. Lucky Jane Austen!) So far no publisher will consent to *read* my mss.--or even respond to inquiries accompanied by SAS! (Even though my name was well-known back in the '60's. Librarians then regularly asked when 'another Sally Watson' was coming out!) Evidently the publishing industry has changed since 1970.

I wrote to my old agent, who for years took 10% of my royalties for doing very little--but at least *they'd* know me and read my mss, wouldn't they?

Well, sort of. When Mary Feltrop finally remembered me, she was all effusion, and said I must send something to her. Some day.

My love to you and the kidlets--and to keep me posted about how you are doing! Fred, I do miss you so very grievously!

Always, Sally

Sienna
August 4,
Dearest Jenny,

Wow! Wish you could've been here last night!

My bedroom looks out on the back garden, but the windows offended me. Just standard windows, unlovely, letting in too little light. (I *love* light!) So, using leftovers from my house sale, I had them transformed into a sliding glass door opening on a lovely new deck. I leave the door open at night to enjoy the air and the cricket song. Two nights ago I woke to a sound of--furniture moving? On my *deck*? Well, there are some boxes and chairs--but no one should have been shoving them around! Still-- the noise was definitely from out there. Some one whimpering, scrabbling. Burrowing behind the boxes? Crying? It was half-trill and half-rattle, but it sounded like weeping. I peered out. Some one, it seemed, about as big as Deirdre (who, with her sister, was firmly hiding under the bed). So I went out.

A baby raccoon! He turned to me, and then rushed up, hugged an ankle and asked if I was his new mum because the old one just sat there and didn't help.

The old one, crouched atop my high fence, confirmed this with a growl. It was plainly not an angry growl, but a 'Do Something!' one. She said Junior had somehow got in to my pestilent garden through my pestilent fence, and couldn't get out.

Well, Junior was very sweet and lovable, but I thought it might be a bad idea to pick him up. I tried to show him the way out the side gate, but he wasn't having it. Finally I went back in--and the bumping, weeping and growling redoubled. So I went out again. Repeat performance except that Mum had moved closer, to the low edge of my roof. The next time, she was lower still, her head practically brushing my ear, saying if humans were so smart, why couldn't I Think of Something?

Eventually we established some sort of communication. I kept going around to the side gate and opening it wider, calling loudly, coming back, talking to them. And at last I saw them depart, Mum virtually frog-marching Junior, presumably out of my life.

You'd love raccoons, Jenny! I've started feeding one in the cemetery, along with his buddy, a feral cat. When I feed Jetsie, Haggis stands upright and says she's hungry too.[6] She takes my fingers in her tiny black ones and sniffs and delicately tastes. I know they're really very wicked--

---

6   See cover

according to human standards--but they are adorable. Beautiful, friendly, clever, diabolically mischievous, have a nasty defensive bite, but seldom feel constrained to use it. Raccoons *are* destructive, but just for food or fun. Like ferrets and monkeys. No human vices. Never malicious, corrupt, hypocritical, arrogant or untruthful. Unlike humans.

And supposedly so clean that they wash their hands before eating.

Mmm. I don't think so. Not quite. I suspect this is as accurate as the one about hair turning white overnight, and color-blind cats. How much dirt can get on those wee black hands? I've seen the dishes they use, far from any loose dirt (in my kitchen, for example, all the way through bedroom, hall, living room and dining room) about *half filled* with mud. Say, a half-cup of dirt per dish? If they carefully trotted back and forth (on two legs?) with *handfuls* of dirt, it would take many many trips. And they'd spill rather a lot on the way. Which they don't.

So--*how do they do it? And why?*

Always and always, your baffled
Sally

2 Obersdorfstr. 2a
53340 Meckenheim-Ersdorf, Germany
3 August, '90
Dear Sally,

I WANT A RACCOON! Please send me one at once, telling him that there is nothing to worry about, I will happily be his new mum, and will fix the fence so he can get in and out as much as he likes, and also have all the dishes of water and free earth to make as many mud pies as he likes. His first mum is invited, too.

The way they transfer all that loose dirt is either to roll in it or fill their mouths, I haven't decided which. The reason is a deep family secret.

My Black Paw Gang wish your twins a very happy Michaelmas.

Love, Jenny

Sutemi
19th Sept. 1990
My Dearest Sally,

Sorry its taken me so long, my writing machine suffered a terminal illness & it's taken me quite a while to get another.

Woke up to a pouring wet morning, Tig took one look out of the window & came straight back to bed, both of the kids were given a Bank Holiday present by Bert the milkman, a little carton of Devonshire cream, he plays with them when he comes, no wonder he is still on his round at 5 PM, when his relief is on. I get my milk at 7 AM. They love that ball you sent but I've noticed at the end of playtime Tig takes it back to his bed & hides it.

The kids have been very loving, they are going through a face-rubbing stage with furry head or wet nose against whatever bit of me they can reach. Lucy's paw is ok now but she is always going to have a little scar across the pad from the ingrown claw, & I always keep her claws trimmed now. Tig has not stirred from his bed all day, most unusual for him. I've been in to see him several times as such a long sleep normally means he is not feeling too well, however he seems all right, I get a bit worried when either of them change their routine. Milk up again today, now 39p a pint & I have just heard on the wireless that petrol will be £4.00 a gallon before long.

Lots of love from Fred, Lucy, Tigger

Oct. 1,

Dearest Jenny

Fred's milkman gave his kidlets some *Devonshire Clotted Cream* for Bank Holiday! Omigawd! I'd trade almost any food there is for clotted cream! There ain't no justice!

Did I ever tell you about my musical cats? Probably not. Well, back in England, I got an ocarina like the one I sent you, and Domino simply adored the sound of it. Would rush up, climb me and press her little cheek next to mine--for the vibrations, presumably--and do a little humming purr along with me. Especially if I played *Once in Royal David's City*.

Deirdre shrugged and said she could take it or leave it.

Now I have an electric keyboard. Domino says *she* can take *that* or leave it, but Deirdre waxes ecstatic. Streaks all the way across the garden and through the house, leaps up on the bench beside me and listens with the inspired expression of saint hearing a message from heaven. Has her preferences, too. *Fur Elise* is her favorite, even the ham-handed way I play it. The only thing she doesn't like is *Jesu, Joy of Man's Desiring.* Dunno why: it sounds ok to me. But she stalks out every time I play it.

It still amazes me, the difference in wildlife in the two hemispheres. The birds are vastly different: even the ones with the same general name. (You know about the robins.) I used to ask neighbors excitedly what this or that was, and they'd say "Why, that's a kingfishers or jay or woodpecker: don't you have them?

Well, yes--but not recognizably. Our kingfishers aren't gorgeous peacock-blue, but sort of blackish with fuzzy heads. Our jays are *blue*jays: totally different! Much smaller and all-blue, with crests, no stripes across tails. Woodpeckers are unrecognizable as such except for their wood-pecking. But we we have humming-birds, everywhere you look. (One crashed into the glass doors last week and fell to the ground under Domino's sleeping nose. She startled, looked up at me anxiously, like Scrooge's housekeeper. "For *me*?" I told her it wasn't, and picked it up, fearing the tiny neck was broken. But there seemed to be a heartbeat--fast as a vibration--so I just let it lay in my palm for the longest time. Then it stirred, raised its head, looked at me--perhaps wonderingly?--pulled itself together, said it felt peckish, and flew off to sup a snack.)

Sorry this is short. Love you very much,
Sally

CHAPTER TEN

FAREWELL TO FRED

30th Jan, 1991

I know, I know, I KNOW!

I am the lousiest letter-writer in Western Europe. I am very very sorry. The trouble is, writing to you goes to as many as 14 pages and usually takes up the best part of one day if not several, and I never seem to have them. Several days, I mean.

Let me give you an example. The twins have been chucked out of the Gymnasium, apparently because German isn't their native tongue (though they were four when we came, so they've been fluent for most of their lives now.)

Lee's teacher asked me to make something called a devils-food cake. Have you ever read a recipe for the thing? It uses every bowl and saucepan in the kitchen and takes hours to prepare, and then when I opened the oven the bloody thing was stone-cold!

So I used the sort of language mothers Aren't Supposed to Know and shot across the road to ask my neighbor if I could use her oven. She said sorrowfully that hers won't get hot enough for cakes. Another neighbor, though, laughed like a drain, said of course, switched her oven on, and to my horror popped the poor devil's food straight in without letting it heat up.

Oh well, it was pretty flat by then, anyway. I went a bit lavish with the icing, and, when I delivered it, mumbled defiantly that it was an American recipe. What the hell are allies for if you can't stab them in the back when necessary?

They all loved it. Thank God for uneducated palates.

Love, Jenny

Feb 16, 1991

Sienna

Dearest Jenny,

Good grief! I've known of devil's-food cake all my life (though I've never made one because I'm no cook and they're too chocolaty for my palate) but I never dreamed they were so complicated. Are you sure that wasn't a German idea of an American recipe?

Anyway, I enjoyed your description! I've been distracted, after the endoscopy--

Ah yes, the endoscopy! I let them do one on Domino last month. I had misgivings at the time. But anything that might help my darling! Now I'm so sorry! It was all a mistake (not to mention a waste of $500.00). Nothing showed up, and when I went to pick her up, she felt so betrayed, she wouldn't even look at me until I'd pleaded and apologized for ages and then only when I said hello to another cat. When she spoke to me at last, it was at great and angry length. I'd *promised!* she said all the way home. It turns out--and they hadn't thought to mention it--that with renal problems they couldn't give her any kind of anesthesia, so she had to endure it all, fully conscious!

I don't want *ever* to put her through anything else! When the time has come to lose her, I want it to be with me loving and cuddling her, and not with her last conscious moments of fear and loneliness and betrayal. I've promised *not* to make her life miserable just to keep her alive. (As I'd want for myself.) But it's so hard to know! She's now been with me for eight years, (four or five since they said two more was her limit) and feeling fairly good, mostly. I do wish I could ask her opinion!

Don't boys have to be nine or ten to get *in* to the Gymnasium, which I gather is a type of school? Are you trying to tell me the twins *are*? Rubbish! Can't be more than seven.

Or-- Were they born in-- uh-- Nov. '79?! Oh! Oops!

Love to all, always, Sally

17th March, 1991
My dear Sally,

This will be only a short note, I am too upset & miserable to be able to settle to write properly. My Tigger went out as usual last Tuesday 12th & then seemed to vanish into thin air. I alerted all of the neighbours when he did not come back at his normal time but nobody had any sight of him at all.

Marjorie has checked all of the garages, sheds & greenhouses the whole length of Fairview Road but no trace of my little boy.

It is getting to be a long time now that he has been missing & I am beginning to give up hope that I shall ever see him again.

Feel too rotten to write any more now, I can only hope & pray that he will in fact turn up again but I'm fast losing any hope. I know quite well he'd come home if he were alive and could, so I very much fear I'll never see him again.

Lucy misses him, of course, and she is behaving very strangely to me. Won't let me out of her sight for a moment.

Hope that you & your kidlets are keeping ok, will try to write again when I feel a bit more settled.

Love, Fred X X X

March 24, '91
Oh, my dearest Fred!

I'm so terribly sorry! What else is there to say? Yes, I must agree: he would certainly return to you if he could. We can only hope that someone fell in love with him and kidnapped him, and is pampering him, and sooner or later he'll escape.

As for Lucy, *of course* she clings to you! One of the only two beloved people in her life has vanished, and now she's terrified of losing you, as well.

Oh dear, I suspect you're feeling much more ill than you are telling me, too. Even though you have your home help (I wish our government here was that caring) I worry that you won't tell them if you feel ill. (I *know* you, dear friend!) I wish I could be in two places at once. I could be your live-in housekeeper, and we'd shock the grannies by apparent impropriety. Would that worry you?

Dearest friend, how I *wish* I could do something! You know my prayers and love are with you, and with Tigger, wherever he is. And with Lucy, too, poor love. I need not tell you to give her all the love and reassurance you possibly can!

Always and always, Sally

Sienna

March 24

Dearest Jenny,

Poor Fred has lost Tigger, and I suspect is very poorly physically, besides. Not that he's *said* a word--I just think so. Enduring in silence like a cat. Shy, too. Wouldn't tell a virtually strange woman about personal matters like pain--much less, where! I feel so guilty for leaving him even though I know his neighbors are watching over him. All the same, I know he's lonely a lot, and probably in more discomfort than he ever lets on. Aside from grieving over Tigger...

Thank goodness I insisted he adopt two cats the last time!

Always, Sally

That summer of '91, Fred became completely bedridden without ever complaining in his philosophical letters. I only learned later. And on Sept. 12, six months to the day after Tigger disappeared, Lucy's worst fears were confirmed and Fred was taken to hospital. The Strides phoned me, and again a few days later to break it to me that it was cancer of the liver.

*Oh, **no!***

At least that was in England, where the best possible care is automatic and unquestioned, and no bill ever presented. They have National *health care,* and that's exactly what it means. For starters, England is appalled at the very notion of hospitals for *profit*: they're *expected* to lose money, just as schools, police, the fire department and libraries do. So instead of *competing*: they *cooperate*. First they took Fred to Basingstoke, that being better equipped for the terrible bed sores he had carefully never mentioned to anyone. Then, learning that his neighbors could visit him more easily at Alton, they transferred him *and* the equipment there, and pampered him gorgeously. Anything he fancied, night or day, he had only to ring.

Two days after he was taken away, Kate the cattery lady rang me. She believed in keeping track of the cats she adopts out! Nearly nine years after Domino and Deirdre, six years after Fred adopted Lucy and Tigger, she somehow got my number, 7,000 miles away, and phoned!

"Kate here. I just heard about Fred. *Who is taking care of Lucy, and why wasn't I told?*"

(So she knew about Tigger, too!) I said his neighbor Marjorie was taking care of Lucy. Kate promptly rang the hospital to request permission for Lucy to visit Fred--and received it. Then she drove all the way up from Liss to fetch Lucy, and then all the way to Alton to see Fred.

He lived long enough to see Lucy a second time, and be reassured that Kate would find her a new and loving home--but he died the day before my birthday parcel to him arrived.

I had never quite forgiven myself for having left him so cavalierly. Now I thought I should at least do something for some one else in his name. Community service? Naw. He didn't care all that much for the

Needy. Just me and cats. So I tried the Humane Society. Just the thing for Fred. And me. Unfortunately, they discovered almost at once that I knew the alphabet, so they made me a file clerk, in a building far from any animals. Well, filing is something I refuse to do even for pay, so after a couple of weeks, I looked for a place to be with animals.

I found a small animal rescue group in a nearby town, but when I arrived to meet them, they were holding a trap upside down, with two terrified cats clinging to the sides as high as they could get.

"What *are* you doing?"

"Getting them out, of course. They're feral."

"Well, if they weren't before, they are now. Are you expecting them just to fall out or something?"

They said yes.

I said they were *cats!* They'd *never* fall out! Not while they were remotely conscious.

They said of course they would, puppies always do.

I said cats weren't puppies; and how about letting me take the trap to wherever they wanted to put the cats--and by the way, what had they planned to do if these feral cats *did* fall out right here with the door open? They said not to bother my head about it; they knew what they were doing; and I should go back wait in the car for a few minutes..

And when I went back ten minutes later, they told me briskly that everything was fine now: they'd euthanized them.

So that was the end of *that* lead.

Next I found a bird-lovers club, also out of town. Misnomer. They proved to be a trio of ailurophobes who told me darkly that cats are evil filthy creatures whose saliva is deadly poison and who are wiping out the entire bird population. Being a stickler for factual accuracy (and never having met an ailurophobe before) I innocently tried to correct these erroneous beliefs. I said that cats--unlike most animals including humans--were forever washing themselves, that their saliva contained a natural healing agent, that more birds (like cuckoos. hawks, crows) kill birds than do cats. And that cats kill far more rats, mice, gophers and voles than they do birds--

The Trio denied this.

I told them that research in England showed cats got over 20 mice and rats per bird. They said See? They killed birds! So I told them Jenny's story about the Finnish quail and the virus.

They accused me of verbal inexactitude. (Not quite in those words.)

I reminded them that dogs kill cats-- (The Trio said Good for them!) --and that man kills everything he can aim a gun at-- (They said that was different).

"I said, all right, how about the Black Death?" They said the which? I said Bubonic Plague, in 1350 or so. Wiped out a quarter of the population of Europe, probably because witch-hunters had wiped out most of the cats that would have killed the rats that carried it.

They said good for the witch-hunters, and it sounded like a whopper, and what was a boob-whatever, anyway?

At this point we found something to agree on. None of us wanted me to come volunteer there. So I departed, to the great relief of all four of us.

Pokey brought a ball of fluff with a cat's face to see me. I thought at first she was a sea otter. Linda and Chuck, Pokey's humans, said her name is Whisper and they'd got her from a new cat rescue group called Catnippers, who seemed very nice and why didn't I look into them? Wary by now, I went to a meeting. Half a dozen enthusiastic people sitting around on hard chairs explained it to me. The idea was to trap ferals--

"*Trap?*" I bleated in my ignorance.

They said Well how else would you catch a feral? and it didn't hurt a bit, and they covered the trap *at once,* so the cats instantly felt all snug and safe in a small space.

I said Oh. "And then what?"

"--and get them neutered, return them to the colony and feed them daily; and some could be fostered and socialized-- "

A cat carrier in the corner said it was socialized already, and what about a lap?

Well, this sounded better--but I wasn't committing myself. Not yet, anyway. I explained that Domino and Deirdre were so bonded to me that they wouldn't tolerate anyone else, man or beast. Some one said Never mind, there was lots else to do: yard sales, publicity, getting donations, organizing, filing--

Euh! Not bloody likely, Mate! Fred wouldn't have asked it of me! I smiled a few times at a vivid and pixie-charming member named Constance, one of the founders, whom I liked on sight and whose answering grin radiated caring, determination and humor--but I sat firmly on my hard chair volunteering for nothing.

That was early October. A couple of weeks later I woke up early on a Sunday morning unseasonably hot even for California. I took the Sunday paper out to my deck chair, but there was such a strong--and hot!--(In October!?!)--wind blowing that I gave it up and came inside, where my radio was nattering away unnoticed.

Presently something caught my attention. Tone of voice? Key words? I listened. It sounded like a fire. A big one! *Where?*

"It's coming!" said a shaken voice. "I'm on the the corner of Florence and Elrod, and there's a 30-foot wall of flame bearing down on me. I'm off!" The mike went dead and I sat rigid with dread. My second-longest friend--since Reed College days way back in the '40's--lived on precisely that corner in Oakland. And her husband had a bad heart--

The whole day and the next we watched the horror of that fire burning a good portion of the Oakland hills and scores of homes, and I worried about Betty and Jack in particular, but presently Dad and Marilyn too, as the fire got ominously close to them. Phoning was of course impossible for days. I got Dad at last, but Betty's line was predictably dead. I eventually learned that they had been in San

Francisco for an opera matinee, and were spared the immediate shock and danger--though their house became a mere smear of ashes.

Jenny, predictably, went bonkers.

Oct., '91

SALLY!! STOP SCARING ME LIKE THIS! This is twice in two years! The news of that horrible Oakland fire on telly is terrifying. Isn't that where you lived with your Dad and sister when you first went over? Are they all right? Are you far enough away to be safe?

I just got your letter about Fred, too. And it makes it worse that he never found out what happened to Tigger. I am so very sorry! I know how fond you were of him. And of course any cat-lover-- No, that's not necessarily true, is it? Some of the ones who want to buy or stud mine are NOT nice people. But Fred really loved them, didn't he? I feel that he had a lot of love to spend and not many to spend it on.

If I don't hear soonish, I'll try to phone. Frantically, Jenny

Dearest Jenny,

Sorry to keep scaring you: I didn't *plan* the fire, actually. Am sending you a detailed report as it affected me and mine. Dad *et al* are fine if scared. No personal harm or damage. It was further from Sienna than Headley Down is from London. Well, slightly.

Yes, you have Fred exactly, bless his heart. I'll miss his letters abominably.

How is The Blacksmith of Anford going? I'm still discouraged. Mary Feltrop didn't return the ms. she had requested, or even the return postage. Or answer my query about Haunted Schoolhouse. It figures. All they ever did, even in my salad days, was to forward my mss. on to the publisher *I* had found for myself in the first place. Sometimes. When they got around to it. One May, Ann (my editor at Dutton) came to London, treated me to lunch, and asked me when *Hornet's Nest* would be finished. I said, dismayed, that I'd *mailed* it to the agent *in January!* The only copy fit to read! Ann had to phone and give them hell and demand it at once. Presumably it was stuck in a drawer somewhere. *And they still took 10%!*

So if *she* approaches *me*, fine; otherwise--

I've finished <u>Haunted Schoolhouse</u> and am trying to get someone to read it or even tell me why not. I think it would be ok for juvenile *or* YA. (But I've no publisher or agent to tell me.) In the meantime, I've sort of started the earthquake one, which I might call <u>The Angry Earth</u> or maybe <u>Demented Earth</u>? If I can get enough info. It was *only* 180 or so years ago: you'd think there'd be more known! And I don't know whether to bother except for my own amusement. And getting accurate information might prove a nightmare. Being bloody-mindedly stubborn, I'm still trying. For one thing, my block is gone and I'm hooked on writing again. It would be more encouraging, though, if I thought anyone would ever read the results--

Deirdre's been in the wars again. When she produced her tail for me to 'groom' (which I'm sure is how they see it), I ran my hand under her belly for her massage--and felt something Very Wrong. Like ragged and sticky.

"Deirdre! Let me look!"

She said No ruddy fear: I *knew* I wasn't allowed Liberties. A session in the bathroom did no good: as I once mentioned, she's stronger than I, not to mention wigglier--and this time I was afraid of hurting her. So down we went to Dr. Patrick, and she let *him* look without a murmur.

"Oops!" he said, looking shocked. "Stitches!" And picked her up, unprotesting.

"What *is* it?" I begged, as he started for the door. He said grimly that another cat had apparently got her. "And when she was in submission, too!" he added, outraged.

Pokey, of course! **And** on Deirdre's own territory, which she never leaves! (And it's no use complaining to Linda and Chuck: they can hardly lock them up any more than I could keep mine from going to Grace's. Cats have their own ideas of territory.)

Following Dr. Patrick as far as the doorway, I could hear them in there, and wished I had Jenny's power of demanding that she stay with all her cats at all times in the vet's. They were murmuring. In fact, they seemed to be--cooing?

"Aw, the little sweetheart!" "Isn't she a dear?"

When he brought her back, I looked severely at them both. "Were you lot by any chance cooing over *Deirdre*?

He said they were. He said she was a little doll, purring the whole time.

I said he knew perfectly well she always purrs in trauma. Since the first day I got her.

He smirked. "And *kneads*?"

She's fine now. So, alas, is Pokey, who tends to swagger a bit. Won *that* one, didn't he? Don't deserve Sally, do they? Let the Winner take the spoils. He can't understand my attitude.

I love you very much--and also your family even though I've never met the Black Paws except for Toot when she was a wee kitten.

Love, Sally and the Girls

PART TWO: CATS IN THE BELFRY

2012	1040	US	Rental & Royalty Incor

Please enter all pertinent 2012 amounts. Last year's amo
expense column should only be used for vacation hom

DIRECT EXPENSES (continued)

Direct expenses are related only to the rental activity. These includ
rental agency fees, advertising, and office supplies.

Pest control. . . . .
Plumbing and electrical . . . .
Repairs . . . .
Supplies . . . .
Taxes - real estate . . . .
Taxes - other (not entered elsewhere) . . . .
Telephone . . . .
Utilities . . . .
Wages and salaries . . . .
Other:

_____
_____
_____
_____
_____

OIL AND GAS

Production type (preparer use only). . . . .
Cost depletion. . . . .
Percentage depletion rate or amount. . . . .
State cost depletion, if different (-1) if none. . . . .

CHAPTER ELEVEN

CATNIPPERS

Sienna

Jan. 28, 1992

Dear Jenny,

Guess wot!

1. I've met another New Old Friend. Name of Arlene. Teaches the 60-hour Master Gardener class I've just started. She has a son with the usual reading problem. (Seems to come to a head, about 90% of the time, with highly intelligent 9-year-old boys who need reasons. Like *why* those squiggles should say 'Oh oh, look look' and who had at least been fine in arithmetic until they came to 'thought problems'). Well, I don't usually brag, but I *can* teach phonics better than anything--and I know it better than virtually anyone. Been doing it forever. Mother taught it to her kindergarten pupils so I just picked it up as a baby and began teaching siblings as they came along. Later, for fun, I figured out aspects of it I've never read anywhere. Not just basics like hard and soft C, but things like *why* there's a D in *dodge, ledge, badge, ridge, smudge,* etc. Reasons. So as soon as school is out. I'll teach Dan, who's a charming lad, and piteously discouraged.

2. Arlene mentioned casually that she Communes with animals. I didn't know if she meant it, and if so, whether she was (a) offering or (b) just commenting; which so confused me that I said nothing, and she didn't volunteer more, but I think I'll ask. One day. It somehow seems a bit cheeky. Like telling your symptoms to a doctor you've met socially. But--what if she could ask Domino how she feels, and why she keeps piddling *and* pooping around the front door--

3. I received a letter from Fred's solicitors. I was more right than I suspected about his being alone in the world! He has divided his entire estate between the Cat Protection Society in England--and me! I'm unbearably moved! Oh, it probably isn't much, considering how frugally he lived--but that's totally irrelevant, bless his heart. Whatever it is, I'll probably spend it on cats. Which is why--

4. --I've sort of joined Catnippers, after all. No, don't get your tail in a knot: I *won't* do fund-raising or filing, and I shan't be fostering or anything. (D&D wouldn't hear of it). But I do think Fred would like me to do something for cats, and the Humane Society didn't pan out, and this sounds worthy. Anyway, I won't decide quite yet. After the next meeting?

5. Today I am--good grief! 68?!

Love to you and the Blackpaws.

Germany
Feb, '92
Dearest Sally,

My poor foolish Colonial Cousin, do you really believe you can keep your eager little paws from carrying those poor cats home? You'd better have Arlene Talk to Domino and Deirdre and warn them!

Mall Madam is taunting Percy, who's not allowed out at night, and she is. I have a tiny space for her at the window, too small for Percy, but

Toot loves working the wedges out and dropping them to the floor with a satisfying clatter, leaving a big enough gap for Percy. She wouldn't dream of going out herself into the nasty cold, with all those ghosties and ghoulies, so she virtuously retires to her nice little electric blanket, and finishes off Percy's supper, and Percy ends up in the sin bin, which has no electric blanket. Also, he knows perfectly well why he's in there, and Madam making big eyes at him and telling him he's absolutely wonderful doesn't mollify him a bit. She's a bloody nuisance and a brat, a typical example of the Younger generation, and she ought to be spanked. If it weren't for the fact that he's a perfect gentleman, he'd give her a hiding himself.

I'm laying bets about how long you can hold out.

Love to your kids, poor little sods.

Jenny

I went to some more meetings of Catnippers; largely because of Constance, actually. My gut says she's a Kindred Spirit. She was urging an adoption program.

"They'll be much better off, and we'd get some return on our expenses," she pointed out practically. (Seems they're so non-profit, not only does no one get any salary, they reach into their own pockets when they run out of donations.) "Adoption fees will help pay the vet bills."

I liked it. Began to bargain about my role--if I joined. My choices seemed limited. I positively declined anything that didn't involve hands-on with the cats. No fund-raising, publicity, paperwork, even being on the Board (which in these beginning days all the half-dozen or so organizing members seemed to be). I'm no good at hands-on democracy, though I approve in principle. All that argument! No, no, no. I wanted only to work directly with cats, who don't argue. But if I couldn't take then home to foster-- I was promptly invited to Trap. Since I had never even *seen* it done, I said I thought not. Not yet, anyway. Negotiations continued. What about Feeding the Colonies--?

I said *that* sounded splendid.

Oh, good! they shouted almost in unison. They needed feeders--
and in my area, too. So I was presently given five colonies. Four of them
had fewer than ten cats each, but the big one at the near-by parking
lot contained nineteen. Lovely! The more, the better! I was hooked
and they all knew it. The previous feeder had offered them horrible
moldy food from the Safeway dumpster--which was left untouched,
of course, cats being fastidious. So Constance and I cleaned that all
away, and brought proper dry food (which they gobbled thankfully);
and I carried on, rejoicing as they began to trust me, marveling at
how quickly they learned to recognize my car among all the others,
and come to meet it.

Three of that big colony were clearly lost or abandoned pets, badly
missing the human love they had once known. The small gray loner
who lived in the northwest drain, I named Shadow. And there was a
pair of buddies whom the last feeder had called Bert and Bobby. Big
orange Bert was bouncy and loving.   Bobby was a stately black and
white Angora-type long-hair of such massive dignity that he needed a
name to match. So he became Lord Robert. Alias Lord Bobbin--or just
Bobbin when we were feeling informal. He responded to all.

The other cats were definitely feral. They had had either unfortunate
human contact or none at all. Still, most of them ventured nearer and
nearer. There was a wily pale gray and white I called Mia, gorgeous
golden-tortie Amy, and Nimrod, a burly battle-torn male whose tail
was not only truncated but had a 90 degree bend in what was left of it.
This fellow was a professional fighter.

I realized that cats are not all loners: they just aren't pack animals.
But they all got along. Bert and Bobbin were inseparable best friends;
so were Amy, Nefertiti, and Seven-Toed Tansy. That charming blotched-
tabby was the first to come to her name and let me stroke her. She didn't
wear her extra toes all neatly alongside the others, as some polydexters
do: hers jutted out comically at her wrists like large double thumbs.
She would come galumphing to meet me, comically over-toed, pause,
wait for me to kneel, then rush forward to rub ecstatically around me.

At the other extreme were dilute-calico Nefertiti who took eighteen months to let me touch her, and then adored it; and Amy, who held out until 2007!

I had been feeding for hardly a week before Shadow, Bert and Lord Bobbin were totally in love with me. Shadow rushed to greet me with hoarse little chirps, Bobbin leaned against my shins, and Bert dogged my heels, talking loudly.

Almost at once I began to think in terms of homes for those three, especially after Bert developed a rodent ulcer and submitted with total tranquility to a carrier and a visit to Dr. Patrick. By the time I returned him next day, he had fallen even more in love with me, and followed me all over the parking lot begging loudly for me to Kidnap Him Some More.

So Constance rushed around and located a farm home for three outdoor cats, and told me to bring them one by one to her empty aviary, to wait for their vet checks. Back I trotted with the carrier. Bert first, I decided, since he'd taken it in his stride, before.

But Bert had changed his mind. Spread-eagling to brace his feet firmly around the outside of the door frame, he explained earnestly that it would be better, after all, if I just moved in with the colony. I didn't yet know the trick of tipping the carrier on end and lowering them hind feet first, so I gave up on Bert for the day, and it was Shadow who went in like a lamb, only asking small anxious questions on the way to the aviary. Once there, he found the special heating-pad-for-cats and settled down blissfully. *Ever* so much nicer than the drain, he said.

Next day I took Bobbin just as easily. He sat in trusting silence all the way.

Then the problems began. I still couldn't catch Bert. He was, in fact, pretty upset. He Wanted his Buddy back! he'd bawl from a safe four feet away. I was to return him *at once*! I promised to reunite them, and find a lovely new home, if only he'd get in the nice carrier, but Bert wasn't having it. Clearly, the Kidnapping would have to wait.

It waited two weeks.

Shadow loved the aviary, spending all his time hogging the heating pad. Bobbin hated it there. Felt imprisoned. Sulked about Bert. Unfairly regarded poor Constance (whom cats usually adore) as his jailer, and wouldn't let her comfort him. Well, he saw me as his sole connection with Bert and Home, didn't he? He'd sit sweetly on my lap and say he loved me in spite of everything and when would I take him back to Bert? Once I had left without him, bedlam would break loose. He complained loudly all night every night, and the neighbors complained about his complaining.

Then Constance took him and Shadow in for their vet check, and it turned out that Shadow had advanced renal failure, and was unadoptable. I sighed and gave up the whole project. Bobbin went back to Bert and the colony. It astonished me that he let me bundle him back into the carrier without protest, but he did, and again sat trustfully all the way back to a joyful reunion with his comrade--after which he wouldn't let me touch him for a full six months. No more of that Kidnapping lark for *Him,* he said. He relented only after Bert vanished (as do so many ferals) never to reappear. So Lord Bobbin became sole Patriarch and a very dignified one, too; again pacing grandly forth to greet me: portly, silken, imperial. Even when he decided to trust me again, you'd never catch *him* scampering to meet me. Not *Dignified,* he said, his thick coat just brushing against my legs. After all, he *was* Lord Robert, wasn't he?

But as for Shadow--Jenny's dire prediction was fulfilled. What else could I do? You don't just kill a cat merely because he's going to die anyway: he was entitled to a bit of quality life. Not in the colony: not now, to die unpleasantly, alone in his horrid drain. Nothing for it but to take him home with me--to the incredulous dismay of Domino and Deirdre.

CHAPTER TWELVE

REQUIEM FOR A SHADOW

Shadow had lived an unknown time in that drain, apart from the rest of the feral colony: a thin little shadow of a cat with long gray fur holding faint overtones of apricot, and one ear rakishly and permanently bent.[7] He stood on his back toes to butt his little head against my hand, purring and drooling rapturously. From the start, it was love he wanted. And where was he going to find it? With all the healthy kittens around, who would adopt an elderly waif with only a short time to live? So there was no alternative, and I took him home, after all, hoping it would be all right with Domino and Deirdre, after all...

It wasn't, of course.

They were shattered. I didn't love them any more! I was *Replacing* Them, they wailed. Deirdre hid behind the brown armchair and moaned. Domino first got instant acute diarrhea-- (Yes, that quickly, said Dr. Patrick. Distress.) --and then bravely confronted him, growling like a hysterical dog. Shadow instantly threw himself placatingly on his back, paws dangling limply: unthreatening and benign. It was, of course, useless. Domino remained resolutely unplacated, intolerant of his very existence.

---

7   See cover

Shadow took it all in his stride. And what an extraordinary little character he turned out to be! His small face was wise, alert, filled with roguish intelligence. He chose to give me unconditional love, trust, and *obedience* (!!) as he did everything else: in full awareness. I had only to tell him a thing once, even disagreeable things like "You must *stay* on *that* chair when Domino and Deirdre are around," or (later, when the desolate Domino nearly went into a Decline and Shadow had to move outside) "*Don't* come in the cat door."

He understood instantly and perfectly--and *chose* to please me. On a wild wet night I got home to hear piteous crying from the back garden, and found him drenched and miserable, pressed forlornly against the wall beside the open but forbidden cat door!

After that, I gave him a soft warm cat-nest in the garage--which he ignored, to stare wistfully through the clear plastic of the inner cat door at the friendly warmth inside, and poke a hopeful head inside now and then to see if Domino had relented. (She hadn't.) So he began sleeping on the top stair where the door pushed him off every time I opened it.

But I hadn't forbidden the window, had I? So in he popped one morning, head cocked, pausing to eye me in mischievous hope.

"Sorry," I said with infinite regret and one eye on the agitated Domino. "Out." He instantly outed--but to curl up beneath the window instead of over on his Very Own deck chair.

Meanwhile Deirdre and Domino, feeling very sorry for themselves, refused to set foot in the back yard at all. He could *Have* it, then, they said bitterly. They'd just Stay Inside and Get Sickly for want of sunshine. Especially, they added sadly, since Pokey now Lurked out front.

Obliging as he was, Shadow had a mind of his own--though he was never impolite. His kidneys made him picky about food, and he indicated rejection with a long firm stroke of his paw diagonally alongside the dish. If I didn't remove it after precisely three repeats-- (he could count, too!)--he would rush around gathering leaves, trash, anything else he could carry, to pile it all in a little mountain on top, to make the symbolic burial literal.

He spent most of that summer there. Usually he stayed on his deck chair, watching for me to come out, purring up a storm the moment he saw me, following me devotedly around the garden making little comments in a hoarse chirp that sounded like a cross between sheep and frog; climbing to my lap the instant I sat down. Still drooling. His body really wasn't fit to live in. But he was so *happy!* Couldn't remember *ever* being so happy, he would tell me rapturously through purrs, pressing his forehead to mine in a long love-pose that felt like communication. He was Remembering about play, too, he would add, tumbling kittenishly after a ball.

Timid with most strangers, he had adored Constance from the start. Now he added supposedly incorrigible seven-year-old Tommy from across the street, and Arlene's Dan, whom I was now teaching to read. But he lived only four months: more than long enough to steal my heart before breaking it. Despite my desperate pampering, tempting him with one food after another until the fridge was full of untouched cans of KD, people-tuna, baby-food, chicken broth--*anything* that might tempt him--he slowly failed. Constance gave him subcutaneous fluid. For two days, I hand-fed him a teaspoon an hour of ground turkey in water. He rallied, ate jubilantly for a week until his tummy fairly bulged--and stopped.

The day came when he couldn't manage even to bury his food symbolically. He climbed laboriously to the uninsulated loft over the garage, and lay limp in the intense heat he seemed to crave, still purring, but more faintly now. Presently he no longer enjoyed life. He huddled and shivered, and Constance and I agreed in anguish that it was time to set him free.

I let him sleep that last night where he had always wanted to be: in my bedroom. On my bed if he liked, I told him. He climbed up on it to show he understood, pressed foreheads for a moment--and returned to his chair. I'll never know why.

Previously when going to the vet, Shadow had curled up in the carrier philosophically. This time he sat upright and intent, eyes fixed unswervingly on my face the whole trip. I'm sure he knew: he seemed to acquiesce. I hoped so! It was the first time I had ever faced the awful responsibility of a decision like that!

It was the first euthanasia I had ever seen, as well: Fred's vet had sent us out of the room. Dr. Patrick knew I couldn't have borne not to be with Shadow at the end! He lay still, watching me trustfully. I stroked his head and looked into the loving golden eyes, holding back my tears. Presently the little gray head fell sideways, too heavy to hold up--but his gaze, wide and still infinitely trusting, was still on my face...

And then--*his eyes went out.* There's no other way to describe it. They didn't close. Their light and love and intelligence simply blanked out, seconds before his heart stopped.

I hadn't known it was like that! I couldn't stop crying.

Domino and Deirdre were delighted, the brats! They instantly repossessed the garden and loft--until the third morning. Halfway out the window, Deirdre froze, glared, yowled with lashing tail at Shadow's apparently empty deck chair. A few moments later, quite independently, Domino started out the garage door near the same chair, stalled, bolted bushy-tailed back into the house. Though I never saw him, I couldn't doubt that he had returned. Especially when I saw a little mountain of dead leaves piled on his empty food dish. I could hardly believe it--but there it was!

For two days, they insisted that he was there, and refused to go outside. Then they sallied forth again and began re-marking the deck chair.

Gone, now, they said contentedly.

--Except in my heart and everywhere I looked.

He was a constant worry, a dreadful expense--and my life was unbelievably the poorer without him.

Little Tommy said it best, in the carefully handwritten card which he gave me the day Shadow had finally departed.

"I still love him forever."

CHAPTER THIRTEEN

THE RUDDY 'ORRIBLE HALF-YEAR

"Sally? This is Catnippers. You still prefer hands-on working with cats to fund-raising?" I should have recognized Figgy's style. As usual, I didn't. She was probably chuckling.

"Oh, absolutely!"

"Good. You can be a foster-mother. Cathy's at the vet now, picking up a cat who needs one at once. We'll be right over."

"But-- I can't! I *told* you! Domino and Deir--" It was too late: she had hung up.

And so I fostered One-Eyed Jackie. I sneaked her into the study, came out, closed the door behind me, and was confronted by two pairs of accusing feline eyes, green and gold. I'd Done it Again, hadn't I? they demanded. Just like That Shadow. I Didn't Love Them any more! And they supposed I was planning to drive them out of their Very Own Garden *again*, and let Pokey attack them some more, they added illogically.

I assured them that I loved them most of all, that Jackie would stay shut in the study, that I would go on chasing Pokey from their Very Own Garden, and wouldn't let him Get Deirdre again, cross my heart; and anyway, it wouldn't be for long.

It better not be, they said ominously, and went behind the big stuffed chair to groom each other in mutual sorrow.

Jackie proved to be a sweet little all-black cat with an empty eye socket. She was adult, unbeautiful, virtually unadoptable. I was asked to keep her while we tried to find a Need home--which usually means food and shelter but no love.

But this wouldn't be enough for Jackie. Like Shadow, she was *starved* for love! She accepted all the pain and the visual handicap as animals do: with patience and serenity, untouched by fear or self-pity. Didn't really mind, she said, pressing her little cheek against mine. Didn't even need food, really--if only I would love her? And how could I not?

I almost kept all my promises to Deirdre and Domino. Just once Jackie got into the living room and played hide and seek with a totally confused Dierdre while an even more confused Domino lurked in the dining room demanding to know why there were two of her.

I took Jackie back to the vet for more tests one day, in the carrier in the front seat. She was yelling her head off. Wasn't Going! she wailed. Going to Stay With Sally Forever! she screeched. So, to comfort her, I reached my left hand across as I drove, and put a finger in the carrier. I often did that with mine, and rubbing a cheek on it makes them feel better.

But Jackie promptly seized it in both paws and tried to drag me into the carrier with her. Her Very Own Human! she bawled, digging in with all her untrimmed claws. And I was in the left lane, and couldn't pull over, and hadn't a third hand to signal a move into the right lane. Nor could I pull my hand back, of course: my fingers would have been ripped open. She was just clutching, not attacking, so once I had somehow managed to hang on to my anguish and get into the right lane and pull over and persuade her to let go, there was little damage. But we were both very relieved when at last I got her home again.

Deirdre said disappointedly that she'd thought I was taking her away to join Shadow. In the long run, I was. When, later, Catnippers took Jackie back for more tests, she was diagnosed with Feline AIDS, and euthanized then and there. And I wasn't with her, to love her on her way!

Deirdre and Domino were not mollified. This was Twice, they said. There'd be More, wouldn't there? they predicted accurately. They had feared ever since Shadow that if I spared any love for another cat, there'd be less for them; and they knew darn well this was true of my time and attention. So they deeply resented every fosterling who came through. No matter how small or sweet or helpless, Deirdre would go and moan behind the brown armchair, while Domino sat in the middle of the room and imitated dogs. (She had learned that trick when Shadow was here.)

I received Fred's bequest. Lots! About $13,000! Over a year's income for me! I didn't really *need* it, for my Economic System still worked fine, and I had enough provided I didn't squander it on luxuries. A clothes dryer? Nonsense. Never had nor needed one in my life; nor a cell phone or any other technological gadgets, except a computer. I virtually never ate out, eschewed beauty parlors, credit cards, automatic garage doors, preferred books to movies. The only thing I needed more money for was vet bills and dentist--on which one doesn't stint. So I just treated myself to something called a sun-pipe to lighten my rather dark study ($600.00); and decided to make a BIG gift to Catnippers to please Fred and me, and save the rest for the cats.

So--never having given a larger sum than $25.00 in my life--I presented them with a check for the staggering amount of a thousand dollars! Shocked at my own reckless generosity, I waited for them to be bowled over. But this was no longer the Thirties, and no one lives frugally any more, and they naturally assumed that I must be Rolling In It, and there was more available where that came from, and where was the rest of it? And Catnippers' need was always urgent, wasn't it? We wanted to open a thrift shop so finances need not depend on erratic donations! I ended up giving it all to the cats--even the $5,000 I had planned to save for vet bills.

Well, that was what it was *for*, wasn't it? Fred would have approved. And I *can* manage my own vet bills, and even those of my colonies--just--so my Economic System still works.

August 1, '92

Dearest Jenny,

Long time no write. Busted my wrist in June. *Not* judo, which I have given up. But Judo *training* probably saved me worse harm. It was a pratfall on concrete that would have damaged my spine, but *muga* took over. (You know: the automatic *appropriate* physical response while your mind is going 'Duh!') Wrist better than spine, it said, so my hand went down to catch me.

Ironically I was just getting back from S.F. to see Mary Feltrop, who actually phoned me last month and said she'd be in S.F. and why didn't I come down and meet her, and in the meantime she'd *love* to see my cat book draft at once--so I sent it. When I saw her, she complained bitterly that it isn't Caras! Of *course* it ruddy well isn't Caras! Why on earth should *I* try to write *Caras?* Or any other author? Even if I could? How *could* one author write another? And *why?* She got all huffy and said she didn't want it if it wasn't Caras. I didn't *quite* tell her to get knotted--only that One Doesn't imitate other writers. And but for that abortive trip I might not have busted my wrist. The right one, too. And I'm so very right-handed that when I try to sign checks with the left, I write backwards! Like Hebrew, right to left!

The bank, who didn't see anything remotely resembling a signature on my cheques for weeks, was bemused. (It's a small friendly local bank, where everyone recognizes my voice over the phone--but not, lately, my signature.)

But I have definitely established that the American publishing business has gone insane since 1970. No longer do you write a book and send it in and they read it and let you know. Everything not 'requested' gets tossed unread. (*And* they steal the return stamps!)

I have recently met a private editor who told me the Facts of Life. Very enlightening and revealing and discouraging, it was! It seems you must spend several thousand dollars *hiring your own editor* to put it in some sort of pre-ordained format--*just to get it read!* Maybe. If they feel like it. *You then get a list of places you might try sending it.*

I tend to believe him. It would explain a great deal.

He didn't even suggest that I hire him. Just said the ms. I sent him was good, and suggested that I self-publish. But in my day that was Vanity Press, for stuff too bad to be published properly. I'm not really ready for that! Yet...

Still-- Something to think about. Long and hard! In the meantime, I've re-written *Poor Felicity* (which is OP) and improved and polished it, added animals and re-named it *The Delicate Pioneer*. I expected that at least one or two of my old publishers: Viking, say, or Dutton, Holt, Knopf or even Doubleday (who published the original!)--the publishers who did so well on me before--would *read* it. Nope. Didn't even remember me. Aren't even the same publishers.

And I was speechless at the only response I've had from any of them: the *editor* of Dutton (who published <u>Linnet</u> with praise, prizes and Jr. Literary Guild Selection) thinks my writing "too *diffuce*". [sic]!!!

I received that letter the same day that (A) a Supreme Court Justice presided over the Chicago Art Institute's TV mock trial of Hamlet, in which they explained that he "*murdered his own father, Polonius*", (B) a teacher was fired for using the word '*niggardly*'; "Racist Language", said the school board. And (C) a TV educational program went blithely on and on about ships regularly sailing from England to Oregon *around South Africa*

Love to all, Sally

14th Aug,
Dear Sally,

Well, education in the States sounds quite a good thing. Sailing from England to Oregon around South Africa is entirely possible, Sally, if you don't take the short cut across the Atlantic, and what's an oregon, anyway? You are just getting fussy in your old age, but then you hasn't done the English language proper. Being colonial, like.

Love to you and your cats, Jenny

Sept. 20
Dearest Jenny,

It's been a bad summer, seeing Shadow out, busting my wrist, and then learning that my brother--my favorite remaining sibling--had died alone in his Seattle home, of a stroke; and that my darling Dad has untreatable prostate cancer, Of course now I drive down to Oakland to see him as often as possible (though, alas, no longer bringing him home to visit for a few days), while not neglecting my babies or colonies or class or Dan--and quietly grieving inside.

I can't write requiems to Dad or BZ: this cuts far too deep. I don't even want to write or talk about it anymore, luv. So I'll change the subject fairly violently, mm?

I have realized that calico and tortie cats are *always* girls! Why? It's hard to find the answers, as color is of no medical interest in vet training. Are any other species color-gender-related? So far, no clues: just the fact--but I increasingly mistrust these Experts. Like those who know--a priori!--that only humans have personalities, and it's foolish anthropomorphism to imagine that animals can possibly feel any of the same things that we do: affection, anger, joy, jealousy, contentment, loneliness or even fear or pain! (Words fail me.)

Love you all, Sally

Oct. '92
Dear Sally,

Summer has come and gone, and Germany, like the US, thinks that summer starts at midsummer and autumn at the equinox. I just write it off as lack of genuine culture, everything adjusted for expedience, never mind tradition, history, or even garden or plain astronomy. Politics leave me baffled, too; and American more than European. This activity you call lobbying? What's the difference between that and common bribery?

School has started. Ho hum. And Max is in India (I talked to him on the phone and he sends his love) so I'm on my own again. The Blacksmith of Anford has been desultory. Would like to finish. The idea for a sequel--sort of--is prowling around waiting for a go.

Weather in Germany can be filthy when it chooses. Today it chooses.

Love you, Jenny

Nov '92
Dearest Jenny,

Well, at least Bush is out--presumably forever. And at least his rotten crooked son (the younger one--Neil?--who took a savings and loan bank in the recent scandal for several zillion and got off scot-free) is unlikely to be elected for anything. And at worse Clinton will be better. *Much* better than Reagan! Although I have a feeling that, that if America had any idea what a Rhodes Scholarship *is*, Clinton wouldn't have got seventeen votes? America tends to feel resentment and contempt for brains. "Elitist!" Our idea of a Great Leader is "some one you could sit down and have a beer with." Honestly! (An example of worshipping brawn over brain: a popular car sticker these days proudly declares *"My kid beat up your honor student."* Please don't tell anyone else: it's too embarrassing.)

Clinton's going to try to get a National Health plan passed. *Here?!?* Take the obscene profit out of Health Insurance? Ha! The vultures are already gathering, screaming Socialized Medicine! We should be so lucky! (Sorry. When I'm disillusioned I take it out on America.)

Dan learned to read splendidly over the summer. He's a very bright kid. Very! But the private (!!!) school had told him he was stupid, so he believed it. When he asked anxiously what 'reading level' I'd bring him to, I exploded. "That's a nonsense! Once you know the basics and the special patterns and the irregular common Anglo-Saxon words like *two, women,* and *of* (which is 100% irregular, but we all know it by sight so no one notices) *you can read anything!* You might not understand it yet, but you can ruddy well *read* it!" Now he's back at school, able to read anything as I promised--and is doing it with a vengeance (though the school so far won't admit it). He's a delightful child! I shall miss all of them badly! Did I tell you? They're moving in a few months--to the British Virgin Islands!

Aw--bugger it!

Arlene says that she really *can* Talk to Cats and at any distance! I asked her to ask Domino how she feels, but she said Domino didn't want to tell me if she felt poorly because she was 'afraid of the knives again'. Astounded, I protested she'd *never* had surgery, but Arlene was adamant. "That's what she *said.*"

Then I remembered the endoscopy they gave Domino last February! *She's remembering* **that**? Aw, the poor baby! I told Arlene to tell her how sorry I am, and promise never again!

(Arlene said both D&D wore human bodies not too long ago. This blows my mind! Fingers! The way Deirdre stares at her paws in bafflement when they refuse to grab things properly! I always *said* she thought she should have fingers! And Domino's vocabulary and understanding of communication-- *What if it's true?*)

Love, Sally

The rotten four months extended to six. Dad died in December--peacefully, thank goodness! I was glad for him. His mind had stayed sharp, but his body, though only 95, had let him down, and he was more than ready. Three weeks later--on January 3rd of '93--Domino died too. *Exactly* ten years from the day Fred and I drove her and the still-unnamed Deirdre home to Sutemi. (They loved each other, Dad and Domino.)

In a way it was harder to lose Domino. I had to watch her suffer, for one thing, while Dad was kept pain-free. And though I miss my darling Dad grievously and always will--at least I had him for a long time--and have no guilt. We loved each other deeply, comfortably, with virtually no criticism. I had been allowed no say in his care or death, so all I needed--or was allowed--to do for him was to be there when I could, and love him. I drove down often and talked to him for hours those last days when he was presumably out with morphine. I knew he feared death and I was convinced that he could somehow hear me, so I kept telling him the option *wasn't* hellfire or annihilation, or even harps and streets of gold; but a reality that would rejoice his heart, like Mozart and cats and golf: just wait and see! I feel sure it has.

But I was entirely responsible for Domino! And it was not peaceful. And I could neither help nor talk to her. I felt to blame for not preventing it coming to crisis. I had expected it for years--but that didn't make things easier. At the end, it burst on us without warning. Oh, she had needed Sub-Q now and then, and she began drinking more water, lost her appetite--but gradually. Until that Saturday afternoon. Suddenly her thirst became insufferable. She kept crying her word for 'water', and going from tea cup to water tumbler to flower pot to sink to bathtub; and at each place I produced fresh water and she stared and cried, and hung her face over the water that she could not drink--and pleaded piteously for me to help her: utterly certain that I *could* make it all right if only I would! That broke my heart so that I'll never quite get over it.

Dr. Patrick was away that week-end. So was Arlene. I finally went to an emergency vet--but he refused to consider anything but prolonging her life--and pain. That wasn't what she wanted! She needed to die! Finally I demanded that he ease her suffering, and I took her home, left an urgent message for Dr. Patrick--and cuddled her at last, all night. He rang back early Sunday morning, and told me to go straight to the clinic. Came and opened for me. And then and there--with no nonsense about forcing my darling to live longer in pain, he eased her out of the body that had become an enemy.

I went home, sobbing, and wrote to Jenny.

She replied at once.

20 Jan., 1993

Dear Sally,

I wasn't surprised when your sad little card arrived this morning, but I do grieve for you. Not for Domino, who must have loved you very much to have held on to stay with you for so long, but who finally had to let go. Every time I got a letter from you for the last several years, I have wondered if it was going to bear news of her death, and each time I have been relieved but increasingly astounded, that she was not only still there, but still relatively healthy and certainly happy. I have never heard of a cat with faulty kidneys living so long. Not only did you clearly give her the best possible physical attention, you seem to have added some sort of holy magic of your own which held her together.

Sally, will Deirdre be lonely? Would you like a Siamese? I will gladly give you one if you think it would work out--and if you could pay the air fare. I know you've always longed for a Siamese. The only thing is--these are very aristocratic and arrogant, and I'm not sure how Deirdre would take it.

Actually, Sally, I knew about Domino a couple of weeks ago, but just wasn't sure enough to contact you. I don't trust my instincts that well. I certainly knew she'd made it to New Year, and was mildly surprised. I should have known it was true and telephoned you--but sometimes the telephone just adds pain. I couldn't talk about Sam when she died, and telephone calls made it worse.

All my love, Jenny

Jenny wrote a poem for Domino.

DOMINO
Domino saw love and took it, thankfully.
She gave it back carefully, anxiously [is this right?] generously.
She stayed beyond her time, for love,

And left, when she had to, not gladly, but taking love
And leaving love, and living on,
Apart, belonging, and always, always loving.

Little black and white cat, I never knew you, but I thought of you,
And I hoped for you, and in the end,
I, too, cried for you.

(Yes, 'carefully, anxiously' were the exact words: the essence of my little Sobersides!). I cried all over again, at that, of course--and still do--but it helped heal the grief. Except that Deirdre and I were so bereft! Thank goodness I had her! Imagine losing your one and only! As Fred had done--twice!

As to the offer of one of Jenny's champion pedigreed Siamese-- Ooh, how I was tempted! But if I had harbored any hope that Deirdre would now be lonely, and welcome another friend--especially an aristocratic friend--I could forget it, she said, contracting her tummy, putting her tail forward over her back, stiffening it into a figure S, and quivering it at me lovingly. Domino was Still Here, she said: Right Over There, in fact, and it was Just Us Three forever, now, wasn't it? She became even more possessive than before, and I didn't seriously consider another cat of my own. Or even any more fostering. Not yet. It had been too hard a six months. For both of us.

CHAPTER FOURTEEN

THE CATACLYSMIC SUMMER

Marilyn, after selling Dad's house, packed up his cat Cosmos and all her belongings, and moved to Sienna, which was quite nice and very complicated. She got panic attacks driving, and trustingly assumed Big Sister would take care of all transportation. Which I did. She was feckless, helpless, loving and lovable--and my sweet sister.

In the big colony, all were safely neutered--except for the perverse and triumphant Mia. All trusted me within reason--except Mia. I got more colonies and became an experienced trapper--and Mia was still flicking a scornful tail at me. I had tried for the whole of '92 to trap her--which was excellent practice, but that was all. Not even the skilled Constance could catch her. She simply sneered at us, knowing perfectly well what we wanted but not playing that game.

My only consolation was that no one else had any better luck, not even the most experienced trappers.

I do hate being made a fool of--even by a cat! She would simply sit down out of reach, and sneer, daring me to do anything about it. I certainly tried! I would bait the trap and hide behind a tall fence. She would spy me spying on her. Once she slitted her eyes at me, and deliberately minced her lithe gray and white self into the long trap, nibbling daintily toward the pile of tuna which lay temptingly at the far end just over the trigger, while I forgot to breathe. Eyed me sideways, she did, and smirked--and then just short of the trigger, she stopped, backed out, and virtually bowed to the watching golden-tortie Amy. Be her guest, she said.

Amy didn't, of course, because only a kitten or a very forgetful, insouciant or hungry adult cat will go into a trap twice, and Amy was none of those. Mia wouldn't do it even once. But they do know how to rob them. Creeping in flat and wary; reaching out a long delicate paw to tease the food--ever so gently--around the trigger. Nefertiti sprang the trigger once, knew it instantly, and her swift little body reacted so quickly that she actually got out before the door could finish closing.

I had told Catnippers about the time Mia went halfway in. "Great!" they said. "We've got her now! If she went in once, she will again."

She didn't, of course. She never went near the trap again. It was back to square one: twenty feet, and laughing at me. She might well have had a litter in '92, but I never glimpsed a kitten. The apartment dwellers across the side fence might well have killed them: they were cat-persecuting cretins. Any sudden noise from that direction provoked a tide of terrified felines streaking the other way. It was no place to risk having kittens. I told Mia so, and brought the trap again. She leered at it.

Then one February morning in '93 I looked at Mia, looked again, and narrowed my eyes speculatively. Nothing showed: it was just a hunch. "Mia! Are you pregnant?" She gave me a deeply offended glare, stalked off, and I literally did not see her again for months. I really thought she had gone the way of Nimrod and poor vanished Bert. But my Ruddy Horrible Six Months were still afflicting me: and-- well, I shrugged. I'd done my best. And there was no way I could possibly have found her. One can never find a cat who doesn't want to be found. In fact, they consider watching invisibly while you hunt for them to be the just about greatest game they know. (All mine, it turned out, are past masters of it, relaxed and grinning.)

My busy summer of '93 began at the March meeting of Catnippers. A score of cat-lovers sat in a ground-level lobby talking about having a thrift shop, when we heard a cat crying outside. We stared at one another wonderingly; then Constance opened the door to the deep darkness. Without hesitation or diffidence, in limped a large amber and white cat. He paused, one paw lifted. The Orientally slanted eyes that were to give him his name gazed around with infinite trust.

We *would* fix his broken leg for him, wouldn't we?

Constance came up to me at the end of the June meeting, with the melting look I could never resist. No, let's be fair. I have never *wanted* to resist. She's a lovely person whose greatest sin is too much loving kindness for all.

"Sally? I wonder-- Well, I do know how Deirdre feels about other cats--but we're desperate! We have three kittens--two months old--who need fostering *just* until Monday, when they can move into the adoption program. We can lend you a lovely three-story condo. They'd be out of the way there, and Deirdre wouldn't mind *too* much, would she?"

Deirdre would, actually, and I knew it. But I couldn't say no, and didn't even want to. Not to Con. Or to cats In Need-- I sighed.

"Maybe she-- Just until Monday--?"

"Oh, Gwen says *absolutely*--!"

So Constance brought the tall cage with padded shelves on three levels, put it in the dining room, dangled some kitten toys on string from the top of it; deposited a large carrier, gave me one of her pixie smiles, and departed. I opened the carrier, reached in blindly, and found my hand filled with a wriggling orange tabby imp who instantly tried to climb the curtains. "You are Scamp," I announced with sure instinct, putting him in the condo where he instantly climbed to the top shelf and severed the string of a dangling toy with one snip of his sharp teeth. I reached again. This time it was a flirtatious dark tortie who wriggled sensuously and sang a long aria. "Siren, you are," I told her, and put her in the condo, too, where she promptly sat down at the water dish and began splashing with both paws like a baby in a bath.

I didn't reach for the third; she came to me. Out of the carrier appeared an ivory-white scrap with huge ears, gorgeous blue eyes, and a sharply wedged little head with pale gray points just starting to show on ears, face, feet and tail.[8] The face peered up at me winningly. Was I her new Mum? she wanted to know.

I looked at her and lost my heart. "Your name," I told her, "is Felicity, and you're mine! No matter *what* Deirdre says," I added uneasily, glancing across the room to where my ebony girl was regarding the proceedings with shocked disbelief before heading for the brown armchair with heartbroken moans. Felicity cocked her diminutive head to one side and regarded her with grave interest.

Thereafter, inside the condo, Felicity watched while her siblings rampaged. Siren went on splashing and singing. Scamp bit the strings off the toys as fast as I hung them. They wrestled vigorously. Felicity, odd girl out, still watched, appraising. She was, she told me, Studying Life. Predictably, three days turned into ten. I had to let the triplets out of the condo. Siren and Scamp proceeded to drive Deirdre back behind the chair with a lively game called Gotcha while Felicity sat atop the scratching post like a tiny elegant sphinx. And then I got another phone call.

"Sally? Help! Fuji-- Oh. Remember the cat with the broken leg? We call him Fuji for his slanted eyes. He desperately needs a foster home! Just temporarily."

I was by now discovering what 'temporarily' means in cat rescue speech. Deirdre had known all along. Hadn't I learned *anything* yet? she wanted to know. But Fuji really needed a home, and every other member of Catnippers was bulging at the seams (as usual), and--like the others--I could never refuse a cat in need. Especially that one.

To my surprise, he began carefully making up to Deirdre. He would lie down, a huge soft buff-and-white cushion, patently unthreatening, just in line of sight from behind the chair, but at a safe distance--and simply sleep. It worked, too. To my surprise, and doubtless her own as

---

8   Photographic Felicity is all *over* the cover

well, Deirdre began to find him acceptable. Felicity helped. She posed, tiny and vulnerable, beside Fuji, and purred softly. And Deirdre gave in! She came out of hiding, touched noses, presented the top of her head to be groomed, and suggested an alliance against those two hellions who were energetically ruining the curtains and drowning the carpet.

The alliance worked quite well and was endlessly diverting. Felicity proved to be a gymnast. I took many photos of her in mid-air, just by holding my camera up and waiting. Fuji developed a comical habit of getting on the chair I sat in, standing alongside my thigh and simply crashing his hugeness sideways in a solid slab, coming to rest along the center of my lap, where he would settle with no adjustments at all. Felicity used to observe this with thoughtful blue eyes. And at last one day she came up on the chair beside me, and tried it too. The problem was, Fuji weighed thirteen pounds, Felicity two. She merely fell an inch or two sideways and came to rest, still nearly upright, against my thigh. Then she'd squeak in frustration, try again, and at last retreat to the top of the scratching post, still Contemplating--and trying to figure the thing out.

And actually, she did. Came up one day and stood on *top* of my thigh, looked up at me ("Watch this!") and crashed over, heavy as a potato chip, to land neatly and accurately down the center of my lap just as Fuji did. He watched with astonishment. One day he tried it from Felicity's position atop my leg, and naturally crashed clear across and off the other side. I don't think he ever figured out why, but at least he went back to his old way.

And Deirdre? She observed it all noncommittally, but never even tried to change her own style, which was to drape herself firmly *across* my thighs and never mind the gymnastics. Leave that to the young'uns, she said, casting a tolerant eye at Felicity and a jaundiced one in the direction of the endlessly cavorting Hellions.

Then the two Hellions went off to be adopted, and Felicity took over their role. She played Cougar, hide-and-seek, Cowboys-and-Indians and Gotcha with her new aunt and uncle. She also grew. At three pounds, when she hurtled across the room at her elders she had merely bounced off them, and they had hardly noticed. But a month passed (no, of *course* Fuji hadn't moved on to a new home!) and, now four pounds, the little catapult was fairly knocking them over. They were *not* happy about it, either. Deirdre squalled while Fuji--big gentle pussycat that he was--would roll Felicity on her back and growl ferociously about how he was *really* going to tear her limb from limb *this* time, at which she would grin and try to bite his nose. [9]

Then she started playing Gotcha all over the house with me.

Gotcha got pretty complicated. It was basically cops and robbers, but with lots of hiding, lurking, pouncing, chasing, leaping over chairs and on to tables, and shouting Gotcha all along the route. Fair wore me out, she did!

Deirdre and Fuji, retreating to my bed, said thank goodness for small favors. And I, who ten years ago flinched from the thought of two cats, now had three.

Jenny and Figgy both leered at me knowingly: I *know* they did!

That catatonic summer continued busy and confusing. Cats kept arriving, like the oysters in Alice in Wonderland: "And thick and fast they came at last, And more and more and more." First Felicity and the Hellions. Then Fuji.

And then along came Elinor.

---

9   See cover

CHAPTER FIFTEEN

THE COMING OF ELINOR

Elinor Chose me. With panache, drama and incredible determination. She first appeared as a dark shadow streaking across the garden. The shadow definitely ran like a cat, so one day I shouted at it. "Hey, you! Come back here!"

It instantly stopped in mid-stride, became a gorgeous Persian cat, paced over to rub a plush cheek on my leg, sat down, and studied me carefully. I returned the compliment. Her coat was fine, fluffy, and the best-groomed I'd ever seen. She was--um--Dilute-tortie Medium-long-hair? Blue-cream sort-of-Persian smoke? Something like that. With a fabulous ruff. A beautiful face (not flattened, thank goodness!) made bizarre but charming by one blonde eyebrow and a half-blonde chin. The lush fur on her hind legs made a full-bloomer effect. She was well fed and a stranger to the neighborhood.

"Where did *you* come from?" I asked. She groomed my ankle a little and said never mind all that; she was going to live here now.

The Hellions had only just left, and I still had my hands full with Deirdre, Fuji, and Felicity (who could at the moment be heard playing Gotcha inside the house). Enough was enough. I told her I was full up and to return to the good home she clearly came from. She said no. I said I wouldn't feed her. She said she'd eat my gophers, then--and did. She and Fuji teamed up on it. So what could I do? Having advertised in vain, I finally said she could stay. She said that was already established, wasn't it? I said all *right* then; and I'd take her down for her vet check, and a spay if necessary; and her name was--um--Elinor. She said she knew it was, and now get rid of the other cats. Meant it, too. She swanked into the house, swatted Felicity (who at first seemed to think it all a jolly new game), picked fights with Fuji, and in no time at all, Deirdre was right back behind the brown armchair.

Elinor proved to be a willful, flirtatious, amusing, temperamental, winsome little tyrant. One minute she'd be on the back of my chair devotedly grooming my hair; the next, cursing me up one side and down the other for goodness-knew-what. She'd come to me in the garden, all purrs and cheek-rubs, following me around sociably. She was clearly very fond of me, and--eventually--she accepted the others. But I think (like Kipling's Cat) she was too independent ever to give her whole heart to anyone.

My friends adored her, especially Arlene and Dan. She was their favorite of all my cats. Well, she would be, wouldn't she? She flirted with them outrageously, and regularly had Dan giggling on his back on the floor so she could groom him better. Especially his longish hair, which put her into contortions as she *stretched* back and up to reach the full length of his hair with her busy tongue, trying to do it in one pull. She really was an expert on managing long fur. Groomed mine every chance she got, waiting outside my shower daily, hoping I had washed it and would kneel in front of the hot air vent to dry it, so she could help.

She had only two basic sounds. Noisy purrs, or lurid profanity. The latter happened for any of a dozen sins; but particularly touching her paws. It was mostly sound and fury, actually. She never extruded a really *malignant* claw or fang. Well--almost never. Except when a vet came to give their inoculations at home. Not on *her* territory! Elinor yelled, activating all her teeth and claws; and it took a net, a large bath towel and four hands to get the injections into her. (But when Constance came to do it the following year, Elinor said Oh well, friends were Different, and swore only enough to preserve her reputation.)

On the other hand, *nobody,* not even Dr. Patrick on *his* territory could trim her claws. Not properly and not safely and not alone. Having some sense of self-preservation, I didn't even try. My Master-Gardener friend Joan said she was sure *she* could do it--but a brief discussion with Elinor left her blinking. Joan said she learned some brand new words from that.

Still determined to be an Only Child, Elinor repeatedly went for the others. Felicity thought it was just a new version of Gotcha, but Deirdre and Fuji hated it. Elinor got into real fights--or at least wildly noisy ones--with Fuji in particular, twice chasing him squalling across three neighbor gardens--and at least once being chased. (And her untrimmed claws were like scimitars!)

Elinor *always* started it. I chucked her outside over and over, until she got the message so well that after a while she'd start the fight, march to the door on her own, and wait for me to open it. (She hated cat doors. If she was to go out, it must be on her terms.) She was so awful that eventually I banned her from the house, put her food and water outside and told her to go home. She ate for a few days, but she was a very proud lady, and stopped coming around. I was sorry, because she was very loving and a character, but assumed that she'd indeed returned to the good home she obviously came from.

And by then I had other things on my mind. Fuji went missing.

I hunted, called, ran ads, put up posters, recruited young Tommy and his friends to scour the neighborhood, remembered Fred and Tigger, and wept. The only thing we turned up was Elinor. Tommy and I had been searching Fuji's favorite haunts in the unbuilt three acres behind my house, and there she was, curled up in a nest of long grass, just Looking at me. Not begging to come back, mind: she'd never so abase herself. Just quietly waiting to be invited.

I melted with remorse, brought her in, and told her this was her home as long as she liked, but *please* would she try to be just a *little* nice? She seemed to know exactly what I was saying, and actually did reform a bit. For a while.

But I found no Fuji. Then Arlene visited just before they moved to the Virgin Islands, and offered to try to locate Fuji mentally. (She had never pushed this talent at me--nor had I asked. I was afraid to believe in it. *Could* she, *really?*) I agreed of course--but with hope and skepticism warring. Because she hadn't met Fuji, she asked to hold my hand to help with the contact. I went over to her--and was rudely pushed aside by Elinor, who jumped up to Arlene's lap and stared at her.

"She wants to do it," said Arlene in surprise.

I said that was ridiculous: she and Fuji hated each other.

Arlene consulted Elinor. "Love-hate", she reported, and proceeded to make contact with Fuji, using Elinor. "It's dim," she said. "He's got a new home--says it's a fat and happy life--no competition--" I was frowning, wanting desperately to believe that he was indeed happy in a new home. But-- She suddenly looked at me, her dark eyes eyes wide. "You never told me you had banned Elinor from the house!"

It was the first of Arlene's many Clinchers. I *had* to believe she had indeed talked to Fuji, and that he was too happy ever to return.

After her new virtue wore off, Elinor concentrated on Felicity, who soon joined Deirdre in martyrdom. She inevitably fled behind the sofa and shrieked for me to rescue her. I'd rush in to find Elinor simply sitting beside the sofa washing her paws a little: smug and saintly. Butter wouldn't melt, and all that.

"Elinor! I *saw* that, you little wretch!"

She'd look down her nose at me, give her paw a last dainty lick, saunter to the door, and wait. And so--well I still had three, didn't I? Deirdre, Felicity, and Elinor. And of course all the colonies I was to go on feeding for years and years--

How was I to guess what that summer still held?

CHAPTER SIXTEEN

MIA AND HER CHILDREN

In August Mia showed up again. At first she just sat, well out of reach, staring at me speculatively over folded gray paws. After a week of this, out she swaggered one day from a gap between fences, followed by four kittens, none of whom resembled her in the least. She had really been a busy girl, Mia had! Two vivid calicoes[10], a gorgeous black and white Angora, and a tawny, white-muzzled boy who looked like a tiny agouti cougar with striped tail--white muzzle and all. I promptly named him Ariel: Lion of God.

Back came the trap, for the kittens this time.

And did Mia warn them about traps? Nope--thank goodness! She'd birthed 'em; her duty was done and it was my turn. To my infinite relief she simply sat and watched complacently while her hapless offspring pranced in for the tuna, led by the impetuous Ariel. In fact, it was Ariel who walked into the trap twice: the second time when it was set for his brother Tuffet. (Mia had also neglected to instruct him about that.) He said the first time was interesting and the food was very good.

In any event, they were four months old, and any enterprising female can become pregnant at that age. (It's why so many vets have

10 See the calicoes on the cover. Both of 'em.

lowered the minimum age for spaying.) So I took Ariel and one of his calico sisters to the vet and then regretfully returned them to Mia, as there were no vacancies in our adoption program. Then Tuffet, a black and white male. Marilyn, visiting me, offered to foster him for a few days, and then phoned to say that she was keeping him. So now there was just the other calico to catch.

I unpacked the carrier and set it on end, (I'd learned by then about putting them in tail-first) and looked around. At that instant, *somebody* did *something* beyond the fence to cause general panic. Cats fled in all directions. *Somebody* caused a small terrified calico to come virtually flying through the air in my direction. I reached out a hand in a virtually random grab--and *something* caused it to seize her *en passant*. (As I later told Figgy. it was one of her less subtle efforts, and a bit hard on my too-too-mortal flesh, as well.) Though by that very suspicious miracle I caught the kitten correctly by the scruff, my good luck stopped there. She simply twisted frantically around inside her own skin and chewed my thumb and forefinger to the bone in a dozen places. I changed hands, and she promptly put more holes in that one.

I'll say this for my determination! I knew if I let go now, I'd never in a zillion years have caught her again, and she'd be doomed to be a feral mother for a relatively short and miserable life, at the mercy of the cretins. With maybe up to three litters each year. More? So I hung on grimly, got her into the carrier and home, washed and peroxided my bleeding hands, took her to the vet, and *then* got myself to Emergency for treatment and antibiotics and a good scolding.

When I went back for her next day, the vet's assistant looked at me reproachfully. "Why didn't you tell me she's had a broken leg? It's knitting, but it'll never be quite right."

Well, *I* didn't know, did I? We had only just met! But of course that settled that. Kittens don't break their own legs, as far as I know. Nothing would induce me to take her back to the cretins over the fence! Such a lovely kitten! Bright calico saddle, head and tail; snowy face and underpinnings. And what a sweetly pretty smiling face she had! *Really* smiling. (In profile, cat's mouths turn down or run straight or occasionally curl upward. Hers was a delightful smile.) I named her Cameo and gave her to Felicity to play with. Since her siblings departed, Felicity had seemed a bit bereft. Now she was first puzzled, then delighted. Her very own new playmate! Within two days the kittens were inseparable. They were the same age and size, so it was perfect.

Now I had four!

But what of the rest of the litter among the cretins? I got the other calico and named her, after much deliberation, Allegro. She was larger than her sister and with the same general pattern---except that where Cameo had vivid fist-sized splotches on her saddle, divided down the center like mismatched wallpaper sections, Allegro's was brindled black-and-orange. She had one orange ear and a piratical black patch over the right eye that belied her placid personality. She was the one who, as soon as she got big enough, loved to sit on the back of my recliner, stretch her neck over the top of my head and blissfully snuggle her chin in my left eye. It was her sweet-faced sister who, if I inadvertently moved so much as a toe in bed, would leap straight up into the air and come straight down again teeth-first. All in fun, of course, she would assure me when I yelled.[11]

Five! Allegro, Cameo, Deirdre, Felicity and Fuji. Good grief! Constance smiled approvingly. But there was Ariel still out in the colony, with all his siblings adopted. I decided to save him, as well--especially after seeing his portrait in *Pedigreed Cats,* under Caramel-Silver-Ticked Oriental Short-hair. Each hair ranged outward from smoke through shades of cream and dry sherry, he had tabby markings only on forehead, legs and tail, with black or champagne ticking evenly on his torso, giving him a lovely iridescent look. A beautiful boy needing a loving home that so far was all girls.

---

11   Ten years later, I put her into a book: *Loyal and the Dragon*--under the pseudonym of Caprice

Ariel didn't agree. He was now Best Friends with Stubbins and Amy; and though he adored love-ins, rolling ecstatically on his back to let me rub his cream-sherry tummy--he was his mother's son. Given a glimpse of a trap, or even a carrier, he hid for a week.

Mia vanished for good that winter.

I saw a mini-documentary on calico cats about that time. It said that unless a female has orange on her own coat, she can not possibly produce calico kittens.

Mmm. A pity no one told Mia! That ignorant, infuriating little pale-grey-and-white cat never suspected that she couldn't--so she did. Two of them. (What's more, though Tuffet and the calicoes probably had the same father--not Ariel! Not ruddy likely, Mate!) I wondered whether I should tell Allegro and Cameo that they really aren't calico at all: they just look that way?

The experts were dead wrong, of course. Gray-and-white moms can perfectly easily produce calicoes if Dad is orange. It requires merely an orange gene on one X-chromosome, and a black on the other. I finally tracked down that fascinating color-sex relationship--and not easily! It turns out that *orange and black genes ride separately, one to a chromosome--and only on the X,* never that itty-bitty Y. So a cat needs two X's to have both black and orange on her coat. QED. Males have only one X and one Y. And the reason most orange cats are boys is that it needs only the one O gene on their one X chromosome. Again QED.

The kittens proceeded to grow, as kittens tend to do. The twins, of course, retained their calico coats. But Felicity--

It was clear from the start that with those huge ears and long legs, the wedge-shaped face, blue eyes and slinky build, Felicity was at least half Siamese. But as her points started to develop, I began to wonder what kind? Seal on cream *or* blue on silver, yes. But gray on cream? With shadowy stripes developing on her flanks? Naturally I wrote to Jenny. *Her* Siamese were all Grand Champions and things, and what she didn't know about Siamese breeds probably hadn't been invented.

"Her body is cream but her ears are smoky gray; and she's developing blue agouti stripes on her legs and tail and face, and a narrow ivory outline around those very blue eyes," I wrote. "I think her mother must have been frightened by a UFO."

After many letters and photos, Jenny replied: *"Felicity, so far as I can see, is a blue tabby-point (lynx-point in America) Siamese, and we don't ask personal questions about her mother, okay? If her nose-leather and paw pads are pink, (well, pinkish) I'm right. If they're black or blue-grey, I'm wrong and she's a right odd mixture. So glad you've finally got your Siamese, you deserve one."*

So I had a good look at Felicity's nose and paws. and wrote back: "Hmm. Well, she has news for you. How about pink nose leather *and* charcoal-grey paw pads? Gotcha!"

Answered Jenny: *"A Siamese judge and I have been looking at Felicity's photos again. She is blue tabby-point. Her nose is pink (a) because she's young (b) because of contact with some sort of Colonial chemical in the cat litter, and (c) any other unlikely idea we can hit on. Tell her please she has not 'gotcha' and this is no language for an aristocrat to use, let alone royalty. I have been baffled by experts. Often."*

Me: "Okay, I'll settle for Blue Lynx-Point, which sounds more exotic than tabby-point. But Felicity has one more message. Why, she wants to know, if she's Siamese, that at six months she still has a voice like a three-week old kitten?"

"Gotcha!"

How was I to guess the changes a few months would make? Little by little, so slowly I hardly noticed, she became a blue-eyed gray tabby with a *tiny* Siamese head and paws, and a silken amber pate to her head: quiet, gentle, usually invisible. Ecstatic when I spotted her and stopped for a love-in--but she gradually stopped coming to demand Lap and Love and Under the Covers. Too much competition? Instead she slept on the bed lying across my left shoulder with that silken amber head snuggled blissfully under my chin.

A year later she was a lazy Tubby Tabby with blue eyes. [12]

And a picky eater!

---

12 Felicity virtually stars on the cover.

CHAPTER SEVENTEEN

SCALLYWAG

2 Feb, '94
Dearest Sally,

I love the photos you sent of Elinor and the twins, but your use of colour terms baffles me. We don't know 'calico' over here; how do you Colonials define it? A tortie with white? We'd call them all tortoise-shell.

I think Elinor is probably a pedigree cat, but as she seems to have a proper nose as opposed to a squashed bit smeared on to the front of a flattened face, I doubt if she was a show cat. Not over there, anyway. (Most European countries won't allow those poor flat-faces in cat shows at all.) But what lovely colours she is! If you ever find out where she came from before arriving in your back garden, let me know.

Cat shows. Yes, well. I couldn't show Scallywag last month, as he wasn't fully inoculated against leukaemia. Wouldn't take the chance. (In Europe alone over a million cats a year are dying of this.) But I entered him last week end, and he insisted on my sending a letter from him to Felicity.

Dear Felicity,
Allow Me to Introduce Myself.
European Grand Champion International Suryasun Excalibur, five

times Best Variety, once nominated Best in Show, three times chosen Best In Show, once deprived of Best of the Best due to Nepotism and Intrigue.

Scallywag to my friends, Stinkpot to my Mum, Excalibur the Mighty to the next door dog. (Excalibur the Rather Small when my Mum is cross with me, as she is at the moment, rather. Well, how was I to know I wasn't supposed to spray on it? Whatever it was?)

I have a Grievance. I have been called a Jinx. On cameras. You see, me being so Incredibly Handsome, photographs are required to impress my potential harem. Dad, who is quite extraordinarily brilliant, has a camera. A terribly expensive one. And sometimes Mum tells him to photograph me, and she goes out and buys film, and sets to work polishing perfection (grooming Me) and then stands back and waits for results, and they are hopeless. And Dad's are worse. And Mum gets very cross, and says Other People With Cameras... and so on. So then she buys more film, and says Get out that stand thing I bought you with the lights, and then it turns out that one of the lights is broken and can't be mended, so they try with just one light, and the photographs are hopeless, and Mum says Other People With Cameras... and so on.

Well, Dad is in India, so Mum sneaked off with me to a professional photographer.

Now, I really was very good. I mean, how would you like to be plonked on a strange carpet and have bright lights all over the place and some odd woman pushing a camera into your face and saying the "Ooza Pretty Boy" routine in German? It was all a bit boring, so I just got on with life and had a good wash. Or the odd yawn. I was perfectly polite, mind you, purred when stroked, tried to explore (I do feel guests should show an interest, don't you?) knocked over only one of the lamps, and only one of its legs got broken, and it's got two more. I don't know why they made such a fuss.

So this woman with the Camera kept saying could I be made to sit up and sit still and just slant up my eyes and lower my ears a bit, and HOLD IT FOR MORE THAN TWO SECONDS, and Mum was asking, in that slightly dangerous tone of voice if she'd ever photographed a cat before, so I thought I'd leave them to it, and went to look at what was on the desk, which was a lot of papers, and then there was more trouble, and then the odd woman got what Mum said was "Smashing! Marvelous! JUST what I wanted!" and the odd woman said yes but the flash hadn't worked. And Mum said JINX.

So when we got home, Mum said I'd cost her her a Bloody Packet Again, but she supposed I'd been quite good for a Siamese, so I was allowed into her work room. Well, I had been GROVELLING AROUND ON THAT BLOODY CARPET for about TWO HOURS, and then she got annoyed because I had just a small spray against something on her desk.

I think it's VERY UNFAIR, and I want to come to California and live with you.

Is it true your poor voice is broken?

Mum says I am not to ask you how to play Gotcha because we think up enough trouble without any help from Abroad, but I really would like to know.

Scallywag

Sienna

Dear Scallywag,

I'm Felicity the Incredibly Adorable, and my mum says I'm not to tell you how to play Gotcha even if you ask, because if you and the Black Paw Gang are proper Siamese, you've already figured it out for yourselves, and if by any chance you haven't, she doesn't want your mum mad at her. So I'll just say that nobody is to stop, ever, except just to reverse direction or leap on or over something, or hide *just* while the other one shoots past; and then you go after them *at once,* and nip their heels or yell, to make them run faster and knock more things over.

There's nothing wrong with my voice! It can be simply *terrifically* loud sometimes when I get Excited, like when Elinor is bullying me and Mum hasn't noticed yet. But usually I don't need to bellow, so why waste all that loudness if you don't need to? When Mum plays with that thing with shiny white and black paws sticking out, that make noise when she pushes them, I sing along. She says my voice is lovely and sweet, and quite loud enough.

But then she says for goodness sake, why don't I Speak Up? That's when I'm outside and that wet stuff starts playing Gotcha down from the sky, and when I hide under the roof of the garden shed and call for Mum to come carry me in and keep me dry, and she doesn't hear, and I'm not Excited enough to Bellow. But now she knows where I probably am, and comes anyway, so that's all right.

There was a cat with a black face and tail and legs and a terrible voice, all yells and yowls, on the TV one time, and Mum said that was like you. If it's true, how can you possibly think *my* voice is broken? I do feel sorry for you, but never mind, not everyone can be as beautiful as I am.

Felicity

PS: from Sally. I've lost track again. How far down has your alphabet got?

Germany
'20 Feb.
Dear Sally.

Quick reply before I forget your question.

We had the J clan, but it coincided with an outbreak of ringworm, the one and only time, for which I thank whoever is responsible. I had sold Jamaica and Jinda to a nice young man, then discovered ringworm, then he telephoned me to ask about these marks on the kittens' faces, so they had to come back. I couldn't sell them until the ringworm had cleared up completely, of course, and I grew very fond of them (as one does!). But I fell for a sob story where Jinda was concerned – a Dutch woman whose old Siamese had just died at the age of sixteen or something, and who was bereft, so Jinda went to her, and that was a bad mistake. Jinda was almost immediately sold on, and was killed by a dog owned by her next owner, who telephoned me, completely distraught to do her justice, but who opened the conversation by asking when she could have another kitten, so any potential for a for a beautiful friendship died on the spot.

Jamaica stayed. For good. She and Scallywag adore each other, and hate to be separated. They should have lovely kittens, and they send love. (Well, Scallywag does. Jamaica doesn't. That's Jamaica.)

I've got them in Scallywag's run. She's indignant about it, and says keeping her confined is an abuse of Feline Rights. Stopping her beating up her granny (Toot) is also an abuse of Feline Rights. She's a seal point pain.

It would be lovely to have friendly cats leading a normal life in this house, sitting on laps watching TV in the evenings, curling up together on the sofa during the day, basking in the sunshine in the garden. But Scallywag has taken a binding oath to murder Percy, and Percy's hobby is insulting Scallywag, and Jamaica is going to be My Only Cat if it kills her, or, more likely, everyone else, and my poor old granny cat Toot finds the whole situation completely bewildering (which isn't difficult for Toot, she's always been a bit hazy on most subjects) and frankly I could spank the lot of them.

Love to the kids.

And to you.   Jenny

In the meantime, Elinor now had four girls to persecute. Deirdre, of course, virtually lived under my bed--a bit smug, actually. Elinor seemed to know that was strictly off-limits for her. Felicity spent half her life sitting bolt upright behind the sofa, looking very displeased indeed. But the twins weren't as much fun to bully. The peaceable Allegro just lay down when chased, while tiny Cameo, after a few weeks, decided *she'd* like to be the dominant cat, and chased back, small as she still was. Her dog-growl became quite impressive after while. Just as well, because Allegro seldom made a sound at all, Deirdre chatted only to me, Felicity's voice wouldn't scare a mouse--and *some* one had to talk back to Elinor.

It wasn't exactly a peaceful household, though. Elinor still wanted me to get rid of the others, who heartily returned the compliment. At

Christmas, Arlene visited from the Virgin Islands, had a mental talk with the cats overnight, and arrived next morning looking shocked.

"It's that little Cameo! *Isn't* it? The smallest calico, with the pretty face? She's *fierce!* She doesn't *want* to be friends! She wants to tear Elinor limb from limb!"

I wasn't at all astonished. That was Cameo, all right! Allegro was the placid but cunning twin. If I went out to bring her in, she'd lay her front half down, cheek resting innocently on the ground, twinkling sideways up at me with butter unmelted in her mouth-- 'Here I am: come pick me up!'--but with her sneaky back half still standing firmly on its feet so that when I got almost within reach, she could take off instantly. But Cameo was definitely the feisty one.

Arlene begged them all to try to come to terms. Allegro said she already had, and the others said they'd think about it. But, having thought, Elinor decided the solution was for her to subdue all the others. This naturally reinforced the Felicity-Cameo bond. They formed a pretty powerful Defense Brigade and took the war to the enemy--at least whenever Mum was handy in case they needed reserves. Things got quite exciting for a while, and *then* began to settle down.

Little by little, over that winter, the balance changed. Elinor slowly stopped using that menacing, flat-eared, low, out-to-kill pursuit. It became a teasing bound, ears and tail high. She said it was a new game called Pounce, and more fun than Gotcha. Felicity denied this passionately. She still fled abjectly if I wasn't visible, but got very confrontational if I was, wanting to take turns being Pouncer, which was against Elinor's rules.

It came to a head every breakfast time. The Defense Brigade-- increasingly militant--Lurked at Elinor's dish. Felicity, bold with all that support, would march over and swat at Elinor a few times. I'd yell at her. She'd back off and wait for Elinor to start eating--at which point- -every morning!--she sauntered over and deliberately, insolently sniffed under Elinor's tail.

I didn't need Arlene to translate that one!

CHAPTER EIGHTEEN

ORPHANAGE FOR SKUNKLETS

Sienna

May 12, 1994

Dear Jenny,

Well, I've had an exciting spring, so far, with my five and Mr. Mockingbird, who has suddenly become very aggressive about his nest again, dive-bombing my cats. They all tend to watch the trajectory with narrowed eyes--but particularly Cameo. I did warn him again--but, man-like, he ignored me. And yesterday I came home to find all five sitting in a prim circle in the middle of the living room, like the Nuremburg judges, surrounding a very tidy and very dead mocking bird. Not a feather out of place. I asked how they managed that, but they wouldn't say: only that he'd asked for it. Which, undeniably, he had. So I buried him, and that was that.

Only it wasn't.

The next day I arrived to find a tighter and more alert circle around an equally undamaged but very lively fledgling. Fell out of the nest, they said, and they couldn't put it back, so they saved it for me.

Oh, thanks, kids! Muttering, I put it in a small box, took it furtively along to Bird Rescue--fearing to see that trio of ailurophobes there--

and hurried home thankfully. Alas, my cats, carried away by their own virtue, presently produced its indignant sibling. For dear Mommy, they said, because she liked the last two so much!

Back to Bird Rescue, who this time bent suspicious eyebrows on me and asked what I was doing. Enough was enough! The third fledgling was more fledged, unintimidated and shrieking for Mama. So I grounded the cats, took him outside and looked for his mama. Fair frantic, she was. Her Husband and Children had been Kidnapped! she squawked, and was patently grateful to have this one back. Practically came and took it from my hands. And until she had got Junior to fly away with her to a safer territory, my poor abused little girls, who may really have saved them and certainly had not harmed them, had to stay inside. So much for virtue being rewarded!

But *why* did they do it? I simply don't understand this at all--but it's true.

Last night was very warm and balmy, so I opened the sliding door in my bedroom wide and read in bed for a while with the twins on my legs as usual. But suddenly last night they all began to show a deep interest in Outside, going to the screen door and staring out. (I'll explain about screens one day: they're to keep out flies, and I can't *think* why you stubborn Brits don't adopt them, even from us mere Colonials. After all, you've acquired the hamburger--though I *never* got used to hearing it called a Wimpy--and even--*quel horreur!*--tea bags.)

Anyway, presently Felicity joined them, and then Elinor. (Deirdre went under the head of the bed.) I shone my flashlight (torch to you) out there, but couldn't see a thing. Heard some rustling, though, so I went out through the garage, shone my flashlight again--and there were three baby skunks, bushy tails aloft, just puttering around the garden. Fearlessly, of course. You don't have skunks in Europe, but you must have heard of them. This animal fears nothing, and with good reason, too. The original chemical warfare. I watched them for a while, wishing I could see them better, but not knowing where their mum was, decided not to go closer.

Back inside, I found the girls still staring out, fascinated. I hated to spoil their adventure by closing the sliding door, but I did. Because every so often I'm awakened in the middle of the night by echoes of skunk stench drifting in, which is an experience I prefer to do without.

I don't suppose you've ever smelt skunk? Lucky you! It's quite indescribable. It can be smelled for a quarter of a mile, and the oil drops stick and refuse to come off, and no one will have anything to do with you, so that you feel like A. A. Milne's Bad King John. ("--And sometimes no one spoke to him For days and days and days.") So I very much hope those young'uns and their mum will realize what an affable and harmless soul I am. (And the cats.)

We get all kinds of wild life here, right in the middle of Sienna, including several I've never told you about. Like chipmunks, gophers, and 'possums (who have got to be among the most charmingly unlovely things God ever made, along with warthogs, poor dears) and mockingbirds and scrub jays, and cardinals (but not on the west coast). Like you, we have deer, who regularly go into my neighbors back gardens to munch their flowers. (Not mine, as I have a non-see-through fence, and they sensibly like to look before they leap. Instead they come to my front garden for the roses. 'Very tasty,' they say; 'Very nice.' Last year we had an affable brown bear ambling down the middle of a street during morning rush hour; and cougars occasionally visit back yards (gardens to you) and come up on porches and peer through the windows--and once, alas!, one assumed the family pet was on the menu and had it for dinner.

<u>May 18.</u> Next chapter on skunks. Went out to the garage for something last night, and here was a little skunk busily exploring the place. Cute as a button! I feel sure in my bones it's a girl: so I named her Little Dorrit. She had got shut in when I closed the door for the night. But she said she didn't mind a bit. It was interesting here, wasn't it? she added, busily sniffing around. I watched for a while, and then went and opened the cat door and told her she could leave if she liked.

She didn't. Instead she came over and sniffed at my bare toes for a while, and then sat down on them with her hot little bottom! It was all quite amiable. Then she went back to the corner, burrowing herself right out of sight behind the boxes.

Oh, well, all I could do was leave the door open with food and water outside and give her the options. This morning the dishes were turned over, the contents gone, and presumably the skunk too. I'm a bit sorry. Dorrit was a real darling...

May 24. Yesterday evening my next door neighbor Grace sat at her back window and watched my cats romp all over her lawn with a skunk. Having a ball, they were. And last night, the twins again left my bed and went to sit at the screen silently conversing with a small moving thing outside. It didn't at all mind my spotlighting it with a flashlight, just ambled around, nosing at grass or garden now and then. I do hope it was eating the snails, who invade and eat like a plague of locusts! I wonder if skunks do like escargot?

May 30. And have I been a busy little girl! I was wrong about having a skunk or three: I am actually a whole nursery school and probably an orphanage for *thirteen* baby skunks. Went out at dusk, to the back corner of the garden where tansy, honeysuckle and Shasta daisies make a lovely jungle. Heard a rustling. Called. Out popped a little black striped head. And another. Soon eight of them, with plumy tails fanned straight up (not forward), had appeared. They shuffled around a bit, came to investigate me, and finally ambled across the back of my garden. A few minutes later five more dived through the fence from Grace's and scurried after them. 'Wait for us!'

I haven't seen any adults, and this surely must be two litters. At least? I rather think they lived in the empty land behind, where bulldozing has just begun, so that their parents may have perished, and the orphans came here because I've lots of lovely grubs, worms and snails. My cats have welcomed them, explaining that I'm an affable if eccentric auntie who's good at playing, cuddling and producing goodies, and always speaks kindly except to Pokey.

Which is more than some people do. The other night, I looked out the open front door to see one of them hightailing it up my drive and around by the side gate to the back yard. I went to see what had scared her, and there were half a dozen neighbor children *led by* that bloody man Roger from next door (the one who insists that all my cats run around his house turning on all his outside faucets--taps to you). Now he was in hot pursuit of Little Dorrit.

"Sally, did you see--"

"Yes!" I snarled. "She's come back home to be safe; and how *dare* you chase her like that on her own territory? Now bugger off and leave her alone!"

He stared, totally nonplussed, like someone whose big scary firecracker had gone "pfff".

Last night I went out at dusk and called. Out they tumbled, about seven of them, playing, wrestling, sniffing at Auntie's ankles. But I do worry. Are they safe roaming out at night with idiot humans around? Might Fish & Wildlife come after them? (Recently they executed a raven named Colin, unable to fly, who had been living happily, but, they said, illegally with an animal rescue family.) Are there are too many for the resources of the area? And though they have given my runner beans a chance to grow up uneaten by snails, what happens when my corn gets ripe? (They get first whack, that's what, and welcome.) Probably as they grow up they'll spread out into new territories, some staying to keep the snails down. They are charming little things, with little to fear from anything, who now come when I call.

Next day. They have a new game. I think it's the New Gotcha. They tumble and toss like kittens, and then, one by one, turn their backs on one another and me, bring tails forward, aim their little well-armed butts, and pretend they're in earnest. So far, they haven't been. It just *came* to them they say, as something fun to do do. If Roger harries them any more, I'll tell them to use live ammunition.

<u>June 15.</u> Aw, I've been and gone and scared my poor little skunks! I wanted photos. I don't think they minded the flash, any more than they did the flashlight. I think it was the sound of the automatic re-wind that did it. Not at first. I took four shots of Little Dorrit leading two others toward me. She paused uncertainly, scuttled away, came back. I got another. Same thing. The fourth time, while she was bravely walking all by herself straight toward me,[13] I thought she was used to it now. But when the film wound, she streaked away and didn't return.

I'm *sorry!*

Wish I could send one to you. You and the Black Paw Gang would really love it, especially Chandi and Toot. And Scallywag, says Felicity.

Luv, Sally

Obersdorfstr. 2a
53340 Meckenheim-Ersdorf, Germany
Dear Sally,

I want a skunk! Please send me one at once, telling him that he can be a Unique Visitor and live in the garden and the house and be my friend, and I will love him to bits. Did Little Dorrit ever forgive you for the scary noises? Poor little love! Just coming up for a friendly chat and somebody throws a growling grinding bolt of lightning at her; no wonder she left in a hurry! I had thought they were bigger. I always imagined them about the size of a badger or a spaniel. But how pretty they are!

I now have eight resident cats in the Blackpaw Gang. Scallywag is still collecting high titles and growing fame, never beaten in nineteen shows, stunningly beautiful and one hundred percent loving, but Percy sprays like

---

13   There she is, on the cover: the photo that scared her.

a demented skunk (I assume). Would Arlene like a word with him? Tell him to stop fighting Didi and picking on Chandi and spraying, and then he can come into the living room where it's a lot nicer. Chandi will be happier, too.

What has Pokey been doing lately? And Whisper?

Love, Jenny

July 8

Dearest Blackpaws and their mum,

Well may you ask! (In fact, has Figgy been whispering in your ear?)

A few weeks ago, Chuck and Linda moved a few blocks down the street. I had mixed feelings. Would miss them--but not, particularly, Pokey. Still, from the depths of my new expertise, I told them to be sure to keep them inside for at least six weeks, so that they'll realize that's their new home. They said oh, both cats loved them more than they did the house. I said (my own theory) that that wasn't it. Cats see no reason why their beloved humans couldn't still be at the old place *as well as* the new, and they go for both. They didn't take me seriously. A few days later, both cats showed up, saying I was now their new human. No matter how many times Linda fetched them back, they returned. Now they just hang around, not sure where they belong but fairly sure it's here. Whisper on the front porch, Pokey all over both yards. Chuck and Linda have given up and got a couple of new kittens.

Love to you and yours, Sally

CHAPTER NINETEEN

A BURMESE VIRAGO

Sienna,

July 17, '94

Dearest Jenny,

Constance has brought me a beautiful little Burmese to foster. Perhaps even to adopt? she wondered. Elegant little thing, obviously pedigreed. People heard her crying and watched her lurking forlornly behind Safeway's for weeks before anyone thought to phone us. She spent two weeks in Con's bathroom while ads and posters went out. Amazingly, not a twitter, so now she's One of Ours--and here she is. In my study.

I knew when Con described her that she must be an aristocrat. Now I see she's a goddess. I asked if her name was Bastet, and she said it wasn't. Turned her back on me. So I asked if it was Lady Burma and her head snapped around as if on springs and she told me loudly and at great length in that hoarse bellow (as opposed to Felicity's kitten squeak) that it is. And that I'm her new slave.

Sept. 20. I could get quite fond of this one... I think... Only she's so ruddy arrogant! If only she gets on with the others-- (Hollow laughter, thinking of The Doughty Elinor.) And I do suspect Lady Burma wants her new human slave all to herself. But while Elinor now makes only desultory efforts to become an Only Child, Burma--who is still shut in the study, of course--has started shoving her elegant nose under the door and roaring that if there's Anyone Out There, they must *all* leave *at once*. Or Else! And since my lot have never heard such sounds before, it dismays them considerably.

Sept. 22: I was wrong: Burma isn't at all like Elinor. She makes Elinor look like Jimmy Carter making nice to the Arab terrorists. I let her out yesterday--just to test the water--and suddenly had something like Bosnia on my hands. Talk about ethnic cleansing! That six-pound scrap utterly routed not only Deirdre, Allegro and Felicity, but even my feisty dog-growling Cameo!

Especially Cameo, it turned out. Because the chase tore through the house several times at speeds you wouldn't believe, until finally I seized Burma in mid-air, hurled her back into the study, slammed the door, and went to look for poor Cameo--

--and couldn't find her! Finally a ghastly thought occurred to me. I went to the study--and heard a despairing growl from inside! Cameo had taken refuge there before I threw Burma back in! The poor little sod was glued against the wall under the desk, being Menaced by the virago, scared quite literally spitless and shitless. Great ropes of saliva drooled from her mouth and she'd soiled herself. It was ages before I could pry her loose, and while I washed her off in the bathroom, she was limp with shock. Poor little thing! I tried hard to comfort and cuddle her, but that could not restore her self-respect. All the feist has gone out of her.

And the next time I inched the door open, Burma shot out between my feet and confronted Elinor. I had given up any notion of adopting her--but I confess I did think briefly that it would be nice for Burma to get her come-uppance--and who better to deliver it than my intrepid Elinor, who had proved a match for everyone, even Pokey and the large dog down the street? So I warned Burma that this was my Doughty Warrior, and she'd better not mess with her!

Ha!

They saw each other. They froze, three feet apart, staring, for probably six seconds. Then Burma hurled herself straight at Elinor, silent and sinister as a laser beam--and Elinor, without the least thought of self-defense, fled incontinently.

Once again I had to catch the wriggling, murderous little demon in mid-air. And Elinor's dought is, for the moment, lost along with Cameo's feist.[14] Now I'm desperately trying to find someone to take the valuable and inimical goddess off my hands. Soon!

I no longer wonder why she was abandoned at Safeway!

Halp, halp!

Love, Sally

Jenny phoned at once, not waiting to write. She said didn't *any* of us know *anything* about Burmese? That's the way they *are*, she said: fighting cats. Feline rottweilers: seldom tolerating any other animal unless brought up with it from birth.

Actually, we *hadn't* known. Any of us. Or at least, none I've talked to.

So that was that. Unadoptable by me or any of the rest of the well-catted members, who prudently refused to take her even in temporary fosterage.

Meanwhile, Burma bellowed under the door that she was Coming Out to Get Them. They profoundly believed it. With good reason. Allegro looked haunted, Felicity cried a lot, and Cameo wouldn't come out from under furniture. Deirdre (though she alone had escaped the Hunt) was in her usual refuge, and Elinor, still smarting from shattered dignity, wasn't fit to live with.

The siege went on for days, until we had an incredible bit of luck. An elderly couple showed up, he an invalid, both grieving for the Burmese

---

14 The dought returned almost at once. The feist did not.

they had just lost. And they had no other pets! They took her off at once, all three deliriously happy.

So were my lot. Provided, they said, I never did it again. And, they added, they expected me to compensate them with a diet of tuna and people-chicken. With corn-on-the-cob, asparagus and broccoli for Cameo. Oh yes, and salad with bleu cheese dressing, which she has just discovered.

CHAPTER TWENTY

BOOTSIE

Nearly two years after Domino died, I lost her sister, too. Deirdre, apparently happy, had learned to accept the assorted newcomers and get on with them. Even Elinor--more or less. She seemed well. Her coat was black and glossy. She still, after twelve years, didn't like to be picked up--but that was due to her feral kittenhood, and I humored her. If her idea of a cuddle was stand on my lap, turn her back, shoot her tail forward along her back and invite me to sniff her little ass-hole, fair enough. But when I did pick her up one day, I realized in shock that under that thick black fur she had lost weight. A lot of it.

Tests showed the kidney failure I had learned to dread. Deirdre, saying she didn't feel well, went to live under the head of my bed. Purring. Any treatment, said Dr. Patrick sorrowfully, would just postpone the inevitable. Did Deirdre want that? Could Arlene find out for me? Could she contact her from the British Virgin Islands?

!!!

Dear man! How many vets would (a) accept my stories about Arlene's psychic powers (b) conceive of her doing it at all that distance--which she could--and (c) be sensitive enough to want to consult Deirdre?

I hardly needed Arlene's report, though. I remembered Domino's endoscopy all too well! So now, with Deirdre sick--Deirdre who simply loathed even being pilled, and rolled her eyes in frantic denial no matter how gentle and skilled I was-- I phoned Arlene in the Virgin Islands, already knowing the answer.

Arlene, it turned out, already knew the question. "Sally? Deirdre says **NO!** She says she doesn't want any more pills, either. (Another of her clinchers: I hadn't mentioned pills.) "She says she wants to be with Domino." Sobbing, I hung up, wondering how soon. Right away? I would never knowingly keep a cat alive against her will...

At that point, Deirdre came into the living room and began to play. Not very vigorously, but the idea was there. Not yet. She'd spend a little more time with me first.

And so I waited. I watched and loved her, pampered her and played with her for three weeks. Then she went back under the bed, and when I came to find her, she climbed painfully up to my lap and butted me in the stomach.

To be sure, I rang Arlene.

"Hi, Arlene: this is Sally--"

"She says Now."

I missed her terribly, my little Quivertail Fingers Greedygut-- The way her short legs looked like turtle feet, flashing out and in beneath her when she ran scared, low as a beetle. The way she hid under chairs if a newcomer entered, followed me outside to hide under bushes and call me, rushed in and sat ecstatically by my electric keyboard when I played.

That winter, cats started appearing at my door one by one, inquiring brightly "Is this the place?" I became a way-house. Provided food, shelter, names, love and spay-neuter trips to the vet; but with no room in the adoption program, I could do little more. (A few left rather quickly after the vet, but at least they were safe from parenthood.) I put a large drawer on top of a cupboard under the high working shelf in the garage, with just space for little visitors to get in. (Actually, they found and appropriated it themselves: I just added nice soft toweling.) I'd go out before bedtime with a dish of supper, reach in blind, usually to find my hand full of soft purring cat fur. I'd caress and scratch ears and jaw for a while, present supper, and go in to bed.

Still, I did find good homes for some on my own. Whisper took up semi-permanent quarters on my front porch, where I finally put a little 'cat house' with beds both inside and on top. (She has never yet come inside.) McGregor went to live with my friends Ann and Richard; and of course there was the twins' brother Tuffet--

--Ah yes, well, Tuffet. I had growing doubts. When I visited Marilyn I inevitably found him huddled under the bed. Not deliberate cruelty: Marilyn was incapable of that! But he hadn't been that way when she took him. Something was wrong, and I didn't know what to do about it.

Catnippers still didn't have enough money for the shop we wanted. Not nearly. They had a board meeting about Ways and Means, Constance told me later, and some one came up with a winner. "I know! Sally can mortgage her house!" Con flinched and determined to warn me, but the others beamed. What a good idea! Well, it seemed logical. I had given Fred's All, hadn't I? How were they to know about Sally's Economics System? So, innocently confident, they phoned before Con did, to tell me what I was going to do.

I gawped, incredulous. *"Me? Give you my equity? **Go into debt?**"* I brayed, and then fell about laughing for a while.

They took it quite well, I must say, and no hard feelings. (Later they gave me a gorgeous new unabridged copy of Roget's Thesaurus which I've used every day of my life since.)

By now I worked two afternoons a week in our adoption room in a local shelter. In the summer of '95, the county suffered an epidemic of FIP (Feline Infectious Peritonitis.) We at Catnippers had been paranoid about cleanliness and prevention, and got off easy--but it was nerve-racking. One sneeze and off to isolation in some one's garage. Little black Bootsie--who sported four silly looking white toes on his right hind foot--went on sneezing, and stayed in quarantine at Con's until he was totally de-socialized and unfit to return to the adoption room. Moreover, Halloween was coming, and we never adopted black or even mostly-black cats in October, just to be on the safe side. Bad things could happen to them! (Interestingly, England considers black cats to be *good* luck.) All the same, I was utterly taken aback when Monica suddenly turned to me with a sweet purposeful smile. "Sally, since Deirdre died, you're short a black cat, aren't you? And we have a glut of them. How would you like to--er--foster Bootsie?"

I gaped. "But-- But you *know* I can't foster!"

"Deirdre and Domino can't object any more."

"Yes, but-- The cats always *bond* to me! And then they're unadoptable--"

"Yes," she beamed, not quite smirking (although I strongly suspect that somewhere in *peri* land, Figgy was). "Thank you."

It was beginning to be a habit. Oh well, so I had another black cat, my first boy (I still refused to count Pokey) since Shadow, and a B to fill in my alphabet, all in one. The girls accepted him quite easily, saying that they didn't mind a little fellow like this...

Well, actually, only Felicity and Allegro said that. Elinor expressed her displeasure by piddling on the floors--though, considerately, only on the bathroom and kitchen linoleum. But presently Cameo began complaining bitterly that Bootsie first stole and then broke all her toys.

This was quite true.

Of all my cats, it was Cameo--the pretty calico with the smiling white face--who most loved toys. And everything (except, astonishingly, Christmas tree ornaments!) was a toy to her. She would seize anything I was holding or had held: pen, pencil, scissors opening and closing entrancingly, comb, fork, nail file, toothbrush, even a knitted doll which she carried around carefully and lovingly. (She always took perfect care of her toys, hiding them so that the rest of us couldn't play with them too roughly.) Most of all, she loved the little real-fur mice. They were Hers. She would pick one up ever so delicately in her bared teeth, and then, head high, not to drag it, prance around the house with it, virtually singing.

Bootsie changed all that. He didn't, she pointed out bitterly, just *steal* her mice; he didn't just kill them. He *eviscerated* them, she wailed, displaying an undeniably empty skin.

The others were more tolerant. (After all, it wasn't *their* mice.) Be patient, they seemed to tell Cameo. He was still young.

True. At three months, weighing just the normal three pounds: he was an unsocialized little guy so frightened of the Big World Out There that he instantly accepted me and the study as his only security. And the moment he graduated from the study, the first thing he did was ransack the house for hiding places. First the inside lining under a recliner, where he made a small warm lump. When he outgrew that, he found another: around, behind, *and* under a cupboard in the kitchen, through a too-small space at the side.

It surprised me a little when he and the other calico, laid-back Allegro, became Best Friends. It shouldn't have. After all, Cameo and Felicity were a twosome, Elinor a loner, and Allegro had lacked a buddy. And she and Bootsie loved to wrestle...

Bootsie's Little Operation, though, seemed not to have removed certain instincts. He would push Allegro flat on her face, take her scruff in his teeth and pause uncertainly. She would roll her eyes back to peer at him. Was it a new game, and if so, what came next? He would say he wasn't sure, and go into normal wrestling. If he got too rough, she would simply swat him.

They agreed on one thing. Let anyone even *think* about coming to the house, and both vanished: she as silently as the dawn, he with sound effects like Armageddon.

And he grew.

He apparently took the standard 'a pound a month' for kitten growth rather too literally. At eighteen months, he weighed eighteen pounds. He wasn't fat: he was *big!* From collarbone to groin, he and I were the same length. (Granted I'm short-waisted--but all the same...) He had to find new hiding places one by one when he outgrew the old ones. (He did it very well. To the end of his life I could never find him when he was hidden. And it's a small house.) He couldn't understand why he could no longer curl up on my lap comfortably while I worked at my desk: his legs, shoulders, tail, head and rump all draped over the sides. He was a Growing Boy, he'd explain to me.

This was blatantly true. I kept wondering when he planned to stop.

Then he decided to become a Big Game Hunter like Elinor. This came to my attention when he brought me his first trophy, strutting inside with it, his head up and back so it wouldn't Drag on the Ground, and laid it proudly at my feet. All for me, he said, because he loved me.

I looked at it.

It was a smallish earthworm.

He had bigger game in mind, though. He took to arranging himself across my desk (squashing or dislocating everything else, of course) with his nose virtually pressed against the printer. Waiting. It was a new kind of mouse hole, he explained. Flat white mice came out at him, and if he didn't back away, they *hit* him. He'd catch them *all* for me one day, he promised, as soon as he was quite sure they didn't bite.

Felicity finally taught him to play Gotcha properly. This was a relief to the rest of us, who were not up to what she considered Scratch. Scratch is something to see! Forget cops and robbers! This is more like the battle for Iwo Jima: mostly airborne and extremely fast and noisy. We watched in awe--except, of course, Elinor, who licked her paw offhandedly and said she could do that all by herself. She probably could.

Obersdorfstr. 2a
53340 Meckenheim-Ersdorf, Germany
Dearest Sally,
   I'm telling you first.
   Little, Brown have accepted Blacksmith*! I'm now trying to write*

"Glory", the sequel, which I call a paraquel. Yes, she's Ann's beautiful half-sister, superficially spoiled, actually a genuine split personality, and I'm sorry I can't discuss her yet. You know why.

Love, Jenny

Sienna
Dearest darling Jenny,
   YAHOO!

CHAPTER TWENTY-ONE

CHANDI

Sienna

June, '95

Dear Jenny,

Oh, super! Yes, I think just <u>Blacksmith</u> is a better title. When is publication? I can't wait to read it! Is it another gut-wrencher like <u>Nemesis Club</u>?

I'm glad *one* of us is getting published again. I got almost to the climax of <u>The Angry Earth</u> but it refused to be finished. You know how it is! Something's Wrong, and you don't know quite what. Actually, I do know I haven't enough historical information, for one thing, so Characters--and in this case, earthquakes as well--just sit and sulk, and if I push, the result is unfit to read. Won't write itself *or* let me do it, and I sit glaring at the keyboard muttering "Well, what do you *want* to do, then?" Such a good idea, too! And Virginia Carson of the New Madrid Museum sent me such good material! But not enough. Too many basic unknowns about the original town and surrounding land, for one thing. And there seems to be a gap in history between long enough back so that everyone agrees on events--true or not--and so recent that there was good coverage. Especially in a scantly-populated frontier area.

And it's crying to be done! The only novel I've ever found about that quake is so unbelievably bad I can't even glean any background material from it! I've tried over and over--but it seems to have no bearing at all on historical events or place or people: it's as if he did no research, just invented everything but the fact that there were quakes. And the characters are--sludge. No, sludge has some depth. A coat of thin mud? Ah well, I'll hibernate it again.[15]

Tell me as much as you can about you next one. A sequel? About Glory? Not to kill her by premature exposure--but is she Ann's rotten spoiled sister? And what's a *"Paraquel"*???

I told you--I think--about my little guest-room in the garage for visiting cats? Not in the house, mind: I have my quota. Five, maximum, not counting extraneous boarders. Quite enough for someone who once balked at the idea of two.

Well, a few nights ago I went out at bedtime as usual, to say good night to any guest who might be in that open drawer under the shelf. Reached in, found some fur, began stroking-- Good grief! Some one needed a shampoo! I scratched a bit more, around appreciative ears--and then pulled the drawer out a bit for a look--

--And a long toothy snout turned to me, saying ooh, that was lovely: just down and to the left a bit, and what was for supper?

Well, it's the first time I ever found myself caressing a 'possum!

He came back the next night, but I haven't seen him since then.

When I tell people, they say "Oh, weren't you afraid he'd bite you?"

Certainly not. Why on earth should he?

---

15   Took another 14 years, it did!

Germany

July '95

Darling Sally,

Now I want a 'possum AND a skunk and a raccoon: do they get on well together? Also a few snow leopards to breed.

I've given up breeding Siamese. Scallywag and Mall Madam both had their ops last week, and when I've sold the two lunatics I'll be down to five cats, too, because my darling Chandi died two weeks ago, from kidney failure.

Well, at least it was quick. She collapsed, obviously very ill, so I dashed into Bonn with her to the emergency vet. We tried antibiotics just in case it was an infection--but I really knew it wasn't. The next day she was so miserable, and there was obviously nothing but a long death ahead for her, so I sadly took her back to the vet.

In the waiting room she lay on my lap telling me she loved me but everything hurt. When she lay on the table she stretched out her arm for the strap, looking up at me, long loving blinks of those incredible blue eyes, and then just a little gasp, and she was gone.

I do so miss her - she was such a funny little character, always pushing her nose into whatever was going on, and if I got annoyed with one of the other cats she'd chatter to them and then smack them on the nose to curry favour with me. She didn't like jumping, she climbed, hand over hand, up anything, wire netting, wood, curtains.

When Mall Madam was sick, Chandi would curry her for hours, hating it, spitting between licks, but doing it.

Enough. Even when they want to go, do you still wonder if there was anything more you could have done! I can't believe I'll never see her again, running along the window sill, jabbering at me, pushing between Boy and Toot to have her head rubbed, shouting her purr at me to make sure I hear her. Really, she did that, opened her mouth and <u>yelled</u> those purrs. Listen to how much I love you!

I can't write any more just now.

Love

Jenny

Oh, Jenny, I am so _sorry_ about Chandi! I wept at your letter, feeling as if I'd known her-- Isn't it dreadful to lose them? Yes, I too always torment myself wondering if I could have done anything more! At least you were able to help free her from pain quickly. (I'll never forget Domino's last day: long hours agonizing for water and unable to drink it, while I tried to find a vet who would do what she wanted.)

And then at the end, how they gaze at you, knowing, trusting. Until their eyes 'go out' seconds before the heart actually stops and Dr. Patrick says it's over. It's--oh, shivery to actually see life leave the body like that. I'm crying again as I read about dear Chandi, and I wish I could have known her.

It's hard to say anything more--unless I just quote the comforting things you have said to me. We love them, and help them out of bodies that hurt, and we know they acquiesce and are grateful--and we grieve, even though both of us know we'll somehow be together again. But we miss the physical body, as well as the personality wearing it: the individual way every cat moves, speaks, even smiles: the shouted purr, the tilt of the head, the Look, the particular voice, all part of an inimitable whole. It's hard to deal with, isn't it? All I feel certain of is that love endures, and in some form or other, they will be with us.

I know what I can do. I can finish the requiem that has started running through my head: appropriate to a Scotswoman. Perhaps it will return some of the comfort your poem about Domino gave to me.

REQUIEM FOR CHANDI
Pipe her home, the incomparable Chandi;
Pipe her home.
Three times 'round the hill:
Three tunes.

A reel for the joy of her being:
Vivid little friend,
Bright chattering companion

Currying love.
Assuming
The grooming
Of sick Mall Madam--hating it--
     With a hiss, spit, lick--
     (Going to be sick!)

A Lament for the warm little body,
Prancing along the sill
Jabbering still.
Small head pushing for attention,
Silken fur,
Shouted purr:
     (Hear how much I love you!)

And a strathspey, gentle and lilting,
For the love that stays,
For her freedom as she plays
With the company who live Beyond the Hill:
     Loving still.

Pipe her home.

Oberdorfstrasse
10th Sept, 1995
Dear Sally,

    I loved your Requiem for Chandi. It's pinned up over my desk alongside a photo of her. I knew her for nine years, and I look at that photo and even I can't believe the blueness of those eyes. But they were true. Some one told me he'd heard a judge in Spain remark that a certain cat had eye colour "almost as good as the Suryasun cats!" and added that Excaliber's eyes are a benchmark.

He probably overheard that. He (so well nicknamed Scallywag) has started lording it over Jamaica--and getting back as good as he gives, by the way. (Jamaica has become very special to me in several ways.)

School has started, and Max is in India. As usual. So I'm on my own again. Little, Brown have accepted Blacksmith, *and I'm sitting at the computer trying to write "Glory", the 'sequel, with the first four or five chapters a repeat, but from the other sister's point of view. (That's what I call paraquel.) Yes, she's Ann's beautiful half-sister, superficially spoiled, actually a genuine split personality, and I'm sorry I can't discuss her yet. You know why.*

How was your cataract surgery? One has heard of Tamara Suslov even over here, so I assume it's all gone splendidly.

I am skiving today. I should be working on Glory, but apart from having read yesterday's effort, I haven't touched it. I am listening to the cricket match. It's a test match, England v Pakistan, and a cracker. Can't concentrate on writing a novel.

Do you find that when you read what you wrote yesterday, it's always bloody rubbish? but when you read it again a week later, it's not? Why do you suppose that is? Always supposing you have the same experience.

Love,

Jenny

Sienna

Oct. 3. '95

Dearest Jenny,

Well, actually I don't, quite. In my case, either the thing is writing itself, in which case my fingers can hardly keep up with 'my teeming brain', and that's usually my best writing; or else it broods and I can't write a sentence that wouldn't give a cat the pukes, by which I gather that it's not at all what my characters had in mind, so I'm reduced to going back and trying to find out (a) where I went wrong and (b) where I *should* have gone. I have little say in the matter.

I've finished the re-write of Poor Felicity, now titled The Delicate Pioneer. *Had* to do it because back then in the '50's I wrote the bit about shooting the cougar in stupid ignorance, and it spoiled the whole book for me. I hadn't known what gentlemen cougars can be if not put on the defensive; and when later I read the old frontiersmen's boasts about how one would came up and politely sit down at the campfire just to get warm, and sit there, trustingly, while a gun was put to their heads, it broke my heart. And on bitter nights they sometimes curled up beside hunters and kept them from freezing to death--and then were murdered next morning, in gratitude. So I introduced several lovely animals--cats, dogs, skunks; and the New Felicity, afraid of practically everything else, has a way with critters, including a puppy Arne acquired, and some feral cats escaped from a ship. When the cougar shows up at the climax, she follows her experience with the ferals, and Chief Sealth's advice, and aggression is avoided, and the cougar strolls off. As our local ones who show up in gardens and on porches inevitably do. It's a much better book now.

Of course, I've yet to get a publisher or agent even to *read* it. And they *still* steal the stamps on my SAE's.

Never mind, I had my innings: now it's your turn, and I'm so very happy for you! Even if our respective Muses don't work the same way.

Love , Sally and the Cats in the Belfry

I used to knit a lot. Then, that autumn-- (This isn't really going to be a non-sequitur) --I noticed that something was wrong with Felicity's picky appetite and then her poop. I took a sample down to Dr. Patrick, went home, and waited for results. As I sat there knitting and waiting for the phone to ring, Felicity played in front of me, with a bit of yarn. (I have fantastic photos of her as a kitten dancing with it.) Now-- I squinted. Funny! If I didn't know better, I'd almost have thought-- I leaned forward, peered harder, reached, grabbed, pulled--

The phone rang. It was Grant Patrick, presumably with the test results.

"Hello? Dr. Patrick? Guess what? I've just discovered that Felicity eats yarn!"

"So," he said grimly, "have I!"

A very expensive diet! The X-ray showed a huge wad of yarn blocking her gut. Immediate surgery! Looked as if everything would have to be opened! And opening the gut is so risky, too! My heart was crowding my lungs as I waited. Not again! I'd lost Shadow, and Domino and Deirdre; and several colonials had simply vanished--

After a few centuries he phoned, sounding very relieved and a bit smug. "This is Grant. She's all right. And I didn't have to open her intestine to remove the wad. Just pushed it along like threading elastic in a trouser waistband. So she's in virtually no danger. And," he added with modest pride, it's going to cost you less than it would have done."

Wonderful! (It only cost one arm and both legs.) I gave up knitting on the spot, gave most of my yarn away, just put some of the posh, expensive stuff like angora and cashmere safely away in a drawer in the loft.

Several years passed. In 2000 a cat named Onyx opened the drawer, got out the yarn and gave it to Felicity to play with. I saw her out in the back yard with it...

Eating it, of course--

After the second surgery *I really* got rid of all my yarn!

CHAPTER TWENTY–TWO

OBOE

Jan 13, '96

Dear Jenny

Elinor has invented a new game. It's called Super-Pounce, and it is, she says, especially for Felicity. There are two versions:

If I'm dragging Felicity's Very Own Not-to-be-swallowed String around for her to chase, an Elinor-colored thunderbolt shoots across the room from nowhere and vanishes into the next room--along with every trace of string. Five seconds later, Elinor reappears, sauntering in with empty mouth and paws and her butter-wouldn't-melt expression, asking innocently Why is everyone Staring, and *What* string?

If no string is being pulled, Elinor sits on top of a table or chair-back and waits for Felicity to pass, at which point she simply drops on top of her like a boulder from a cliff-top. Alternatively, she hurtles from behind like a juggernaut.

Felicity, needless to say, simply *hates* all three versions, especially the last--even though it's exactly what she used to do to Deirdre and Fuji. She rushes to cover behind the sofa, screeching like a banshee and being a totally rotten sport, while Elinor, saying it's *her* turn to be the Swiss Guard, sits smirking and blocking her exit. I don't know which of them is worse.

But the other day, when the screeching had subsided to a growl and Elinor still sat smirking, who should rush out from the bedroom but placid little Allegro. In a furious temper! Stormed right up the the astonished Elinor, smacked her face soundly several times, and sat there asking if she'd like some more where that came from. Elinor retreated in total confusion. From behind the sofa--in Felicity's usual refuge--came incredulous profanity.[16] Allegro strutted back to the bedroom.

I've been working really hard for Catnippers lately, with the five colonies to feed daily, plus trapping assignments night after night. I quite enjoy it, actually. Setting the trap, placing it, hiding, watching, breath-holding--and--yes--? No? Darn! Oh, *please* go in this time! Just one step more-- Clunk! Yes! He's in! Cover him quickly! It's all right now, luv: you're safe. (We cover the traps instantly with large towels, to reduce their fright, poor things. They always calm down the moment they find themselves in a quiet, safely-small space. I'm often shocked at how many official bodies just leave then sitting exposed, defenseless and utterly terrified--and then euthanize them for being too frantic to handle!)

The young and trusting ones in the colony rush right in to get the goodies, sometimes two at once. The wary ones hold back, and see their mates taken away one by one--and cats aren't stupid, you know. So even if their mates return, they get warier the longer it goes on. But I enjoy that challenge, too.

I'm supposed to trap precisely two a night, no more, no less; because Catnippers makes specific arrangements with the vets. Once, trapping in deepening dusk, I thought I glimpsed a kitten going in. Then another? But no clunk of closing trap. (Sometimes kittens aren't heavy enough, and they gobble the food and saunter out.) I crept nearer, not wanting to scare it--or them--out again. Tricky, this bit! Was that another going in? Ah! *Clunk! Did* I have two? I peered through the dimness and saw two shapes for sure moving inside. Good! That was my quota. So I covered

---

16   Pictured on the cover.

them, took them right home, put the trap in the bathroom and had a good look inside. Six kittens peered back at me!

I phoned Constance, and she lost her cool. "*Sally*! How *could* you? *Now* what--"

Pretty upset, myself, I yelled right back. "Well, I didn't *plan* it, you know! So what do I do now? Go put four of them back?"

What, and never be able to trap them again? Not likely! We pulled ourselves together, decided to keep the extras in the garage, and start phoning other vets first thing in the morning. On the whole, we decided, it was a useful mishap. Well, two days off trapping, for on thing...

What's the latest on cat shows and your unbeatable Black Paws?

Love 'n hugs to you and yours, from Sally, Alphabet (A,B,C,E,F,) and--sort of--Pokey and Whisper.

Oberdorfstrasse
Dear Sally,

Last week we had one of our best shows. It wasn't too far away, for one thing, so I didn't have to get up in the middle of the night and drive half way across Europe with Tigger grumbling in the back and a couple of kittens happily fighting each other and very probably ruining their chances by getting a claw in an eye, and Scallywag snoring gently. This took about an hour to get there, and I only had Scallywag, so there was plenty of time to set him up and even talk to a few friends.

The competition, and I say this with regret, because it's nice to beat the good ones, was rubbish. Had he not won his class, and his Challenge Certificate, and Best of Breed for Seal Point Siamese, I would have been seriously offended. So we get called up for the class win, and then Best of Breed, so I'm already juggling with a couple of trophies, and then there's the Best in Show, which means the best cat in the show, of any age or class, and that really is worth having, and there's a great big cup on the stand.

Oh, don't be fooled by those. They look good in the photographs, and they don't look too bad on a fairly high shelf, but they do not pass the touch test. *The metal coating is microns deep. You know that nice 'ting' you get when you flick a silver cup with your fingernails? Don't try it with these. What you get instead is the tacky plastic 'clack'.*

Beside the point. Our photograph appeared in the cat magazines, the Runner Up and the Best of Breed winners posing beautifully, showing off all their good points and smirking at the camera. Scallywag, Best in Show, overall winner of everything, European Champion, All That Jazz, appears with his head buried in the cup (looking hopefully for biscuits) and his bum in the air, whilst I, proud 'owner', am clearly grinding my teeth and wrestling with him, and three trophies and an armful of rosettes, and failing most dismally to seem to be in control of the situation. We did not show to our best advantage, either of us.

Oh, what the Hell. He walked it. But he is such a clown, bless him.

Love to you and your alphabet, Jenny

Sienna

3rd March

Happy birthday! And how are you liking it in Germany by now? A long time, innit? Over ten years! Thirteen? Whatever. (*I've* been *here* for ten years now! Amazing!) How long do you think you can stick it?

I'm missing England a lot--and I was there only 24 years all told. And though I wasn't in Germany long enough to make a fair judgment--and some things impressed me, like leaving toys for the tourists unchained along the river bank and being shocked at the idea that anyone might steal them--still, I don't really think I'd care to live there. Especially speaking another language! Me of all people, who am hopeless at foreign languages, especially spoken, and mentally hear *L'amour* as *La Moor*. No brains in my ears. Can't sing on key or do accents, either.

I suspect that although you've never said so, you must like it even less than I would.

Feel like talking? If not, never mind.

Scallywag is just showing his personality and intelligence, rather than docility.

Love you, Sally

That was about the time I broke my left wrist. Same way I did the right one. This time it was a Colles fracture (both bones snapped directly on the joint) that left a weirdly misshapen but perfectly functional wrist and hand. (Well, I can't spread that thumb at all--but it's not a handicap--unless I decide to take up music again and try to reach even a small chord; and the left thumb is the only unnecessary digit for typing, so that's all right, innit?) Still, I thought I'd better not tell Jenny, who always unfairly accused me of breaking bits of myself.

I was still in plaster when a large loving cat named Henry in the adoption room pushed a passionately-adoring head against my right hand as usual--and then suddenly turned and bit it to the bone. *Henry???* Something was very wrong with him! So before going to Emergency, I urged Sandy (Arlene's foster-sister and my second-best friend in Catnippers) to have him checked at once; and at ER, I refused to tell them who or where Henry was, lest they seize and euthanize him.

I was right, too. He had a terrible infection in his ear. (He eventually went home with Sandy and Chris, and Lived Happily Ever After--or at least for fourteen more years.)

At Emergency the doctor finished binding and splinting my hand, placed that arm gently in a sling, surveyed the plaster cast on the other one, smiled kindly, and told me to go along home now and relax with a nice cocktail or something.

I told him none of my cats were any good at either driving or catering.

He didn't get it.

18 March., '96
Dear Sally,

Another blazing row with the twins. There are times I wish I hadn't fallen into the wife trap again, I am truly not cut out for it, which is why I threatened to leave. If they think it's all so damned easy to run this family, they can just try it for themselves. Now I'm sitting here at the word processor, wondering if I meant it. I do love them. And Max.

Max is one of the best people I have ever known. He is kind, and clever, and everything I thought I wanted, tolerant, and genuinely the only man I know who does not believe men are superior to women. Why does the thought of trying to talk to him make me feel so weary?

Germany, too. I don't like it. I know many lovely people, even one or two I call friends, but I don't like this country. I don't like the thinly veneered guilt, although I sympathise with it, I don't like the hellish bloody bureaucracy, I don't like the language, or not being able to speak it sufficiently well to make the many points I want to score! I suppose that's the main problem. The twins speak German better than they speak English, and their English is pretty damned good, but I've never managed to cope with foreign languages. Listen to me! In Germany, talking about German as a foreign language.

Always, Jenny.

May 29 '96
Dearest Jenny,

Writers should never live in foreign-speaking countries: our business is words, and it's too verbally limiting! It's why I was never tempted to settle in places I loved, like Denmark, Israel, France, Greece...

If you should ever leave home, come here! There are lots of things you'd hate--but we could be happily verbal and stand united against barbarism, and feed cats, and form a new rescue group with a bigger adoption program. And you could bring all your own cats straight into the US. (Rabies is pandemic on the whole continent, so there'd be no

point in our having quarantine laws.) Elinor would object, of course--
but that's a habit now. And I think Oboe would--

Ah! Oboe! Must've slipped my mind, somehow--

Did I ever tell you about The Orchestra? A colony I feed. I name my
colonies. There's the Clans, Exodus (Moses, Joshua and Miriam), the
Waifs, the Brits and The Orchestra, who are all more or less tuneful, and
look the parts. Piano is suitably black and white, and Clarinet mostly
black. Silver-gray Flute and brown tabby Viola. And a gorgeous one with
a musical mew, all swirls of cream and copper, bronze and mahogany-
-she *had* to be Melody. Such an affectionate girl! Rushes to meet me,
singing for a belly rub.

An old black bandy-legged neutered male who clearly had been or
still was a pet, began to visit infrequently, and then frequently, and then
daily. I got very fond of him, and he of me. Such a funny looking old
guy! He has a big face, huge ears, wide mouth, long upper lip, long *long*
chin, and a long Roman nose flattened along the top, giving him an
odd profile. What with his color and long lean body--not a white hair
on it!--he really does look rather like an oboe--and his haunting hollow
voice certainly sounds like one.

I still wasn't sure whether he had really joined the Orchestra. But
he and Melody began coming right out the gate and halfway down the
street to meet me. She purred and rolled and sang, he tootled at great
length and very earnestly, his big face turned up to mine as if willing me
to understand every toot. "Right, Oboe my lad," I said last week. "You've
clearly had your little Operation, but if you're really a member you need
a health check and your ear clipped and some injections, all right?"

He said it was, I made the appointment, and he came into the carrier
like a lamb. Dr. Patrick checked and inoculated him, and I brought him
home for a snack and to spend an hour or so isolated in the recovery
room--er, bathroom--before returning to the colony--and that's when
the whole thing came unraveled.

First, I noticed that Dr. Patrick had unaccountably forgotten to
clip his ear.

Unaccountably? Not ruddy likely, mate! But I didn't get it yet. I said oh darn, and I'd make him comfy in the study just until I could take him back to have his ear clipped. And then--

Well, all I did was give him a nice big basket to rest in! How was *I* to know that Figgy was back on the job? His eyes lighted. He knew all about baskets! He jumped right in, stood on the edge with those funny bowed front legs, and looked up at me with his heart in his eyes. Oh! he said joyfully, I had Understood at last! I *was* adopting him? he persisted anxiously. It wasn't a mistake? He *could* spend the rest of his life with me: on my bed and lap, being loved? He knew *all* about litter boxes and cat doors, too, he assured me, and settled down blissfully in the basket.

I sighed. He had fleas, of course. I rang Sandy, who is always incredibly willing to help a friend. She dropped everything and rushed over with flea shampoo. But the stuff--even though sold at a vet's--was horrible. Presently all three of us were wheezing and gagging, and poor old Oboe, miserable by now, had to have two more water baths to get rid of the flea bath. He took it like a cherub, only bleating and hooting urgently at the end, more in sorrow than in anger. So we toweled him dry and cuddled him some more, which he adored, and tucked him tenderly in his basket in the study--

--just until he was fit to return the the Orchestra, of course-- Sure!

Love to all, Sally

11th June, '96
Dearest Sally,

Okay, Oboe. So you've got another one, suckered into it again, surprise surprise. But when you next get a cat that's been over-flea-cured, you might try baby powder first, massage it well in, then brush it out, and you might be able to get away with only one bath. Even better, a bran bath, which they usually like. Warm the bran in the oven, then rub it into the coat, and most of them love it, it's pleasantly scratchy, to say nothing of warm.

He's firmly ensconced by now, of course. How is he getting on with Cameo?
Is her feist still missing? I assume Felicity is more capable of taking care of
herself. I look forward to the next installment.

Love, Jenny

Sienna
June 23, '96
Dearest Jenny,

Oboe is very fatherly to Cameo, whose feist is still absent. And
of course he's firmly ensconced. He was in the study only two days.
Then--

"Ready to join the Cats in the Belfry?" I asked. He tootled and
butted his shaggy head at me--and without Deirdre to start a moaning
session, the others accepted him without comment (except Elinor, who
cursed luridly, first at him and then at me and finally at Bootsie--also
black and even bigger--for good measure). Oboe looked around calmly,
trotted straight to the bedroom, jumped--or rather, climbed--on to the
bed (not without some difficulty: he is pretty old) and settled down
modestly at the very foot. Didn't want to be pushy, he told me. He'd be
Out of the Way down here, wouldn't he? Kind of invisible?

Fair enough. The others hardly seem to notice him--unless they
bump into him nose-to-nose around a corner, when they hiss quite a
lot. Startled them, they say, embarrassed. Elinor grumped a bit at first.
Said she let me have *one* large black male, who is young and gormless,
but now I was presuming on her leniency. Never does more than scold,
though. Perhaps she thinks she'd better not? He's never rude--but is not,
I think, a cat to be browbeaten. Anyway, they seem agreed that Oboe
can stay. He goes in and out with the others, and understands sandboxes
and cat doors, and sticks to his own dish with quiet good manners.

One small problem, though. He's so *very* grateful, so happy to be
here, he says, that he really needs to be on my lap loving me all the time.
The others, refusing to allow monopolies, simply crowd on top of him.

So my chair overflows with felines. And they said it was okay for him to join them on the bed--so long as he stayed down there at the foot and left them their chosen spots up my right and left sides.

He hasn't. After a few days he began to act like the camel with its nose in the Arab's tent. An inch at a time. First he sidled up my left side. For a couple of feet. At about thigh-level he ran into the solid bulk of Bootsie, who weighs half again Oboe's modest twelve pounds. Bootsie didn't even object: he just slept on, oblivious. Oboe, though big-boned, is gaunt, so I think he gave up rather quickly--on that side. So he began insinuating himself up the right, displacing the little girls one by one-- and I awoke in the morning to find Oboe the sole occupant of that side of me, Elinor cursing like a trooper, and Felicity and the twins sitting in an indignant row on the floor.

I didn't scold: not hours after the sin had been committed! How would he know what he was being scolded *for*? I just shut him in the study that night--

--and *he got the idea!* Has never done it again! (Their little minds can't grasp cause-and-effect over more than two minutes, mm? Sure!)

<u>July 3</u>. Remember Pokey? Well, it dawned on me that he hadn't been around much lately. Seems there's a good reason. Oboe may be very old and arthritic and bandy-legged--but it seems he's appointed himself Defender of Our Territory and Chucker-Out of Invaders. And a very good job he's made of it. What's more--*he understands human property lines!*

I heard an altercation and rushed out to see him confronting Pokey on the exact edge of Our Property. Not giving an inch to youth or truculence, he wasn't. Ears forward, he advanced menacingly while Pokey, ears perfectly flat, retreated. Snarling but cowed. Knew it wasn't his territory, he did.

Afraid that Oboe might get hurt (he's limping painfully these days, from arthritis) I shouted at them both. Testosterone up, they both ignored me. Instead, Oboe, as righteously wrathful as Moses, drove

Pokey backwards step by step through Grace's garden back to his old home, up the driveway, and finally to the porch. At this point I told Oboe what a hero he was, and that he'd made his point, hadn't he, and now let's go home in triumph while Pokey was still shaken, mm? And have a nice cuddle?

I do pamper him a lot. He deserves it. And he's a frail old guy. When not on my lap, he's usually in the hot sun on the front porch, craving the heat as Shadow used to do. He's slowed down and aged just in the three or four months I've had him. If these are his last days, I want him to enjoy them fully.

--Though there may not be many if he doesn't stop treating my car with such cavalier brinksmanship. His favorite place to sleep is in my driveway. Waiting for me to come home--right there, however long I'm away. Black on black, invisible in the dense shade of the seven-foot rose bushes along the driveway. He's sleeping on the desk as I write this. When I go to the living room, he'll follow and laboriously climb to my lap. He dozes comfortably, every now and then rousing, turning his big funny old face to stare at me long and lovingly, sometimes tootling a doting honk. Feels very secure now, he says--so long as I don't take him away, please. I did last month for his rabies shot, and he thought I was returning him to the colony. The mournful oboe sound was replaced by a full-voiced Siamese bellow that nearly made me drive the car off the road.

Suddenly several points of his appearance and voice fell into place. Totally black... long and lean... big ears... long face... voice... Good grief, he must be part Siamese! (I'm enclosing his photo.)

Now he's back to the hollow horn sound. Ironic. Lynx-point Felicity, who *should* have had the Siamese voice, sounds instead like a sick kitten.

Love, Sally and the Crazy Cats

17th July
Dearest Sally,

Blacksmith comes out on 7th November. Little, Brown are really going to town. A huge £25,000 publicity drive. I enclose a photocopy of their publicity card, which came in a gorgeous box that looked like chocolates but in fact contained a proof copy of the book and a horseshoe, and I was absolutely thrilled.

As for coming over to the USA to promote *Blacksmith*, I doubt I'll even get to the UK. Max is going there tomorrow for a conference at St. Andrews, and *he doesn't want to go!* There is no bloody justice!

I want not only a raccoon, a skunk and a 'possum, but all seven of your cats. I love them.

Love, Jenny

Sienna
Jenny, luv!

How absolutely super! How I wish I could be there! (I'm not so sure about my menagerie. Nothing personal, they say, but they quite like it here, and why gamble a mouse in the paws for an uncaught chipmunk?)

But love, anyway.

Oberdorfstrasse
Dearest Sally,

Thanks for the photo. Oboe is obviously an Ebony Oriental Shorthair (nearest thing to black Havana), probably pedigreed if he really has no white hairs at all. He has the build, the voice, the eyes, the ears, the coat. The picture in one of my books is a dead-ringer for the one you sent. Look it up yourself. He seems a darling, and I'm glad you're cherishing him.

Love, Jenny

Dearest Jenny,

Oboe is dead.

I cuddled him goodbye as usual before leaving to teach my exercise class. As always, I inched out of the drive keeping an eye on him, stopping once to get out and move him carefully out of harm's way. Unusually, I paused as I drove off to look in my rear-view window at him sitting thoughtfully on the sidewalk watching me go.

It was the last time I saw him alive.

Normally I returned to find him waiting on the porch, limping out to sit directly in front of my car when I got out to open the garage door. Not this time. Not in the garden, either. Not in sight. I felt instant alarm. He was *always* there!

Until now.

I spent most of the day wandering around calling--without much hope. Lost cats usually either return on their own or not at all. But I always have to call. In case. (Once, that saved Felicity's life, after all, didn't it? When tiny-voice was trapped under Grace's house--and managed a fine bellow only when she heard me calling.) This time-- nothing. Except that Pokey suddenly strolled on to My Territory, and up to the porch, ominously relaxed and cheeky. Needed a new boy now, did I? he inquired conversationally. And then Elinor rushed up, all grateful purrs and cheek rubs. Dumped him at last, had I?

My heart sank.

That afternoon I went to trap at a new colony and found one of its members lying dead in the bushes, like an omen, on his side, legs stretching out as if in mid-leap. My heart sank further. I tried to phone Arlene. Couldn't get through. Later I went to a Catnippers trappers' meeting. Everyone assured me cheerfully that I was worrying unnecessarily. "Cats go off like that for days," they assured me kindly. They meant well, so I didn't snap their heads off--but I felt like it. I reckon I know as much about cats' behavior as they, maybe more; certainly more about *my* cats, who *never* go off like that. Particularly Oboe, who never goes off at all. So I muttered a bit and went home early to hunt for him. And call. And brood over unlikely possibilities, as had dear old Fred some five years ago. He had *not* just decided to move on. He would *not* stay away by choice: he loved me too much. Kidnapping seemed unlikely. Which left alternatives that haunted me all night and caused me to get up three times to call some more. By morning I was just praying blindly that he wasn't hurting. I got up early, to go to the back jungle again and and search all the bushes once more, because that's usually where they crawl for privacy when they're dying.

But he wasn't there. He was across the street. Betty came over to ask if I was missing a black cat, because there was one lying dead in her back yard.

Not in the bushes. In the middle of the lawn, also stretched on his side, paws reaching out as if in mid-leap. Nothing to show how or why he died. Except that it must have been quick and unexpected: too quick for him even to get to a nice private bush. Shortly after I looked back at him watching me leave? Certainly before I returned a couple of hours later. A heart attack, perhaps, with no suffering? He must have gone across there as soon as I left and died almost at once, or he would have been here to greet me.

True, I hadn't expected him to live *very* much longer. And I'm relieved that he's safely dead and not in fear or pain somewhere. All the same-- Yes, of course I'm grieving--as I always do, for myself. How I'll miss that big funny face turning to gaze so earnestly into mine, the oboe voice, loving, conversational, demanding. He made everyone love him: Constance, Sandy-and-Chris, the neighbors, Bootsie and the girls--and just by being himself.

Rest in peace, dear.

Enough of that. Change the subject before I start weeping, which I haven't because he was ready to go and had a lovely life with me before he went, and he did it, apparently, quickly and easily. *We* should be so lucky!

Love, Sally

Obersdorfstr.

25 Sept. '96

Dearest Sally,

Oh, I do grieve with you for Oboe. I think it must have been lightning-flash quick, for him to be stretched out in the middle of the lawn like that. I think he died happy, pottering around in the neighbourhood in a friend's garden, knowing he was safe, and loved by you. It's the sort of end a cat like Oboe deserves, Sally. Bear that in mind.

Mall Madam is gone, too. Right up to the last hour, no pain, and then suddenly paralysis. When she was spayed she went immediately from being the Boss and duck-when-you-see-me-coming to being very quiet, and quite gentle and happy. Now I'm down to five cats: Scallywag and Jamaica, Percy, Toot and Patchwork (who isn't Siamese but needed a home).

Love you, Jenny

CHAPTER TWENTY–THREE

TUFFET

Oboe died in September, leaving me with only (!!) Allegro, Bootsie, Cameo, Elinor and Felicity. Well, not counting Whisper, still residing on the front porch, and the ubiquitous Pokey, who, disciplined by Oboe, was now a little less objectionable.

By November I was up to eight. Sort of.

It was three years since I took Mia's litter from the colony. Ariel was still there and doing fine (except that he kept getting in the wars and would never *ever* let me take him to the vet, much less home to live with his sisters. I could doctor him on the spot as much as I liked, but no carrier or trap, thank you very much!) I had the calico twins, and Tuffet was still with Marilyn. She insisted that he only under went the bed when I was there. I didn't believe it, but had no chance to check until--

Nov. 1996

Dearest Jenny,

Remember, I've been uneasy about my sister Marilyn and the twins' brother Tuffet? Well--settle yourself for a saga. She decided to take a friend on a luxurious *(very!)* cruise, and would I come over every day and feed Tuffet? I agreed eagerly, and went up virtually minutes after she left.

Oops! She was really in a tizz-wizz when she left for her cruise! Left the back door ajar, and the litter box contained the Sunday paper instead of litter. Dad's cat Cosmos was looking out the door pensively, and Tuffet--as always--was just a scared black and white growl under the bed.

I decided at once to let them live with me while Marilyn was away. Easier for me, more fun for them--at least I hoped so. And putting Tuffet in a different environment and separated from Cosmos, might tell me something, too. So I talked to the growl lovingly for a bit, took Cosmos home, where he settled down philosophically, and went back for Tuffet the next day. But it was the third day before he crept out and on to my lap, whimpering, begging for comfort. When I got him home, he cowered in my study, terrified, for hours, like Marilyn in a panic attack. When I took them both to Dr. Patrick Tuesday for a check-up, Tuffet went bonkers. He *literally* climbed the wall, using pictures as his ladder, clinging to the top edge of the highest before dropping off and bolting for the cupboard where he imitated the action of a tiger until Dr. Patrick captured him with a noose-on-a-long rod. (He said he'd had to use that a few times on ferals--not on *pets!*)

But now, suddenly, Tuffet has given his entire heart and trust to me, bless him! He's joyously at home here, luxuriating in warmth, cuddles and companionship: fine with Cosmos but delighted to meet other cats! He may or may not have recognized his sisters: it doesn't matter. He loves them all! Whatever was wrong is now very right, and I shall simply have to let Cosmos go back to Marilyn and keep Tuffet here. (Actually, she never did *adopt* him: just fostered and kept him, and we footed the vet bill.) He's already staked out his Very Own Place on my bed: on the pillow near my right ear where he can kiss it easily and often. He's learned to play tag and Gotcha with the others, and he seems to be quietly studying Pounce. Such an eager little fellow he's turned out to be, in love with his new life and companions, quite literally bright-eyed and bushy-tailed. If I speak his name (which he had forgotten if he ever knew) he looks up at once, green eyes wide and black tail aloft, panting a little with excitement and joy. "*Me?* Yes, that's me, isn't it? Here I am!" and rush up to me with a wide silent Meow--the only cat I've ever had who used it--wanting to know what we're going to do now, and is it fun and does it taste good?

He's a comical little guy as well as a beautiful one. His face is as pretty as his sister Cameo's, his long black and white coat is silky, lacking the thick undercoat, so that it flows like Lady Godiva's hair. Adores being groomed: will stretch sensuously on his back, legs wide, so I can do his belly and under-legs, no matter how tangled or burr-filled. He usually sleeps draped on the arm or back of an armchair, with head, limbs and tail all hanging limply over the edges like boiled lettuce. Or on his back, head hanging upside-down. He can't understand why he keeps falling off; but never mind, he says cheerfully, and climbs back on.

His plumy black tail is incredibly full and rich--but it's fastened to a white rump, looking as if the wrong one had got glued on by mistake. It waves with happy innocence when he's up to mischief--and he's the only cat I ever met who eats with his tail aloft like a plumy flagpole.

And Elinor doesn't just tolerate him: she *likes* him! I can hardly believe it.

Still, as the mischief happens more and more often, and he's becoming an incorrigible tease, she's beginning to have second thoughts. (Though she has yet to stick a still-untrimmed claw in his direction.)

Yes, I *know* I said no more cats. This is different. Tuffet is merely family who got kidnapped and is home again.

Arlene, Joe and young Dan (now 13) came back from the Virgin Islands for a visit--and Dan took me to lunch! A beautifully groomed very young man taking me to a posh Chinese restaurant, pulling out my chair, gallant and solicitous of me as very few dates have ever been.

In fact, I can't remember ever enjoying a lunch out as much! I think it was his first real grown-up date--and I adored it. So, clearly, did he!

Hugs, Sally and the Cats in the Belfry

Bonn, Germany
Dearest Sally,

I do like the sound of Dan - I have to admit I've never been taken out to lunch by a thirteen-year-old gentleman friend! What a delightful experience!

Love, Jenny

Thanksgiving (American holiday)
Dearest Jenny,

I received my very own autographed copy of <u>Blacksmith</u>, and thank you so very much! I totally loved it, and couldn't put it down, and now would some one like to come and uncurl my toes? It well and truly unraveled my guts! Good grief, woman, what a writer you are! <u>The Nemesis Club</u> was just practice, wasn't it? Your style is still not merely impeccable but vivid! Compelling. (As opposed to--say--the highly-regarded Ken Follett, whose prose is also impeccable--and as about as colorful and exciting as pablum. I can never get through two chapters.) <u>Blacksmith</u> glued me to my chair. I hardly did anything, even eat, until I finished. It's a brilliant book, luv--and I feel perhaps unduly chuffed at having--in a way--Discovered you. At least, I was the first to realize that you can really write--wasn't I?

And it goes back to that judo course in Brighton in '69!

I love and admire you, dearest friend!

Sally

Oberdorfstr
31 Jan, '97

Sally, I <u>love</u> our presents from you! Including the hanger, which alleviates the eternal problem with wardrobes, and the honey server, which really <u>doesn't</u> dribble. I hadn't believed it.

I'm still in a bit of a whirl! <u>Blacksmith</u> was chosen by W. H. Smith as one of their "Fresh Talent" promotions (six chosen out of somewhere near four hundred!) and that meant I was in London for a week, on the goggle box, on radio, and signing books. Everyone should be a celebrity for a few days once in their lives just for the giggle!

After those few days the joke begins to wear a bit thin, but the luxury hotel! The chauffeur-driven car, with passers-by asking each other who that can be when it draws up in front of the bookshop!

*The USA doesn't want <u>Blacksmith</u>: the heroine doesn't fit. At the party W.H. Smith gave at the launch of the Fresh Talent lot, the head of Warner Books USA spoke to my agent. "**Six foot <u>five</u>?**" he said, looking incredulous.*

Yup, six foot five, and you can lump it, mister I-forget-your-name. Heroines can be feisty, Sally, but they'd better be small and pretty.

Right now I'm waiting on tenterhooks to hear what my editor thinks of Novel Number Two, and she's already cursing me because 'paraquel' isn't really a word, and now I've been and gone and written one. Glory's story (<u>The Black Cat</u>) has the same time span as <u>Blacksmith</u>. As Hilary said, rather bitterly, we started with sequels, we've had the odd prequel, and now we've got.....?

Love, Jenny

March 3rd
Dearest Jenny,

Paraquels, yet! Well, best of British luck to yours! Maybe I'll try one some day. (A pair?)

I'm a bit discontented these days--though nothing as serious as your problems in Germany. It's just that I want it both ways. To have a say in running things without having to go to Board meetings. I want to get my lovely and loving and lovable 'trappee' cats in the adoption program just *sometimes*-- but somehow it's always No Room at the Inn. And two other members, Sandy and Chris, who foster, are fretting because they reckon their fosterlings are put into adoption *too soon:* before Sandy reckons they're socialized *enough.*

I've almost given up trying to get anyone even to *read* any of my new mss. It's like throwing them down a well. I'm writing just for the fun of it, now--and it *is* fun, or I wouldn't do it. Sometimes I can hardly wait to get back to the computer to find out what's going to happen next. (Do yours take over like that?) Just finished a full-length book based on Magic At Wychwood (which was only four short stories) using the same characters plus a dozen more, and hint of future romance. Lots of fun. Ostensibly a juvenile, but too--subtle? Alas, I can't dumb down my wry understated humor, and won't dumb down vocabulary or style, and this couldn't be written straight, and so it's surely 'too hard" for most (I fear) of today's kids. It's not just vocabulary--but what do they know or care about Arthurian England or the Days of Silly Chivalry, or the concept of royal princes earnestly reading books of instructions on it? And my tongue-in-cheek humor really depends on readers understanding what you're poking fun at. (I used to quip if asked my name, "Watson, as in Elementary, my Dear." No longer. Just get a blank stare. One guy said, "Oh, I'm sorry!")

So-- The Wayward Princess is, I fear, just for my own enjoyment. And Dan's. The select few of my ilk.

"How's Glory coming? Is her title definitely The Black Cat? I *like* it! (So does Bootsie, who thinks it's about him, even though I tell him with those four silly white toes, he's not properly a black cat, is he?)

The U.S. is the poorer for rejecting a heroine of 6'5", and serve us bloody well right. I reckon a lot of American men might find a heroine like Ann intimidating. Here, 'heroine' tends to mean not the protagonist, but the protagonist's girl. Beautiful and yielding.

At the moment, Bootsie is sprawled across my desk hypnotizing the printer again. That cat is a feline Li'l Abner if ever I saw one! Oops-- You Scots don't know Li'l Abner, do you? Pity, because you have the best if not the only word in the world to describe him. Gormless! That's Bootsie: huge, sweet, simple (well apparently), and clueless. He strolls half a step ahead of me, so I'm forever tripping over him--and only my well-practiced breakfall has kept me from seriously fatal falls. He sleeps smack in the middle of doorways, and never moves out of the way because he never knows that he's in it.[17] He proudly brings me earthworms and dandelions (Big Game), stalks invisible flies, squashes my lap and stands on my solar plexus and breathes passionately into my face. Gormless!

He is still crouched, watching that flat white mouse as it emerges.

The girls are all sleeping here and there around the study, Elinor snoring. (Did I ever mention that Elinor and Felicity snore?)

A month or so after he joined us, Tuffet streaked out suddenly one day from behind the Christmas Tree and Pounced on the sleeping Elinor, who fled squalling under the coffee table. Then he sat regarding her with cocked head and her very own butter-wouldn't-melt expression. That was Pounce, wasn't it? he wanted to know. He'd been watching how she does it, he said: did he get it right? Fun, wasn't it? Should we play it some more?

Well, he didn't get it quite right, after all. In Pounce, unlike Gotcha, it's only Elinor who gets to do the attacking. I couldn't see her just then, but from the shocked silence under the coffee table, I gathered she was doing some rather hard thinking.

Since then, he's been driving her bonkers at her own game. He Lurks. He Stalks. She'll creep through the room looking haunted, and a moment later, there's Tuffet tip-toeing behind her, tail erect, eager and guileless. Follows through the living room, the dining room, into the

---

17 Bootsie features--as Ab-ram--in The Ivory Cat, and again in The Missing Queen, where he's a major hero.

kitchen--from where comes an outraged yell closely followed by Elinor closely followed by Tuffet. He stands there, sweet innocence and full of himself, tail still aloft and gently waving, while Elinor rushes hissing to Felicity's Very Own Refuge behind the sofa, where she sits and swears in perfect fury.

I don't know where she learned those words!

And of course there's even worse profanity when I sit and laugh helplessly. Poor baby! Keeps getting her comuppance, always deserves it--but never compromises her goal--which is to rule the roost at all times.

Felicity loves it, of course. She sprawls on my recliner, eyes slitted, clearly enjoying Nemesis. In fact, I was photographing her one day on a rich blue blanket that just matches her eyes; when Elinor fled bawling. I'd have sworn Felicity grinned: a diabolical triumphant *nyah nyah!* grin just as I snapped the shutter--and sure enough, there it is on the print.[18]

As for Pokey-- Well, Pokey has changed tactics. He's been and gone and started making nice to my lot, and has won them over! Grace says they sit and chat on her back deck. They escort him into my kitchen to check out the dry food, and up to the garage loft, which, they say, Isn't Taken, and there's that drawer in the garage, and Mum's a softie if you play it right; so why doesn't he quietly move in when the weather is wet or nippy? He says, well, thanks for asking, but he already has, actually.

He has, too. So what do I do?

Let him, of course. Provided he stays nice to mine. Call him in dulcet tones and tell him he needn't run away any more. Give him love and cuddles when I meet him in the garden. Put food, water and scratching post up in the loft. (No litter box: he can go on using outside for that.) But he finally has what he has wanted for-- golly, ten years!

Love, Sally

---

18   See cover.

Little by little that spring I realized that something was wrong with Constance. She sort of almost-vanished, and looked barely-there even when I did see her. No one in Catnippers could tell me anything.

I learned later that she had had a couple of strokes! At her age! Doctors couldn't figure it out, and she was increasingly suspicious that all their guesses were wrong; but, as she says philosophically, "It is what it is", so she just carried on, brave and stubborn. But she was no longer up to doing all the Board work and meetings and organization and trapping and fostering and vet trips and other stuff she had done since helping to create Catnippers. So not only did she feel dreadful, she also felt useless! Especially when someone said, "Well, what *can* you do, then?" and when Con sighed "Not a lot," the retort was "Well, then, you're not much good to us, are you?"

I did not, of course, know any of this for months. Knew only that she looked very ill, that she'd lost that pixie sparkle and *joi de vivre*. I worried, but hardly saw her any more, and it never seemed the time to ask, somehow. When I did see her, she seemed not only ill, but-- extinguished? Almost desperate--which, in fact, she was.

I could tell she was unhappy, if nothing more. With Catnippers? I had no idea: knew only that she seemed sympathetic when I muttered subversively about forming a new cat rescue group devoted mainly to adoptions. And the close friendship that had somehow never quite had time or energy to take that final step into completion--flowed into love quickly and easily. She was indeed the Old Friend I had thought her from first sight!

And our independent rescue *and adoption* group crept fractionally closer.

CHAPTER TWENTY–FOUR

LORELEI

Bonn
18th May '97
Dear Sally,

In a filthy temper lately. It's all getting on top of me. Has been for a long time. I've told Max I want to leave. I want to go back to the UK, which I still think of as 'going home'. I think Max tried to look sad, but he did not quite succeed, and when I asked him if it wasn't, in fact, a bit of a relief, he smiled at me, and said in a way it was.

The fact is, my bad temper does make everybody miserable, and I do realise that. Does anybody ever stop to wonder <u>why</u> I am always in such a filthy mood?

I insisted Max tell the boys I am leaving. They are a little subdued, but they do seem to accept it. Now, I just have to deal with practicalities like finding somewhere to live in the UK, and all that. Jay wants to study special effects make-up in England, and Lee, too, wants to come back eventually. Well, they can face the same problems as I am facing now, like finding somewhere to live, because it won't be with me.

Now I can get on with saving up for the move, and so on. It's all very well my editor saying that if <u>Blacksmith</u> goes as well as they think it should, I'll be all right. That is still in the future--which is always uncertain.

But at least this way Max and I can part as friends.

Sally, there isn't a lot more to say, and despite this all being a relief, I really am feeling a bit shaken. Do you understand? I'll be fine, but I'm going to sign off now and do some practical things, to sort of pull myself together.

Love to the kids. And to you. Jenny

June 1, '97

Dearest Jenny,

Of course I understand! I who rejected marriage not only because I never fell for anyone, but also because I knew in my gut that I was unfit for marriage. No hormones? Anyway, *exactly* this thing would inevitably have happened. I've seen your life start to fall apart little by little, and at first it was only between the lines, and then a few words-- Yes, of course. And I can sort of imagine how you must feel-- but Jenny, I'm also very relieved for you! I've always suspected in my heart that you weren't much more intended to be a mum and *housefrau* than I. I know your new life will be lovely, and you deserve it.

Have you made any plans yet? I'm eager to hear them! Do you know when you'll go? What about the cats? With a 6-month quarantine-- which I assume will cost ££s and ££s--how many can you afford to take, and how can you bear to leave the others, and will Max and the twins take good care of them? Will the twins stay there with Max, then? Really?

Love, Sally

Bonn

15th June, '97

Dear Sally

I'm leaving on 1ˢᵗ February, which gives us plenty of time to sort things out. Max has to stay here at the university: he has a contract. He'll find a flat somewhere near Bonn, but I suspect it will, once again, be a last minute job, and Lee, I think, fears that too. Max does what he thinks is important, and his priorities rarely put the family very high on the list. Lee is a chronic worrier, and I sympathise with that, because I think I am, too.

I love them so much it hurts. But I cannot go on like this. They are adults now, and it is time to cut loose, if you will please excuse the lousy cliché.

I woke up this morning, knowing the answer to my 'where to live?' question. Boat. I love them, I've always had a back-of-the-mind dream of living on one, but it has never been practical. Now, why not? Me and a cat or two, a boat is fine. When people want to come and stay, they can bring a tent, and camp on the bank. My boat is for me, Scallywag and Jamaica.

I didn't really <u>decide</u> to take Jamaica and Scallywag and leave Toot and Percy behind; Percy belongs to Max anyway, and actually Jamaica belongs to Lee, but Jamaica and Toot don't get on - Jamaica's a bully - and Toot belongs to Jay. Jamaica was the obvious one to take. And Scallywag, of course. Quarantine will be fine for Jamaica, do her good, she's almost certainly committed several crimes that would earn her six months in clink. And Scallywag will love it. The only trouble with Valerie's cattery is that cats are inclined to pine for her when they go home.

Oh look, I've got to go, I can't keep nattering on with you! I've got masses to do.

Love, Jenny

Sienna
July 12, '97
Dear Jenny.

Boat? Oh, gorgeous! Tell me more! Where? What kind?

I've been pretty busy, with gardening and writing and cuddling, and feeding and trapping and taking to vets and then back to the colonies, and Constance, and a lot of other things. *And* a new cat: Lorelei. Don't squall: wait until you hear about her!

She is just now settled on a fluffy toilet-seat cover in the corner of the study looking philosophical. She needs to be, poor little mite!

She was caged in Con's garage with some 35 others waiting to be checked by a vet or medicated or socialized or all three. I met her when I went to help out last month--and fell in love. Didn't dream of asking for her, as Catnippers sensibly leave the all-out-gorgeous ones for adopters who go for looks rather than personality (though I did cheat with Felicity: figured Fred's donation gave me the right.) She's an exotic wee beauty with a vivid personality, who bursts into raucous purrs (or snarls) if you touch her. I *think* she's seal-point, with long snow-white whiskers and black-spotted white feet. Constance says she's Siamese cross. Sort of. She has much too short a face for pure Siamese, so maybe she's a short-haired Birman. Or not. Whose odd spots neither breed would be caught dead wearing--so I reckon she's s a mix. A delightful one.

Figgy again. On Monday Catnippers rang to ask if I'd like that Siamese cross at Con's for my very own! Ooh, *would* I!! So two of them took the kitten to the evening clinic for a health check--and arrived, stunned, saying that the three-and-a-half-pound unnamed scrap was very pregnant. And how was I at midwifery?

About as good as Bootsie, actually! I instantly went into the 'Don' know nuffin' about birthin', Missy Scarlett!' routine. They grinned at me wickedly. I held the kitten and discovered that she was leaking wee drops from her rear. They said, oh, that was just the waters breaking. Any time now. All normal. Don't worry, just let nature take its course. And they left.

I did worry. I cuddled and named her and put her with some goodies in a little quilted igloo, where she nested and purred--but didn't eat. I thought she looked sick--but what did *I* know? I just thought so. The next morning she looked worse, and I realized that I did not for one moment expect that kitten to kitten! Something was *Wrong*! So I rushed her down to Grant Patrick, who, bless his heart, takes my hunches seriously. He felt her distended tummy--squeezed--and pus came roaring out of her rear end!

Massive infection! Emergency hysterectomy! Instantly! All three kittens were dead--but he saved Lorelei. I fetched her home this morning, all stitched up with metal staples that can't be removed for ten days. Thank Grant and the cat goddess Bastet she's still alive!

I'll delay sending this, for up-dating.

July 22: Lorelei's staples are out. She removed one herself, which Grant said was impossible.

Not for Lorelei!

She's a Unique. Not only doesn't have a Siamese voice, she has virtually no voice at all. Just a funny little vibrating hum, like a meerkat, when playing or burrowing under a bedspread, a ferocious snarl when displeased, and an enormous purr the instant I touch her. And you know how a cat's whiskers jut forward when pleased? Hers practically cross in front!

She adores tunneling. My bed now features seven furry lumps on top and one lurking under the covers where she can attack anything moving below *or* above. A lovely game--except when Bootsie innocently lies down on the Lorelei lump, causing it to snarl furiously. Her favorite game is Grab, when I seize and tickle her and she bursts into noisy purrs and shoots lively appendages in all directions, like a demented octopus. Well, half-octopus. (Which is rather easier on my hand than ring-chewing and kill-kill, her other games. She plays *rough!*)

She's gaining weight at a huge rate--but is still tiny-boned. I photographed her today with her head all the way inside a water glass[19]. And she still has that leak out her back end, even more than before her hysterectomy. Dr. Patrick is puzzled. Says he remembers my mentioning it when I took her down that first day, but assumed it was part of that emergency. Now it seems not. In fact her entire bottom is always totally sodden now, and she's terribly embarrassed about it. Snarls in outrage when I try to look. Clearly something with the bladder. And she doesn't know where to put all that confusingly uncontrollable piddle. Tries corners, book-case, purses, guests, shopping bags, anything on the floor-

---

19   There she is on the cover.

-but her instinct just won't give her a clue. Con came to visit the other day (no healthier, poor love: just brave and determined) and when she picked Lorelei up she looked shocked and put her down rather hastily. Hadn't reckoned I meant *that* wet!

Dr. Patrick wants to do a dye test.

Aside from the leak, which she can't help, she is in other ways an adorable pain in the you-know-where. Sasses Elinor. Chases 18-pound Bootsie around trying to bite his tail--and does! Swanks through the house rolling her tiny shoulders like a prizefighter. I rang Arlene to introduce her--and after a brief silence Arlene reported in an awed voice, "Sally, she's a *lion!*" She then told both Lorelei and Elinor to behave themselves or I'd stop loving them. Elinor said indignantly (and more or less truthfully) that she *was* behaving. Lorelei retorted, incredulous, that I couldn't *do* that: I *belong* to her.

How are your plans for the Glorious Return coming on?

Love from all, even Lorelei. Sally

Obersdorfstr. 2a
53340 Meckenheim-Ersdorf, Germany
20th July
Dearest Sally,

I've found a boat builder, and I'm having a narrow boat, which I had written off initially because I've never seen one, but they are canal boats. I've never lived near the canal system, never seen a lock, don't know anything about them, but it's all a bit of an exciting adventure. I'm moving to Sudbury first, to stay with the friend who runs the quarantine cattery where Scallywag and Jamaica are to stay for the statutory six months. I grit my teeth about it, but would rather keep rabies out of the UK.

Not much time for writing these days.

Love you, Jenny

Sienna

Aug. 2:

Dear Jenny,

Well, I'm relieved you won't be off on some wild shore like off Cornwall. I might have guessed! I know quite a lot about locks, having grown up in Seattle, where we have huge ones connecting salty Puget Sound to freshwater lakes, (a lovely cheap way of clearing hulls of barnacles), and gone through the one at Panama three times. (Once a few inches ahead of the tsunami from the '64 Alaska quake--which quake I never felt, being at sea!) Wish I could be with you. One of the things I never got around to when I lived there was a trip by canal boat. Never worked out. Now it's too late, as I'm pretty sure I'll never make it back to England. For one thing, too many small kidlets depending on me--plus five colonies.

Oh darn, as my friend Constance would say.

Grant has done an X-ray on Lorelei. He said he's never seen anything quite like it: almost as if the poor little scrap has a deformed pelvis. From infancy? Possible cause of that infection and why her kits died? Catnippers has contacted a specialist in Petaluma--a Dr. Gurevitch--to see if he'll look at her. And they'll pay all costs!

Bless their hearts for still considering her their responsibility!

And if there's nothing he can do, I'll just take up the carpet and put down fluffy toilet-lid covers. I never was house-proud, thank goodness.

Luv, Me

14 Aug., '97

Dear Sally.

Excuse me while I have a small nervous breakdown with a nice cup of tea and a biscuit.

I have just got back from delivering Jamaica and Scallywag to their quarantine quarters in Suffolk, run by my lovely friend Valerie. Jamaica is not used to travel, and does not care for it, as she made clear, for about four hundred miles. Scallywag is, of course, entirely accustomed to it, and slept most of the way, waking only to stare at his travelling companion with an air of amazed disapproval.

Our arrival was no better. Again, Scallywag is used to living in a 'pen', if you will excuse that somewhat derogatory description of the luxury pad to which they were introduced, with heated sleeping quarters, sunning ledges in the outside area, and a lovely view of woodland and garden. Scallywag greeted Valerie with a gracious bellow, Jamaica spat at her. Jamaica does not care for closed doors, let alone locked ones. Not only that, but she complained that the hotel, or whatever it was, was packed with plebs, there's one over there that's a tabby. *Honestly! A tabby! And a black and white thug, look, in that bit in the corner. And why are there bars on the windows? And did that food come out of a tin?*

I left them to get on with it and went into the house with Valerie, who is used to most sorts of cats, including Siamese, but Jamaica has a voice that carries, so in the end we went into the study, with the double glazed windows firmly closed, so the outraged roars were at list a little muffled. But still audible.

I think I can still hear her. I wonder if my friendship with Valerie will stand up to this.

Love, Jenny

Aug. 20

Dear Jenny,

Gosh, yes, it is only five months or so until you go back home, innit! Will your canal boat be finished? If not, when do you actually move to England and where will you stay in the interim? It's all very exciting-- and making me miss England most terribly.

I feel I'm coming to know Jamaica, and certainly recognize dear Scallywag. How I wish I could have met both in person! Reckon it's too late, though. Somehow I can't see either of us ever being able to break away long enough to make the length visit that such a distance would need. (Well, I don't go 7,000 miles just for a week-end, even if some do.) Anyway, good luck to Valerie, who sounds competent to deal with even Jamaica.

Lorelei has been to Dr. Gurevitch, who is darling with her. Rubbed her forehead comfortably before getting cheeky. Says it doesn't look like anything he's seen, either; but it could be congenital deformation of the spine? Affecting the nerves that control the bladder? Says we'll try pills with an unpronounceable name which Grant says is basically Dexedrine without the caffeine. Says it's a long shot, may not work. So far, it hasn't. In fact, it's worse. Next step, the dye test. I'll hold this again, for further report.

Aug. 23: Took Lorelei back down for the dye test--and she's wonderful in the car. No sulks or wailing: just purred all the way, her charming little face and white whiskers close to the bars of the carrier, huge blue eyes looking up at me contentedly.

He administered it, looked at the result--and then kept her there. Seems there's no kidney function at all on the right. He phoned just now to reassure me, and said either it's dead, or doesn't exist. Going to do an exploratory. Said she's fine and purring her head off in the cage.

5 days later. Just fetched her home. The exploratory turned into major surgery (again!) when he found that the right kidney wasn't merely dead: it was just a blob of goop called hydro-nephrosis. And the right ureter was four times normal size and by-passed the bladder altogether. He didn't say if it was congenital or associated with the massive infection, but he removed it all and put a patch on the bladder. (I hope I have this more or less right.)

It was all very traumatic for her, poor lamb. She had stopped purring--and eating, too, they said when I went to fetch her. Just hid in the litter box. But when she saw me, she instantly reached for me, trying to hold my fingers and rub her cheeks on all of me at once. In the car, I found that she has a meow after all. Not Siamese: just a piteous cry if I didn't have a finger for her to clutch. At the moment, she's so happy it breaks my heart. Stopped crying and started purring the moment she got home--a poor little baby with a six-inch incision up her tummy. What did Thurber say in Thirteen Clocks? "I'll slit you from your guggle to your zatch."?

Both of us should rightly be prematurely gray! What do you hear from your children in Quarantine?

<u>Another week later.</u> Well, Lorelei has the all-clear. It's a miracle! Her little bottom is dry. And maybe soon she'll stop that habit of piddling on carpet, shoes, Cameo's toys and the book case? The trouble is, now everything smells inexorably of urine--and to a cat's nose, inextricably as well. So every cat is going to think everywhere is a new litter box!

Uh-oh!

Lorelei was good as gold going down for her final check--though it must have been alarming. She kissed Dr. Gurevitch, but then said she'd rather stay in the carrier if it was all the same to him. But he reached in and caressed and soothed and murmured until she relaxed. Presently she even purred for him--but when he had done, she went firmly back into the carrier and asked when we were going home. Before we left, I gave him his gift. A little cat-in-a-basket ornament--and the cat looks exactly like Lorelei: seal-point Siamese with a very short face.

I've just learned that the surgery alone was worth $3,000.00, if not more; because it was a unique case and he had to invent the cure as he went along. And do you know what he charged Catnippers? Two *hundred!* Bless him!

Love, Sally and Lorelei

Germany
Dear Sally,

Please tell Dr. Gurevitch that I love him very much.

Scallywag is fine. Well, so is Jamaica: eating like a horse, chatting to the neighbours, and telling Valerie that if she thinks she's going to replace my Proper Mum she can damned well think again. Room service, fine. Purring and cuddling, not on your life. 'Being snooty' is what Valerie calls it. Usually cats have succumbed to her by this time, but Jamaica's the bloody-minded type.

Love, Jenny

Sienna

Oct. 21.

Dearest Jenny,

Good grief! Now that Lorelei's well, her fur is growing like crazy. Plush-thick and much longer. Too long for Siamese, too short for Birman, too thick and fluffy for either. Clearly a cross--but what kind? (Not that I care: it's just that I like to know things.)

I got her a playmate to keep her company. From the Catnippers adoption room. Little black Onyx is just under three months and three pounds. He has vivid copper-gold eyes, and his face and build are like dear old Oboe: you know, that long long face with a flat-on-top Roman nose? But his profile is more like that of a baboon. He's a long-hair with a bushy tail that thinks it's a fox--and lies right along his back as Deirdre's used to do--partly why I fell for him. And the fact that he doesn't walk: he struts, head high. Poses like a setter or pointer, chest out and hind legs planted well back. He looks like the Turkish Angora on my calendar--but his bellow is definitely Siamese. Another mix, I reckon.

No one else thought him special. There's a glut of black kittens again this year, so I offered to adopt this one and replace him with one of the gorgeous torties I just trapped... Oh, all right: to be honest, I high-handedly adopted Onyx anyhow, kindly leaving a free place in the adoption room to be filled if they liked (they didn't) by a not-black kitten which I could provide. Because I wanted him and no one else did, so there. We Four have firmly decided to break away with our own adoption group. After Christmas? About the time you go home?

(I've just realized what is so bizarre about that slim Angora-silken body with the bushy tail. The tail has an undercoat to beat all undercoats--and his body virtually none!)

This has been a much-delayed letter, while you make those even more important plans for your future which I want to hear. (Isn't it odd how you and I keep doing major changes at the same time?)

I've enclosed photos of Onyx and Lorelei. They are already Best Friends, and Lorelei assumes she'll always be big sister and Boss. She doesn't understand about Growing. I haven't disillusioned her. She'll find out! (You should see his feet!)

Both send their love. Between chases.

Luv, always, Sally

Oberdorfstrasse
19th Nov, 1997
Dear dear Sally.

I have often had to break the news to novice cat owners that the kitten for which they have paid an awful lot of money is (a) nothing very special as far as show looks are concerned; and (b) almost certainly nothing to do with the pedigree that has been sold with them.

But you, you take the biscuit, you do. You win the prize.

Onyx is almost certainly an Oriental Longhair, and not a bad one at that. They retail at about a thousand marks, and I can just imagine what would happen to anyone who tried to persuade you to part with him. Character, part Siamese sheer cunning and guile, and part Persian soppy daft nit?

As for Lorelei, I can't really tell, because all my books are now packed and I never was an expert on either breed, but she's either a Snowshoe or possibly a Mitted Ragdoll. In fact probably a Mitted Ragdoll.

So how do I find out? I hear you cry, not actually giving much beyond a damn either way, Lorelei being Lorelei and therefore unique and precious even if she was a tabby mog.

You pick her up by the elbows, keeping them tucked tidily and carefully into the sides of her chest; and you swing her, gently at first, backwards and forwards.

If she is a Snowshoe, she will tolerate this for about five seconds and then you will get the 'That's quite enough of <u>that</u>, thank you very much', followed by "Just as well I'm a lady. Try it again and prepare to lose a finger at the elbow joint" reaction. If she's a Ragdoll, the more you swing, the more relaxed and placid and apparently half-witted she will become.

Why? I dunno. Just is.

There you are, Sally. Either way, you've got two quite valuable cats there. Do you want to give me a few more details about the rest of the gang? I'm beginning to wonder about them.

Oh look I've got to go, I can't keep nattering on with you! I've got masses to do.

Love, Jenny

PS: I got a card from Jamaica saying she's <u>not</u> going to make friends with Valerie and I can't make her, so there! It cheered me a bit to hear she's still her old self.

Love, Jenny

Sienna

Nov. 25

Dearest Jenny,

Message from Lorelei: Whatever she is, it's NOT Ragdoll. As well call George Bernard Shaw a romantic poet. I gave her your test, anyway. Just to be fair. I *knew* it was a mistake to tell her why. When she heard the alternative reactions, she narrowed those blue eyes at me and did something different. Stiffened her body and pointed her toes like a ballet dancer, she did, and said, Well, it was quite a good new game but not as much fun as stalking the vacuum cleaner with Onyx or threatening people who come to the door.

The fourth time I tried it, she growled--but only because she was bored with it, and she always snarls when displeased. She certainly has some interesting genes somewhere. *She has become a Guard-Cat!* When the doorbell rings, she rears up on her now-dry rump and growls warningly. If it's friends and I bring them in, she's all sweet friendliness--which is more than I can say for most of my anti-social kidlets--but if it's salesmen, and I stand confronting them at the door, there's Lorelei poised threateningly at my ankle, nattering about guts for garters, confronting them too. And she has taken what you Scots call a scunner to Jehovah's Witnesses. At the very sight of those black briefcases, she snarls so fluently that they've apparently decided this is my Familiar, and now tend to pass my house by, to my great pleasure.

Am sending another photo of her on her very own stool in front of the telly, which she has Discovered. Particularly animal programs. *Most* particularly, David (or is it Richard?) Attenburgh. The TV nature commentator, not the actor. Comes running at the sound of his voice and sits enthralled on her Very Own little stool that lives there just for her. The others aren't interested.

Love, Sally

Obersdorfstrasse
December 3, '97
Merry Christmas

All right, so Lorelei's not a Ragdoll; I believe you. She looks like a sort of Snowshoe Balinese, which hasn't been invented yet.

You've done it again, in fact! Not content with picking up strays that turn out too be Something Very Special in the Way of Pedigree Cats, you've now beaten the breeders to something they've been trying to do for about ten years.

There isn't a lot I can say about this.

And seeing off unwanted visitors ties in, too, Balinese being about 80% Siamese and extremely territorially protective.

Snowshoe Balinese, she's got. Snowshoe Balinese, maybe Seal Point Snowshoe Balinese, didn't even know it.

Lovingly, Jenny

I loved the pedigrees Jenny kept finding for my little waifs from colonies and parking lots! Both of us played the game deadpan, pretending a series of aristocratic parents who kept finding each other by chance, ignoring awkward details like Felicity's mismatched nose-leather and paw pads, Lorelei's odd smoky spots on her feet, Tuffet and Onyx's very proletarian families--and the laws of chance. I did have a remarkably handsome lot, though, some of whom *looked* like champions even if they couldn't prove it. And Oboe and Elinor *might* have been pure-bred something-or-other: I never knew where either of them came from. Descriptively, Onyx was indeed a long-haired ebony oriental-- And Lorelei: a Birman-faced, short-bushy-coated, whisker-crossing, chestnut-and-seal-pointed Snowshoe Siamese? What fun!

Sienna

Merry Christmas!

Well, the die is cast!

We four discontented Catnippers members, Sandy, Chris, Con and I, have made up our minds. There are too many adoptable cats needing homes, and too little room in the adoption program, and life in a colony is very much second-best for them! Us to the rescue! I'll still trap--and Dr. Patrick will do the neutering, and we'll run our very own adoption program--and find homes for *all of them!* It's a very amiable divorce: good will and cooperation all around. (After all, we're all there to help the cats.) Constance will fill her garage with a new lot: ours--starting with that amazing feral orange family. (Every single cat in three colonies in adjacent gardens! Some gene pool!) And we already have our first: a cat who was taken in to a vet for euthanasia simply because he's missing a foot. The vet quite properly won't kill for some one's convenience; so he phoned me, and we took him and Chris (who does think of great names!) named him Tripod. We'll be ready to start--and apply for our Non-profit status--by March, we think. I can hardly wait!

Love 'n hugs, Sally

CHAPTER TWENTY–FIVE

THE CATASTASIS

Obersdorfstrasse
1st Jan, 1998
Dearest Sally,
HAPPY NEW YEAR!

And thank you very much for all my presents. Especially the cat t-shirt and the very pretty kimono which is packed, ready for the boat.

On February 1st, I go. I can't say the boys are dignified adults yet--only that I seem to love them more than ever. They'll come when they're ready. Max continues to do whatever he thinks is important, and it's never much to do with the family, and I still hardly ever seem to see him. But.

I'm on the third book of the trilogy. <u>The Iron Snakes,</u> its called. Written by Ann again. I have to finish to pay off the tax for what I earned on <u>Blacksmith.</u> So I must stop now and post this.

I remember that day in Brighton. Thirty years ago? I'd found a bit of Tatami that wasn't as hard as brick and I was trying to make sure that I got thrown <u>there</u> whenever possible - if I couldn't avoid being thrown at all, that is. You turned up, all friendly smiles, and made me <u>move</u>. Isn't it odd, the way the most unlikely lives sort of plait into each other?

I'm enclosing my English address.

Love, Jenny

Life was a bit hectic after that while we all got our acts together and new lives in order. Jenny moved back to England early in 1998, and for a while she stayed with Valerie, renting a little room at the back of her house, but it didn't work out. Jenny was writing The Iron Snakes at the time, and too restless. When she writes she paces about and goes for walks, and the only way out was through the kitchen/dining room, which was where Valerie worked. So Jenny found a room in Sudbury, six miles away, and rented that until she could move onto the boat. But she couldn't just not see her Jamaica and Scallywag, so she'd cycle back to Bull's Cross every evening to visit them.

Sienna
Jan. 23
Dearest Jenny,

Thank you, *thank you,* **thank you** for my copy of <u>The</u> <u>Black</u> <u>Cat</u>! What a Paraquel! You've done it again, haven't you? I had to have Con come uncurl my toes--and then I had to uncurl hers. Riveting! Did you say there's to be a third? I do hope so!

You asked for an update of my brood. Calico twins Allegro & Cameo, and the third triplet, the engaging Tuffet. Gormless Bootsie. Intrepid Elinor. My precious Felicity. Babies Lorelei and Onyx. The now-civilized Pokey, and Whisper--That makes--uh--ten! (And I once jibbed at having two!)

Onyx says he always knew he was a very exotic breed: he just hasn't decided which one. (Interesting. Con knew his mother and both sisters. Two gray, one black, all short-hair, none remotely exotic. His father must really have been something!) He is One of a Kind, anyhow. And you got his personality exactly. Cunning guile plus soppy daft nit--*plus* arrogant swagger.

He is either a very tidy or a very imaginative cat. Whenever I collect the dishes at mealtime, he has always placed a furry toy mouse in every one. Counted 'em himself, he says proudly. They're the appetizers.

He and Lorelei are always together, loving and grooming and playing, even though the play looks rather more like a battle to the death. Being a year older, (and a lion) she still outweighs him--barely. He's catching up. And I've noticed that when he squalls to Mama for help, and I snatch him from those aggressive little teeth, he instantly rushes back into the fray.

Yesterday she was the one who did the squalling during a battle. It was not for help. It was her war cry. She hurtled out of the tangle, bounced off the nearest wall and ricocheted herself right back in.

She has invented a new game for Tuffet. She'll spot him sitting blissfully in the middle of the hardwood floor, contemplating. A baseball slide sends her shooting on her back to third base right under his startled white nose. A brief frozen tableau. She squalls. If he doesn't react, she scrabbles extruded claws an inch from his face. "Yaaghyaaghyaagh! The moment he reacts, she catapults away, circles the bases, and slides in again. He seems quite bemused.

Well, it's not long before we're officially our own adoption society. Still unnamed.

Love from Sally, Con, Sandy and Chris to you, Scallywag, Jamaica--*and* The Black Cat, and long--and soon--may she sail.

Hugs, Me

Sudbury, England
19 February
Dearest Sally

I tell you what, those cats are keeping me fit. I cycle twelve miles a day to visit them, and it's by no means on the flat. But it's worth it. They are always waiting for me, and I sit with them while they have their tea. Jamaica gave me a bit of chicken liver yesterday, picked it up out of her bowl and dropped it in my lap, with a loving little chirrup. Valerie cannot believe it when she sees us together. Jamaica is the first cat she has ever had that she cannot handle. Scallywag is a doddle, lets her do anything she likes, purrs at her and gazes adoringly into her face with those wonderful blue eyes. I haven't the heart to tell her he did that with the judges, too. She believes she is the love of his life.

I picked them up yesterday. Debbie drove me over, as I had no intention of trying to bring them back on my bike, and Debbie is used to Siamese and Orientals. However, even she blinked a bit at Jamaica's voice, and what she said when loaded into a car. But it was only six miles, even though it felt more like forty.

They've settled in very well. Scallywag approves of my bed, upon which the sun shines in the afternoon, and Jamaica has now found a way of twitching the curtains to one side, looking out of the window, and commenting upon everything and everybody she sees. She's become quite a talking point in the neighbourhood.

Scallywag is a hero! There was a break-in next door, and he heard it and raised the alarm. Well, that is the official version – in fact, he was complaining at being woken up at half past two in the morning when one of the burglars dropped something. Apparently, they thought the noise (which was quite a mild one, for an irritated Siamese) was some sort of siren, so they legged it. One of them fell off the porch and hurt his ankle, and a passing neighbour saw it, and sat on him until the Boys in Blue arrived. He then opted for the easy life by telling them the name and address of his friend, and they caught him, too, before he had had a chance to hide the loot. I ran quite a spiel for the local paper about Scallywag only being eighteen generations down from the Royal Cats of Siam, who were used as guards in the palaces and temples. Scallywag had his photo taken. Jamaica said it was all very silly.

Love to you and the menagerie,
Jenny

Feb. 22
Sienna
Dearest Jenny, Scallywag and Jamaica,

Hail and salutations from The Ailurophiles!

That's our tentative name. Either we'll expand the public vocabulary with it or (alas!) change it to something brilliant but comprehensible like The Sienna Cat-lovers' Adoption Society.

Anyway, we now exist officially, with Con's garage and Sandy's house as quarters for the adoptees. Not mine, except as a love-and-cuddles clinic for cats-in-a-cage. I have a small house, and eleven cats of my own now, (counting new arrival Tiglet from down the street, who recently showed up asking if This is the Place.)

Tripod was adopted at our first Adoption Day, at a near-by pet store. He showed off admirably, waving his stump around with an air of gallant courage that impressed everyone--particularly one woman, who hovered and lingered and wailed that she *did* want him but-- Sighing, she set off for her home about an hour away. Two hours later she was back, distracted. "Please, is he still here? I got almost home and couldn't stand it."

And five others found homes that day!

I do think that's an auspicious beginning for the Ailurophiles!

Love you, Sally

That letter crossed the long-awaited letter from Jenny:

The Black Cat,
England
Dearest Sally and All,

We've moved onto the boat, and I love it! So do the cats. It's a long way from finished, but I flatly refused to move into the caravan, which was offered as being more comfortable. My lovely boat is full of tools and offcuts of wood and sawdust – and, until last night, mice. Well, that kept Scallywag and Jamaica royally entertained all night, and I didn't get a lot of sleep, but we are all agreed that this is the life. There are two dogs here, but they have been put firmly in their place, and now walk rather warily along this bit of the towpath, ready to sprint for safety if there is any sight or sound of either of my two. There are seven cats, too, and this worries me, because Jamaica is getting very shirty with one of them, and there's not much I can do about it.

Take care of yourself, Sally. I love you lots, my dearest of friends.

Always, Jenny

CHAPTER TWENTY–SIX

EPILOGUE

And so-- Well, this isn't The End, of course: that's for novels, where the plot goes uphill working toward a climax, and then has it, and you tidy up the little odds and ends, and that's it. But this is real life, which just bumps along at random. Apparently.

That was twelve years ago, the start of 1998. We never dreamed what was ahead, of course. Began with dire predictions about the start of a new Millennium--the date of which most people, determinedly ignorant, got a year too soon. Forgot how to count, did we? Even a couple of Mensa friends. Didn't even know that in a decimal system one counts from one through ten, not zero through nine?

As it turned out, the predicted disaster happened, all right--at the *real* millennium, a year later, when our election was stolen by the Supreme Court who supposedly have only judicial power. Then, six months ago at the start of 2010, they were earnestly and erroneously discussing how the First Decade of the Millennium went--when it still had months to go. Including BP's possibly terminally lethal oil spill, currently ripping out at a zillion barrels a day.

Ah well. Should be interesting, whatever. As the old Chinese Curse suggests.[20]

---

20 "May you live in interesting times!"

The overt theme of this book was--obviously--cats, but the sub-theme turned out quite unexpectedly to be that strange pattern Jenny and I have played for forty years. Whether by chance, Karma or Figgy, we have independently but nearly simultaneously opened one new chapter after another--similar ones, too--in our lives. Beginning on that Brighton judo course--which, you'll note, Jenny remembers rather differently from me. That was the first chapter of a friendship that ignores separation. The next chapter was cats. Then we both left England: she heading east and I west. Both got writers' block. Then we both started writing books again. And finally the amiable divorces: she from Max and I from Catnippers, and new chapters for both of us.

Twelve years is a long time in a cat's life. Jenny still lives on her canal boat, now with Waah-li who looks rather like Onyx but more so, with ears as big as sails. The twins did follow her back to England, and she is now better friends with all four sons than when she was trying to raise them. She has had half a dozen books published and invented a flood-warning system called Water Alert.

Constance turned out to have Lyme Disease. Symptoms like a combination of AIDS, malaria and syphilis with a bit of arthritis, whip-lash and brain tumors thrown in. We've become very dear friends.

I still have Allegro and Tuffet, now 17; Lorelei and Onyx, 13. Whisper, still living firmly on the porch and refusing to come in, must be twenty. And there are two more, whom I got in '99: gorgeous Maine Coon Vienna (who behaved with attempted adopters much as Jamaica did with Valerie, and told Arlene that it was because I belonged to her in a previous life and she had decided to keep me this time.) And finally my beloved Familiar: tortie-seal-point Balinese mix Sybil, with creamy fur the texture of a rabbit, who follows me everywhere. She would need a book of her own.

Five is supposedly old. With love as well as food, they live much longer. Still, all my colonies petered out, one by one, at remarkably old ages. But golden-tortie Amy outlived all the rest of that first colony. She had always been stand-offish, but in December of 2007, old, cold, soggy, lonely--she came straight into my hands when I held them out. Probably nineteen or more by then, she weighed four pounds, hadn't a tooth left--and when I got her home I realized *she was totally blind and deaf!* Dr. Patrick found that she also had bad heart and kidneys, and he didn't know why she was still alive. "Just keep her comfortable," he said compassionately, "and she might last until Christmas."

But Amy fooled us. Having Discovered the unsuspected heaven of cuddles, soft warm beds, and delicious puréed chicken, she was not about to leave it. She lived another fourteen months, groping her way cheerfully around the house and even--to my alarm and that of neighbors--outside; falling down the concrete front stairs one by one, on her nose, turning smack into the garage door, doing an About-face, down to the middle of the street and along to the cross-street, impervious to honking cars. (They learned to drive very carefully, in this block!) She loved every minute!

Catnippers finally got their thrift shop: a lovely light clean place with lots of goodies at reasonable prices and were an instant success. In fact, they're now a thriving business. I gather they don't really do adoptions, but have a splendid spay-neuter program--which was, after all, the first and primary purpose. We were the adoption people. In a little over three years the four of us found homes for nearly 800 cats--and rescued and neutered a lot more.) Including the one I named Tornado, who might have made a lion quail. She swept through the holding cage like one, demolished food, drink, litter tray and bedding with a few deft swipes. Her kittens were born double the normal size, and she went berserk when we tried to get near them and sat on them every time they showed normal kitten interest in us humans.)

But by the time I was 80 and the others were ailing in various ways, we kind of drifted to a halt. Still on call for trapping, but not much more.

At the end of December 2000--precisely at the *real* millennium, I started writing in concentrated earnest, with the first of two books laid in ancient Egypt. The work was orchestrated by a little song sparrow, who spied me through the window, fell in love, and courted me for nearly four months. I named him Sylvester. He'd fly around the house, peering into every room until he found me; then sing a stanza and hurl himself chest-first at the window. Not beak-first in attack: chest-first, trying to reach me. Then he'd slide down the pane to the sill and pace tunefully, or retreat to the nearest branch, sing again, and hurl again. Thud, song, thud, song, thud-- He particularly loved the study, which has screens where he could cling and walk around, peering in, serenading. When I went outside, he hovered and serenaded, even lighting once on my head and once on my wrist.

The night after I finished the first draft of *The Ivory Cat*, I awoke suddenly at 3 AM, sat bolt upright and bleated "He's gone!"

He was. Forever. I miss him terribly.

The Ivory Cat was followed by *The Missing Queen* and a trilogy featuring Lark and her siblings. In 2002, Joy Canfield at Image Cascade republished seven of my first twelve titles. Last year The Angry Earth finally came out. Currently I'm working on this, an adult rewrite of To Build A Land and on two new Egyptian ones.

Paraquels.

Jenny and I will probably never meet again in person, and we seldom talk on the phone because a cell call to or from a canal boat would pay a CEO's bonus. But never mind: our friendship never did depend on propinquity. We've snail mail and email--and Jenny has psychic hunches about my cats; so we're never really apart, as we never have been since that day on the Brighten tatami.

Breinigsville, PA USA
20 October 2010
247740BV00001B/1/P